continued . . .

Ace Books by Jes Battis

NIGHT CHILD
A FLASH OF HEX
INHUMAN RESOURCES

Inhuman
Resources

Jes Battis

ACE BOOKS, NEW YORK

THE BERKLEY PUBLISHING GROUP
Published by the Penguin Group
Penguin Group (USA) Inc.
375 Hudson Street, New York, New York 10014, USA
Penguin Group (Canada), 90 Eglinton Avenue East, Suite 700, Toronto, Ontario M4P 2Y3, Canada
(a division of Pearson Penguin Canada Inc.)
Penguin Books Ltd., 80 Strand, London WC2R 0RL, England
Penguin Group Ireland, 25 St. Stephen's Green, Dublin 2, Ireland (a division of Penguin Books Ltd.)
Penguin Group (Australia), 250 Camberwell Road, Camberwell, Victoria 3124, Australia
(a division of Pearson Australia Group Pty. Ltd.)
Penguin Books India Pvt. Ltd., 11 Community Centre, Panchsheel Park, New Delhi—110 017, India
Penguin Group (NZ), 67 Apollo Drive, Rosedale, North Shore 0632, New Zealand
(a division of Pearson New Zealand Ltd.)
Penguin Books (South Africa) (Pty.) Ltd., 24 Sturdee Avenue, Rosebank, Johannesburg 2196,
South Africa

Penguin Books Ltd., Registered Offices: 80 Strand, London WC2R 0RL, England

This is a work of fiction. Names, characters, places, and incidents either are the product of the author's imagination or are used fictitiously, and any resemblance to actual persons, living or dead, business establishments, events, or locales is entirely coincidental. The publisher does not have any control over and does not assume any responsibility for author or third-party websites or their content.

INHUMAN RESOURCES

An Ace Book / published by arrangement with the author

PRINTING HISTORY
Ace mass-market edition / June 2010

Copyright © 2010 by Jes Battis.
Cover art by Timothy Lantz.
Cover design by Lesley Worrell.

ISBN: 978-0-441-01884-0

ACE
Ace Books are published by The Berkley Publishing Group,
a division of Penguin Group (USA) Inc.,
375 Hudson Street, New York, New York 10014.
ACE and the "A" design are trademarks of Penguin Group (USA) Inc.

PRINTED IN THE UNITED STATES OF AMERICA

10 9 8 7 6 5 4 3 2 1

For Lynda Mae

Acknowledgments

I completed this book immediately after taking a teaching position at the University of Regina, and I am grateful for the reduced teaching load, which gave me time for writing and editing. I am also grateful for the attention and support that I received from various colleagues during the writing and editing process, including Medrie Purdham, Dorothy Lane, Gary Sherbert, Troni Grande, Rob Rose, and Susan Johnston.

And, as always, I am thankful for the patience, kindness, and brilliance of my partner, Sebastian.

1

Luiz Ordeño's apartment was on the corner of Davie and Pacific streets, where the city became ocean. The building was famous because it had a tree growing out of its roof. The height of the tree was supposed to echo the height of the Douglas firs that had grown all around here originally. Precontact. The building was a tourist attraction, and celebrities haunted it while filming movies on the cheap. Jean-Claude Van Damme was reputed to own a suite, or maybe a whole floor.

The penthouse belonged to Ordeño, and the tree was growing out of his ceiling. It made me think of the baobabs that could take over an entire world with their roots.

The lawn of the building was cordoned off, and strips of tape demarcated the borders of the crime scene. On the inside of the tape, people moved with logic and efficiency. Exterior lamps made the air hot. Colored evidence placards stuck out of the grass like candles on a cake.

A van for on-site forensic testing was parked in the entrance. Two houses down, an OSI tech was checking the integrity of the first perimeter veil. She passed an alternative light source over a patch of dark air, and colors danced within the arc. The veil was working. The street stayed empty.

It takes work to stay invisible. We had to be at every scene first. We couldn't leave a trace behind. We damaged the environment and tangled atomic forces by creating veils. We messed with the equilibrium of the universe. Our tests created pollution, both chemical and psychic. There was a whole section of the CORE devoted simply to erasing our metaphysical footprint, but they were fighting a losing battle.

Often, in order to analyze a substance, we had to destroy the sample itself by annihilating its substrate. We moved over the surface of the event and left nothing but vague organic ruins behind.

The door to the building was open. Clean and bright lobby. Two symmetrical potted bushes framed either side of the door. Their leaves were gone, and the branches looked like naked tendons.

The floor leading up to the elevator was tiled and spotless. A tech stood at the concierge desk, reviewing security tapes and then recording them to a flash drive. She'd snuck in a coffee, which she drank in stolen moments, whenever her ranking officer left the room. There were probably dozens of hidden coffees throughout the scene, pushed behind notepads or snuck underneath chairs. Their steam had to be messing up some of the detection equipment. Someone probably just filtered it out.

The keypad in the elevator had a button marked PH. They'd already lifted a print from its metallic surface, although it most likely belonged to Ordeño. Trying to print the entire lobby was a fool's errand. Maybe 10 percent of what they found would actually be catalogued in IAFIS or its paranormal counterpart, DAFIS. The rest were shadows.

On the top floor, the air-conditioning hissed. Cables snaked across the carpet, attached to various light sources. Multiple laptops transmitted pictures via the CORE's secure wireless network. Flashes lit up the polished concrete walls.

The door to Ordeño's apartment was open. It looked solid. Not the sort of thing you'd break down easily. And even if you managed to pull it off, there'd be a nasty spell waiting for you on the other side. Nasty like explosive decompression.

The suite was floored in dark pine, which looked real. There were knots, gaps, and other indiscernible shapes in the surface of the wood. It creaked under the pressure of multiple boots. The entryway was lit up, and every stray hair and mote of dust burned orange in the halo. The floor looked clean.

Farther in, the hallway narrowed. There was a guest bathroom to the left, dark, except for the purple shadows that moved across its length. Someone was checking the walls with short-wave UV light.

The entryway branched off to the right, opening onto a large kitchen. A tripod was set up on the tiled floor, along with a charging station for cameras and ALS batteries. All the little glowing lights from the battery indicators looked like candles lit for mass. Even the blinking LEDs.

A frying pan sat on the stove. There was cold oil inside of it, and traces of food. The digital clock read 3:03 A.M.

At the very edge of the kitchen floor, someone had placed a marker. There was a blood swipe on the tiles. Something had disturbed the blood while it was still drying, producing an abstract shape with skeletonized borders. A hand, maybe, or the side of a moving body.

The kitchen opened onto a living room with tall bay

windows, all reflecting the same patternless dark from outside. Bookshelves lined the walls. There weren't many paperbacks. The spines of the books were made of leather, hide, moleskin, and other materials. Some were metallic, and one or two books were even pressed between plates of stained glass, like miniature church windows.

One slightly recessed shelf, apart from the others, held something made out of smoke. It might have been a book, or something else. Nobody, as of yet, was willing to examine it further. The vapor smelled sweet.

The living room was floored in darker wood, almost too smooth. You couldn't tell if it was real or laminate unless you touched it.

"Jesus. Look at that."

"What?"

"The couch."

"It's clean."

"I know. It's just so ugly."

"Is it from IKEA?"

"Urban Barn. I recognize it from the catalogue."

"We have an Urban Barn catalogue?"

"Yeah. We got it in the mail."

"When?"

"Thursday."

"Oh, my God."

"What?"

"How gay are you? Did you actually hide the Urban Barn catalogue from me, so that you could read it first?"

"I didn't hide it."

"Where is it right now? Is it in your bedroom?"

"Maybe," Derrick said.

I shook my head and scanned the bookshelves. "Definitely an academic. Lots of books on legal philosophy, Roman law, and civil rights stuff."

"Did you happen to notice the book made of smoke?"

"Yeah. I'm afraid to touch it. They took pictures, though."

"Who's on photography?"

"Becka. And Linus is looking at the blood."

"He left the lab?"

"Yeah. He was one of the first ones here."

"Who else? Selena, right, and Tasha for sure."

"You're so transparent."

"What are you talking about?"

"Oh, is anyone else at the crime scene? Maybe the special investigator who happens to be my boyfriend?"

He rolled his eyes. "Not just him."

"It's okay to enjoy having sex, Derrick. Someone should."

"I guess. I just don't want to appear too happy, you know?"

"That's ridiculous."

"Things go bad when you're too happy. You get distracted."

"You're allowed to get distracted. Men are distracting. You can't just anticipate things going to shit right away."

"But things always go to shit. Look around you."

"I'd hardly compare your relationship to the murder of a high-profile necromancer." I glanced down the hallway that led to the master bedroom. "Not that breakups can't be fatal. Most homicides are domestic."

"Ordeño was supposed to be single."

"That's indeterminable. He could have an army of lovers and we'd never know about it. The guy's a professor and a legal activist. You can't tell me he doesn't know how to cover his tracks."

"But that's assuming this was a crime of passion. It could be an execution."

"No way. Door was locked and armed with something heavy. Nobody's walking away from that kind of magic. He let the attacker in. They knew each other."

Derrick started down the hallway. No pictures on the walls. Just a Doctorate of Law from the University of British Columbia, and beneath it, an undergraduate degree from the Universidad Complutense de Madrid.

"Not much on family and friends," Derrick said.

"Probably too busy. Spent his life working."

"Any relatives?"

"All dead."

"Is there going to be a funeral?"

"On their side, I imagine. But we're not invited."

The door to the guest bedroom was open. It had a leaded pane of glass, etched with two hummingbirds. I looked closely at them, and their edges blurred a bit, shifting to red. I felt something move across my scalp.

"Has anyone touched this glass yet?"

"I think they're going to use cyanoacrylate fumes on it."

"On an active materia cluster?"

He shrugged. "That's what's written in the log."

"Someone's going to get their head blown off."

"They've all got insurance."

"True. The payout must be enormous."

"If you can prove that it was a paranormal event."

I stepped through the entrance. Nothing happened.

Ordeño had a TV in his bedroom. It was a small one, sitting on a night table. I pictured him falling asleep while watching *Dateline*. Red carpet at the foot of the bed—a color that would have been called *gules* in the middle ages, like the kind they used to line the interior of a knight's shield. Edges gilt in gold thread. It didn't look like it had come from Pier One.

I'd only ever seen one other necromancer's bed. Lucian's was big and surprisingly comfortable, with faded blue sheets. Sinking into them was like putting on your very favorite pair of worn-in jeans. Ordeño's bed was a bit smaller, in fact. It had a black duvet, which lay folded neatly to one side. No canopy. Just a regular bed in an ordinary room, belonging to a lawyer who obviously lived alone.

I looked up, and saw something drifting in front of my face, slowly, like a feather. Strands of defrayed materia were floating all around the room, visible as motes of dust. Something had ripped the magic from these walls like dogs tearing flesh off the bone.

"Tess?"

I blinked. Linus was staring at me, camera in hand.

"Sorry. Did you say something?"

His mouth twitched. "I was just asking if you could hand me a bindle. There's some fabric caught in this blood spatter, and I need to tweeze it."

"Oh. Sure—" Derrick was already handing me the envelope. I gave it to Linus. "Sorry I'm a space cadet. Not enough sleep. Too much coffee."

"Don't use that word unless you're willing to go get us some. We've got at least another three hours to go."

I turned to Derrick. "We're missing *Hell's Kitchen.*"

"I don't even want to talk about it." He stared at the bed. "That's a really nice comforter. It looks expensive."

"Man, you're all about capitalism tonight."

"We got salary bumps. It would be nice to spend some money on the house."

"We also have a mortgage. And Mia. That doesn't leave us a lot."

"We're pretty comfortable right now, though. I mean, relatively speaking. We made a huge down payment on the house. And Mia doesn't actually ask for a lot of things. She barely eats."

I looked at him. "Are you trying to get me to approve something? I already said no to the industry-grade espresso machine."

"I was thinking of something a bit more substantial."

"Like what—"

The glass door to the en suite patio opened, and Selena Ward stepped into the bedroom. She looked tired, but not angry. Good sign.

Her hair was different. I tried not to look confused as I took in her appearance. Her arms were bare. She was wearing a black blouse and charcoal slacks, which were covered by a protective nylon apron. I looked at the boots. Charles David.

"Did Lucian come?" I tried to keep my tone neutral.

We weren't talking. Lucian and I.

I mean, that's not entirely true. We watched movies and had sex and sometimes we even made dinner at my place. All the things you're supposed to do when you've been dating someone for a year. Everything was great, except for the fact that we couldn't be seen together in public.

And the sex was starting to get kind of habitual. We could ring all the bells in less than fifteen minutes now. Then he'd get distant, and I'd get busy with something else. Or I'd find myself huddled on the balcony, nursing a beer while I watched him work, getting more and more paranoid until I just wanted to jump up and down and scream: *We're two incredibly hot people. Do you really have to return all those fucking e-mails right now?*

"His team arrived first," Selena answered.

"Lucian has a team?"

"Of course. Lawyers. Techs. A pathologist. I had to keep him away from Tasha the whole time, in case she decided to get territorial."

"What about Miles?" Derrick asked. We both looked at him. "I mean, I heard he was coming, too. There's materia damage to this place. We need someone who can analyze it. Competently. Right?"

She rolled her eyes. "You can stop twitching, Siegel. He's in the master bathroom. Working."

Derrick's eyes drifted toward the bathroom. Jesus. If he

thought he could hide in there with Miles and "take samples," he had another think coming. If I had to scrape blood off the walls, he was going to be right there beside me.

"Where's the body?" I asked.

"Right over here. Underneath the painting."

Ordeño was lying on his side, half-pressed against the wall. He was facing away from us. I couldn't tell if his body had been positioned, or if he'd simply died that way, staring at nothing.

"He's wearing armor," I said.

"Yes. He is."

Ordeño was wearing a delicate suit of golden plate. I could see what looked like wings carved into the surface of the armor. As I looked more closely, I saw that the wings had eyes. Creepy. Some of the blood had seeped into the grooves and contours of the breastplate. The rest of it decorated the wall behind him in rising and falling arcs, like sine waves. Arterial gush. The drying fluid pooled on the hardwood floor, clotting into clumps that browned, almost caramelizing, as the serum and heme separated through oxidation. I saw dozens of large parent stains on the baseboards, scattering out and forming satellites with partially skeletonized fingers. Many of them had been disturbed while drying, suggesting that something heavy had moved across them, creating a swipe.

There was a painting hanging above him, as Selena had indicated. The subject was a small girl with blond hair. At least, she seemed to be the subject. There were a lot of people in the frame, including what appeared to be the painter himself.

"*Las Meninas*," Derrick said. "By Diego Velázquez."

He leaned in closer to the body. Over the last two years, he'd lost some of his shyness and become far more comfortable around crime scenes. And his powers had sharpened. I still had no explanation for what he'd pulled off last year, when Miles was temporarily possessed and Derrick cured him. Derrick's power had etched itself onto the surface of the air in flaming silver lines, and for the first time, I could feel what we called dendrite materia. It wasn't just wispy thought-magic, or the jarring buzz of telekinesis.

Whatever Derrick had access to felt structurally dense and perceptibly vast, like gravity, or a weak nuclear force. I understood it only slightly more than I understood Lucian's necroid materia. I was a miner. I oriented toward earth materia. The earth was something I could get behind. Raising the dead was an entirely different dance, and I wouldn't have ever wished for Lucian's power.

I mean, I'd like to think I'd never wish for it.

"Look at his neck," Selena said. Her voice remained neutral, as if she'd just invited me to check out a new kind of artificial sweetener. I crouched next to the body and stared at Luiz Ordeño's face. All I could really do was stare.

The face was a ruin. Part of his throat had been torn out, and the musculature was exposed, along with the hyoid bone, a white sliver against the dark red of the muscle tissue. There were two visible wounds, both triangular, which had avulsed most of the left half of the jaw and mandible. The skin around the wounds was marbled purple and red; fatty tissue showed through the uneven borders of each wound, with muscle flaring underneath. A clump of black hair was stuck over his left eye, caked in blood. His right eye was closed.

"There's bloody froth," I said, swallowing. "Around his mouth. And the borders of both wounds are jagged."

"What else?" Selena asked.

"Blood around his neck. Spatter on his shirt, and more drops on his face. Looks like contact spatter, mostly."

"There's more blood on his left hand," Derrick said. "I can see it from here."

Grateful for the chance to turn away from Ordeño's face

for a moment, I looked to where Derrick was pointing. There were dried bloodstains on the knuckle of his ring finger, and more on his thumb. A smear on his wrist may have been caused by the larger parent stain on the glass, which would explain the wipe pattern.

"There's multiple splash stains here," I said, "and a possible contact transfer with the glass. None of the stains are over four millimeters in diameter, at least as far as I can tell."

"What does that suggest?"

"I don't know—that you should hire a bloodstain analyst? That's not my field."

"But you took a class on it. Everyone had to."

Her expression didn't change. Why was she busting my ass about this? Maybe she was still steamed about when I'd lied to her about Mia Polanski. But that was two years ago. I also didn't want to mention that I'd missed most of my bloodstain-analysis course because Derrick and I had gotten sucked into a *Gilmore Girls* marathon.

"I guess it suggests medium velocity spatter," I said. "An ax, maybe? But those wounds almost look like they were made with a piece of glass."

Tasha Lieu, our chief medical examiner, made her way across the living room. She looked at the body and shook her head. "Wow. Someone really went to town."

"Can you determine time of death?" Selena asked.

"No. I can take his liver temp and look at his stomach contents. But TOD is an inexact science."

"I don't need you to write a paper on it, Tasha. I just need a broad time frame."

Tasha was looking at the lower wound, closest to the mandible, where the most muscle tissue was showing through. "The blood on his face looks a bit like marbling," she said finally. "But it's mostly contact transfer. Has anyone tried to move him?"

"No."

Tasha placed a gloved hand lightly on his arm. She pressed two fingers against his flesh for a second. Her fingers left two blanched white marks, which took three more seconds to fade.

"Lividity is unfixed," she said. "He's probably been on the ground for less than twelve hours, since the blood is still settling, especially in the areas that are pressed against the glass. He's still in partial rigor, though, which means that it's been less than thirty-six hours. That's my best guess for now."

"Your best guess has nearly a twenty-four-hour margin for error."

Tasha shrugged. "It's all I've got. I'll know more after the gross exam. I'm assuming there's a full media blackout on this case?"

Selena nodded. "We'll have to secure the morgue and the autopsy suite."

"Do you think it was a glass shard?" I asked. "It kind of looks that way."

Tasha looked at the wounds again. Her eyes weren't cold, but they weren't entirely engaged, either. Maybe, to her, it was like staring at an algebra problem, or a jigsaw puzzle.

"Could be," she replied. "Like I said, I'll know more after the post. But it definitely isn't conventional sharp-force trauma." She frowned. "See here? Whatever it was perforated the larynx and thyroid gland. Left internal jugular vein is severed. The borders of the wound-track are uneven."

I pointed at the narrow end of the second wound, where the hyoid and jugular were exposed as a mess of bone and flushed tissue. "There's something like a notch. Just at the bottom, on the side of his neck. Caused by the weapon?"

Tasha squinted. "I'll have to measure it, but the distance

between those two notched points might correspond to the width of the weapon. Has someone already taken pictures of the body in situ?"

"We've nearly filled a terabyte hard drive with digital photos," Selena replied.

"Okay. I think we can move him, then. I'll be waiting back at the lab."

2

I sat on a bench overlooking English Bay, smoking, watching the black water as it moved out beyond the rocks. I could see a few scattered fires across the length of the beach, along with the glowing cherries of pipes and cigarettes, hovering like fairy lights around the half-buried logs. The Rollerbladers had finally left, and were replaced by scattered couples and family pods making their way along the seawall. I liked to listen to their slightly incoherent conversations:

Yeah, but the problem with this *dog in particular is that he keeps* . . .

God only knows why she didn't leave after he fucking went to San Diego . . .

I can't get this app to work even though I paid for it and now it's driving me . . .

What did I say? Popsicles later. You can have them after we . . .

Why does nothing ever change in this city? Why do I keep doing it over and over . . .

People walked by without looking at me. It probably had something to do with the halo of smoke above my head, which made me feel like the Wicked Witch of the West Coast. All I needed were winged monkey-slaves. When was the CORE going to give me winged monkey-slaves?

I took another drag. A patch of shadow to my left rippled, and a man in a black coat and blue jeans appeared. The glow from my cigarette made his face look sketchy, like an afterthought. But his lovely mouth was anything but.

Lucian smiled. *"¿Alguien esperas?"*

We'd been practicing a bit of Spanish over the last few months.

Mostly, I just wanted to be able to decipher whatever he was mumbling when he thought I wasn't paying attention. After looking up some direct translations online, I soon realized that Spanish insults were in an entirely different league, making their English counterparts look positively genteel in comparison. Some of them were textual marvels, combining religion, ancestry, and promiscuity at once into a kind of profane verbal missile.

Derrick's Spanish was perfect, of course. He'd snort whenever Lucian muttered something, and the two would exchange that conspiratorial buddy look that made me want to shoot both of them.

"I was waiting for you," I said, putting out my cigarette.

He sat down next to me. *"Pareces especialmente bonita esta noche."*

"That line doesn't work in any language."

He chuckled. "I had to try."

"And we appreciate your effort."

We sat for a while, not talking or touching. That seemed

to be our pattern lately. I wanted to put my hand on top of his, but it seemed like an impossibly difficult move, something far beyond our current choreography. It made me angry and tired. I didn't say anything, though. I never said anything, and neither did he.

The water looked like black ice. I wanted another cigarette, but I knew that he hated the smell. If I was going to be honest with myself, I hated it too. But I needed something in my hands, in my mouth, and he was no longer available. It was either Dunhills or Junior Mints, and that was an addiction I'd already laid to rest.

"What time did you finish up at the scene?" he asked.

"You mean Ordeño's apartment?"

"Yes. The scene."

"There are lots of scenes."

"But this is the first to involve both of us."

I leaned back on the bench. My muscles ached from processing trace evidence spread across the living room wall. I needed a hot shower and a handful of something with codeine. It must have shown, because he reached over and placed a hand on the back of my neck. His fingers were warm. I closed my eyes.

"I knew Ordeño." He massaged my neck.

I kept my eyes closed. Lucian so rarely imparted personal information that I didn't want to say anything to scare him off. Instead, I leaned forward, letting myself relax beneath his fingertips.

"He was a teacher and a friend."

It's weird. You didn't normally imagine necromancers having friends. Then again, you didn't imagine them having vinyl collections, or eating scrambled eggs with ketchup, or making sublime coffee, but Lucian did all of those things as well.

Just as I was nearing the point of absolute relaxation, with the perfect edge of horniness—the kind that begins as a flutter in the center of your body and spreads out like tisane blooming in hot water—he took his hands away.

I sucked in my breath. Great. Another sleepless night watching TV. On the up side, I could finally tear into that sealed box of Quality Street Chocolates that Derrick had hid under the sink.

I lit another cigarette, mostly just because I needed something to do with my hands. Lucian watched me.

"So you and Ordeño were friends?" I inhaled. The nicotine made me dizzy in a pleasant way. It was probably one of the only things keeping me awake.

"Smoking is a slow, ugly death," he said. His look was neutral, but I could tell by the purr in his voice that he enjoyed ribbing me.

I shrugged. "A pureblood demon couldn't kill me. Neither could an elder vampire. I don't think nicotine really stands a chance at this point."

"Maybe not. But I know a fair bit about death, and all the magic in the world can't reverse the damage you're doing to your lungs."

"Christ." I stubbed out the cigarette on the bench. "For someone who channels necroid materia, I think you're being a tad judgy."

"I just prefer you alive. That's all."

I don't feel alive. Not lately. I just feel tired and mined out, like someone tore up my foundations and left a heap of rubble behind.

I rubbed my eyes. "Thanks. I think."

"Besides. Your breath is sweeter when you're not smoking."

"Oh? What does it smell like?"

He smiled. "Like everything good. Everything that I love."

"Go on."

He leaned forward and kissed me, twice on each cheek. Then his lips brushed mine, and for a few seconds, I didn't think about anything. The fluttering returned, and with it, the ache.

His thumb moved across my cheek. I could feel his nail, and for a moment, I wanted him to split my skin like an orange, paring me down until nothing but a liquid core remained. But he didn't. He played with my hair, breathing, his mouth uncertain on mine. Then he pulled away. His expression was unreadable.

I sighed. "What kind of a friend was he?"

"Ordeño?" Now he was looking at everything but me, as if the entire beach had suddenly become fascinating. "We met a long time ago. I respected him. It's an incredible loss to the community."

You mean to the cult of necromancers?

Luckily, he wasn't a telepath. I tried to comport my expression, to appear neutral, like I wasn't actually interrogating him on behalf of the CORE.

"Selena mentioned that you arrived earlier tonight."

"Yes. I was called to the scene."

"Who called you?"

"A superior."

Right. Circular answers, like always. Why had I expected something else?

"So—did your people get enough information? Will they be returning?"

"My 'people' were satisfied, yes." He smiled slightly. "They'll be sending some of their data to your lab tomorrow morning."

"Some?"

He shrugged. "It's politics. You can't expect full disclosure."

"Of course not. That would signal trust."

"The CORE isn't exactly in the business of sharing information either. You can't expect trust to operate only one way."

"Maybe if we knew something about your 'people,' we'd be more forthcoming with information."

"What do you want to know?"

"An address would be a nice start."

He chuckled. "It wouldn't be called the 'hidden city' if you could find it on Google Maps. Anonymity is part of our lifestyle."

"Maybe that needs to change."

"It's not going to. Not anytime soon."

I stood up. "I have to get home."

"Tess."

I stuffed the cigarettes into my purse. "I'd like to get more than three hours of sleep before I attend Ordeño's autopsy."

Something passed across his eyes. Pain.

Shit. This was someone he'd known. A friend. It wasn't a John Doe demon whose body we were analyzing for trace evidence.

I closed my eyes. "I'm sorry. You knew him, and I'm sure he was a good person. He seemed like a good lawyer, at any rate. But we still have to go forward with this investigation, and it'll be a lot easier if you can guarantee some cooperation from the necromantic community."

He rose, putting his hands in his pockets. "We'll give you as much as we can. We want to see the killer brought to justice."

"We" meaning the community? Or just you?

My shoulders slumped. I was exhausted. I'd have to take a cab home.

"We'll look at the evidence and see what appears," I said. "In the meantime, keep in touch. We may need to conduct a formal interview with you."

"Can we do it at the house?" He gave me a half smile. "Maybe Mia could do it. She's on the debate team now."

"Unfortunately not. It'll be in a room with Selena."

"Ouch. That's scary."

It was strange. I'd seen his power. I'd seen him die once before. *That* was scary. But you could never tell what frightened a person. Maybe when you controlled the forces of entropy and decay, the things that really scared you were impossible to describe.

"I'll be there. Behind the two-way mirror."

I kissed his cheek.

"Good." His eyes fixed on mine. "You can protect me."

I don't think so, I wanted to say. *I couldn't before. I can't now.*

I just smiled. "*Por supuesto.* Of course."

The air was damp, and I could feel the cold in my lungs. Derrick had left. It was just me on the dead street. All the clubs on Davie had closed down for the night. Every shop was dark. Even the convenience store on the corner of Bute was closed. All the sugary snacks and copies of *Maxim* were indistinguishable beyond the black pane of the storefront window.

On the left side of the street, a trolley bus had simply stopped. The cables that connected it to the electrical lines overhead were motionless. There was nobody on the bus. Not even a driver. The front door was open. I kept walking.

Davie was the only street in Vancouver that literally went into the ocean. It followed a steep incline until it hit the beach, giving way to sand, trees, and sunbaked patches of grass. Even a dozen blocks away, I could feel the knife-edge of wind coming from the water. I could smell something on the air. Something burnt or burning.

I kept walking. I could see the Christmas lights that covered the facade of St. Paul's Hospital, winking on and off like holy semaphores in the distance. I turned onto Burrard, then paused by the empty lot that used to be a gas station. Now it was just a gaping hole, an abyss with a Panago Pizza and a Quiznos, both encamped on the edge. Not much of a frontier, really.

I walked downhill toward the hospital. The Christmas display seemed to be the only source of illumination for miles, or at least for the length of the street. But I knew the city well enough to navigate it in the dark. I'd grown up here. It was like visiting your childhood bedroom and knowing instinctively where the light switch was, how many steps down the hall in the dark, how the blue glow from your parents' television set flickered against the walls.

I stood in front of the entrance to the hospital. A sign next to the underground parking said NO SPACES. A row of ambulances was parked off to the side, each one identical, like Hot Wheels. The Christmas lights flickered. There was a nativity scene made of blue, green, and gold bulbs. Mary's mantle was distractingly blue. Baby Jesus was supposed to be made of gold bulbs, but the yellow coating had flaked off in places, so that his face consisted of a few points of naked white light.

The doors slid open, and I walked into the emergency waiting room. All the lights were on, but the entire waiting area was empty. A blood pressure monitor beeped quietly next to the triage desk. The vinyl seats stretched in rows of dark green, burgundy, and puce. I wondered if every hospital in the world used the same furniture supplier. The floor was painted with blue, black, and red lines, demarcating patient zones from staff zones. I followed the red line, which led past the triage and down a hallway with evenly spaced, identical doors.

Pieces of equipment lay discarded in the corridor. I recognized an EKG and what looked like an IV drug dispenser, but there were other random components from different devices that didn't look familiar. I didn't touch anything.

It's like the underworld. Don't eat, drink, or touch anything, unless you want to end up like Persephone.

I could hear something. First a clicking. Then a long, slow sound, like air being pushed through a pump.

It was coming from the doorway to my left. Room number 521.

521. May the twenty-first. My birthday.

I opened the door. The room beyond was divided by a number of floral curtains, all moving slightly. I could feel cold air coming from an open window. A machine beeped. Then I heard the wheeze of the pump again.

A light shone from the curtained space in the corner of the room. I tried to feel what lay beyond it, but all my senses were asleep. I could barely feel the materia in the walls and floor around me. The cold weight of the machinery dulled everything.

You've still got your athame.

But I didn't. The sheath on my belt was empty.

Shit.

I tried to block out the sound of the machines breathing. I reached further down, beneath the rotting linoleum and the foundations of the hospital, into the deep mineral structures that supported the building itself. But the familiar power was gone. All I could feel was lack. It chilled the tips of my fingers and settled around me, a static of snow and heavy shadow.

I exhaled and pushed open the curtain.

At first, the figure on the bed was unrecognizable. His skin was translucent, with veins thrown into startling relief. His eyes were closed. The pump moved his lungs, and clear fluid dripped through an IV. Different screens around the bedside displayed different numbers, but none of them seemed to mean anything. His blood pressure was 19 over 82.

I swallowed. 1982. The year I was born.

Click. Breathe. Click. Breathe.

I stared at his small, white hands, sheathed in wires. I looked at my own hands. There was no resemblance.

"Is it you?"

He opened his eyes. They were the color of dirty ice, with a flare of violet around the pinned pupil. He smiled.

"Tessa Isobel."

"What are you doing in my dream?"

My father's smile widened. "What are you doing in mine?"

I pointed at the monitors. "Are you dying?"

"I've been dying for almost seven hundred years."

"If you need someone to pull the plug, just let me know."

He chuckled. "You haven't got the nerve."

"Oh, I've got the nerve. I'll do it right now."

"Go ahead."

I started unplugging random cords. I flicked off machines. I pressed every red button on every monitor. The numbers flickered and died.

My father didn't.

"You see? You can't do it."

"That's not fair."

He touched my hand. His fingers were warm. Feverish.

"You tried, though. That's what counts."

I stared at him. A thousand kill-sites revolved within his eyes. Fire gathered within them. I felt it on my face. I took it into my lungs, and it seared all the way down like bourbon, eradicating me cell by cell.

"I'm going to find you," I said.

His hand was soft and gracile in my own. Almost liquid.

I looked down, and there was nothing but blood, a spreading, silent pool of blood on the bedsheets. His face rose out of the stain, like hot wax.

You are, the blood said. *You are going to find me.*

3

I woke up disoriented, like something had taken me apart during the night and put me back together all wrong. The comforter and sheets were lying in a tangle on the floor, and my pillow was nowhere to be found. I guess that's what happens when you're wrestling with demons in your sleep. Particularly demonic relations.

I never knew my real father. I'd seen him in visions and dreams, a dark, penumbral presence, like a piece of black sky torn from the middle of a storm. *La tormenta*, in Spanish. Hah. I was learning. Sometimes Lucian called me *la tormentita*, his little storm.

Kevin Corday was the father I'd known since I could remember anything. Twenty-six years ago he was just a stranger on his way home at night, taking a shortcut through Oppenheimer Park. He found my mother lying unconscious, bloody and broken. He brought her to the hospital, and from that moment onward, he was always a part of our lives. Even then, I was a tiny seed growing inside of her, the product of a violent assault. My mother said she didn't remember anything about that night, except for Kevin holding her hand in the hospital room and, afterward, the pain of recovery. But I wasn't so sure. I can't see how you could forget something like that.

And in my vision, she'd recognized him. My "real" father. She'd stared into his ancient, reptilian eyes, and she'd known him.

I could see her, holding her athame with its pearl hilt. Standing before the creature who'd nearly torn her apart years ago, numb to her screams.

You won't see her. As long as I live, you won't ever know her.

But that promise couldn't be kept anymore. I needed to know him, to know *it*, the pureblood demon who'd sired me. He was in my dreams more and more, whispering from some dark, wrecked place within my mind. He could see me. Like a tourist from another world, he was watching me fumble and fall down and try to get through each day without having a complete mental breakdown. And he was enjoying himself, disporting himself and taking his pleasures.

If he was going to reach out and meddle with my life from another world, at the very least I'd get some answers from him.

Of course. All you have to do is find him, and figure out a way not to get killed while doing it. Simple as putting together furniture. Connect h-bolt to c, and then shoot yourself in the head, because it'll hurt far less than what he might do to you.

I stood up. The blinds were half-closed, and rain-filtered light seeped into the bedroom, giving everything the grayish cast of a silent film. I needed an outfit that would go with the rain. Something gortexy. It was bad enough that I had to wear a bra at all times in the house now, since we were living with two teenagers.

I felt too tired to put an outfit together. Too tired to even drag myself across the room, let alone reach the kitchen. I guess having your ass kicked by a primordial demon could do that to you. But that was a year ago, and I still felt like my insides were raw. Like my body was nothing but scar tissue, held together by stitches, bandages, and the dumbass neurons that refused to stop firing. I loved my job, and I loved my family, but all I wanted to do was close my eyes and let myself be washed away.

I stood still for a moment, relaxed, and tried to align myself with the earth.

When I was a little girl, and my power was at its height, I used to be able to hear the convection currents deep beneath the crust. For some reason, they sounded like distant dogs barking to my twelve-year-old ears. Now I could barely feel the layers of mud, sediment, and bedrock beneath the house, creaking and settling within their dark matrix. The power didn't flow through me like I was a naked lightbulb anymore. Lately, it felt more like trying to coax an old transmission into second gear, with every nerve in my body screaming a complaint.

If I felt this way at twenty-six, how would I feel at forty? No wonder mages died young. The golden years weren't much to look forward to.

I threw on a sweater and ventured into the hallway. Derrick was cooking something, and I could smell coffee. My senses perked up. Materia couldn't rouse me in the morning, but coffee was a different story.

The kitchen was a strange domestic tableau. Mia sat at the table, drinking coffee and doing her homework, or at least something that looked like her homework. Even Derrick, who had a flair for handwriting analysis, could barely decipher what she wrote in the margins of her notebook.

Miles was sitting next to her, looking over her shoulder. He signed something to her that I didn't catch, and she shook her head.

"No, I think I'm supposed to solve for y. But I could be wrong. I stared at this same problem for, like, a thousand years last night before going to bed, and it still doesn't make any sense."

"Math never really helped anybody." Derrick put a plate of bacon and eggs in front of her. "Except for bloodstain analysts. But they're creepy."

She tasted the eggs and made a face. "Did you put rosemary in these?"

"I may have."

"God, is there anything you don't put rosemary in?"

"I can think of several things."

"All I'm saying is that, sometimes, you can just let eggs be eggs, you know? They don't always have to be fancy."

"I'm sorry our kitchen doesn't resemble a truck-stop diner. If you'd like, I can make some corned-beef hash for you."

"Mmmm. Could you burn it a little? I love it that way."

He looked at Miles and signed: *Any advice?*

Miles shrugged and signed back: *At least she's eating breakfast.*

"Morning." At least I think that was what I said. It might have been "mgrngrl."

Derrick put a steaming mug in front of me. "You're up early. I thought you weren't meeting with Tasha until ten."

I let the mug warm my hands. "I have to stop by the trace lab first."

"Is Cindée working with the armor that they found on Ordeño?"

"And Ben. He mentioned something about a Teichmann test for old blood, and it got him all excited."

Mia closed her notebook. "Why was the dude wearing armor? Was he in one of those medieval reenactment societies? Because there's this guy in my physics class, George Pearsall, and both of his parents belong to one of those, and they actually put on armor and fight with swords. I mean, she's like a serving wench or something, but apparently his dad—"

"We're not discussing the details of an active case over breakfast." I eyed her mug critically. "Since when are you drinking coffee?"

"Since I started studying for AP exams."

"It hardly seems healthy."

"Didn't you eat, like, a whole box of vanilla wafers before you went to bed last night?" She shook her head. "That's not just unhealthy; it's sad."

"I had low blood sugar. And you're fifteen. You should be enjoying the tenth grade, not studying for college entrance exams."

"They're AP exams. The SAT is totally different, although I'm going to write that, too. It's the only way I'll get into Stanford."

"Make sure to win a few scholarships in the meantime," Derrick said. "We can't afford to pay that kind of tuition."

"Those grants are supercompetitive. That's why I have to ace all of my AP exams and do extra-credit work."

"Isn't Stanford a little far away?" I asked. "What about UBC?"

"What about it?"

"They have lots of great programs."

Mia folded her arms. "Tess, do you even know what I want to study?"

God, I hated when she said my name like that. *Tess, do you even know what I'm talking about? Tess, do you have any idea how lame you sound?* I never talked to my mother that way. But Mia wasn't my biological kid, and she knew it.

Miles made a quick sign while looking at me: He extended the index fingers of both hands and rotated them counterclockwise next to his head, while assuming an expression of vague authority.

"History," I said. "Classics, right?"

Mia gave him a look. "That's cheating. She totally didn't know."

He shrugged and spoke softly: "Just making conversation."

I heard some shuffling in the living room, and Patrick emerged. He looked exhausted. He was pale, even for a vampire, and he hadn't even bothered to use any of Derrick's thirty-dollar hair paste. His five-o'clock shadow made him look older than eighteen, and slightly threatening, which I didn't want to admit even if I felt it. Living with a young vampire magnate had its emotional ups and downs. Mostly, I tried not to think about the fact that he could drain my blood while I was sleeping. If he wanted to borrow the car and stay at a friend's place, I wasn't going to stand in his way.

"Morning." Derrick raised an eyebrow. "Looking a bit rakish, aren't we? Did you sleep in a mausoleum?"

"Funny." Patrick sat down and yawned. "Barely slept at all, actually."

"I'll make some more coffee." Derrick grabbed another filter from the drawer. "Now, if I had my Gaggia espresso machine, I wouldn't need—"

I raised my hand. "Don't even. That matter was already settled."

He rolled his eyes and poured more coffee into the machine.

I turned to Patrick. "Why aren't you sleeping? When I was your age, I could sleep twelve hours a night."

Of course, I wasn't a vampire.

He shrugged. "I don't know. Maybe I need a nicer bed."

"You got my old bed," Mia said, "and I got the futon. So don't complain."

"You can have it back."

"I don't want it."

"Right. Because you stole every pillow in the house anyway, so it doesn't matter that you got the crappy futon."

"Oh, my God, why are you still going on about the pillows? I took one extra pillow from the couch."

"Yeah, the one I was using."

"So why was it on the couch?"

"Just because it's on the couch doesn't make it—"

"Shut it. Both of you." I drained my mug. "As long as you're both living in this house, you have to learn to get along. That means respecting each other's boundaries and actually making an effort once in a while."

Mia laughed. "Yeah, like he totally makes such an effort. Yesterday he ate all the leftover pizza and left greasy paper towels on the counter."

"I asked you if you wanted some."

"Yeah, when you already had two pieces in your mouth. And then you spent forty minutes in the bathroom, doing God knows what."

"It's called—"

"Whoa." I stood up. "I don't want to hear any more of this. I'm late for work. You'll have to figure it out on your own."

"But he can't just hog the bathroom all the time. We all have to use it, and I'm tired of it smelling like Axe body spray."

"You can use the downstairs bathroom."

"There's mold on the ceiling! And the toilet makes that weird noise."

I walked into the living room, searching for my coat. "Then use the bushes. I don't care. In the meantime, Patrick, I'll pick you up another pillow."

"It's okay," he called back. "You can just give me twenty bucks and I'll pick it up myself. You probably don't have time to visit the mall and shop for me."

I poked my head back into the kitchen. "Nice try, but you still owe me for gas, groceries, and those PlayStation games that you rented."

He sighed. "Fine."

"Any preferences for your new pillow? Plain? Stripes? Something robust with cars and women?"

"I don't care."

"Okay. I'll just get whatever's machine-washable." I smiled. "See you all tonight."

"Can you pick up taco seasoning?" Derrick called. "We also need lime juice for the guacamole. It's Fiesta Friday."

"That's never going to catch on, sweetie. But I'll grab something."

I closed the door on his mumbled reply.

I'd never admit it to any of them, but this was the best part of my day.

I sat in the waiting room, thumbing through a copy of *Chatelaine*. The people sitting nearby looked surprisingly normal. I didn't know any of them personally, but I'd seen them working in different departments. Everyone was reading a magazine or sending text messages.

"Tess?"

I stood up and walked over to the desk. The receptionist gave me a friendly, uninterested smile. "Follow me."

The hallway was bland, with white walls and paintings of winter scenes. She led me to an open doorway.

"Have a seat. He'll be with you shortly."

"Thank you."

Her expression didn't change. She simply nodded and walked back down the hallway. I sat down. Had I remembered to turn my cell off? I didn't want to be obnoxious. I started to dig through my bag, but gave up after thirty seconds. It was buried so far down there, nobody would be able to hear it anyway.

I stared at the low desk in front of me. No family pictures or bric-a-brac. Just a computer, an accordion file, and an embossed leather appointment book. Maybe this was what Luiz Ordeño's desk had looked like. Austere professionalism. The brass nameplate read DR. LORI HINZELMANN.

The door opened, and Hinzelmann walked in. He was three feet tall and impeccably dressed, all the way down to his size-five Steve Madden loafers. It was hard to tell with goblins, but I'd guess that he was anywhere from ninety to a hundred years old, which for them was something equivalent to late twenties.

"Good to see you, Tess." He sat down behind the desk, taking a moment to adjust the height of his chair. "Do you want anything before we begin? Coffee, tea, or soda?"

"You have soda?"

"I think there might be a Coke Zero left in the breakroom fridge."

"I'm good. Thanks."

"Excellent." He set down a pen and a pad of paper. "We were talking a bit about your family on Monday. Did you want to start from there?"

"We might as well."

"All right. Go ahead." He smiled. His skin had the consistency of dark wood, impossibly grooved, as if his features had been carved out rather than formed through standard fusions of bone and muscle. I couldn't tell if it was attractive or slightly unnerving. No more so than his yellow eyes with their delicate, felid pupils, which never seemed to blink.

"She's been a little stressed lately. My mother."

"How come?"

"Various things. Money. The usual."

"That's just one thing. What else?"

"I think she worries about Mia."

"Oh?" He wrote something down. "Why do you say that?"

"It's nothing specific. Just this vague sort of thing. Like, she's not saying anything to me, but I can tell what she's thinking."

"What she's thinking, or what you think she's thinking?"

I shrugged. "We share the same DNA. Chances are we think alike."

"Humans share ninety-eight percent of their DNA with chimpanzees. That doesn't mean that both species are identical."

"I'm a lot like my mother."

"Why do you say that?"

I don't know. Maybe because my father's a pureblood demon, and the only genetic trait he passed down to me was a penchant for earth materia?

"We share a lot of the same neuroses," I said.

"Can you give me an example?"

I sighed. This was such familiar territory. I couldn't believe the CORE had any interest in learning about the fact that my mother and I both had short tempers and loved to eat salted avocado spread on toast. But they'd recommended these sessions after I was nearly killed by the Iblis. I didn't doubt for a second that Hinzelmann was sharing everything I said with Selena. Or maybe they just skipped her completely and went straight for her superiors.

Either way, they weren't exactly getting their money's worth. It seemed like the last interesting thing I'd talked about with Hinzelmann was my persistent fear of aromatherapy. I always started perspiring the moment I saw one of those elegant white potpourri diffusers in a store window.

Still—if the sessions were so boring, why hadn't I told Derrick or Mia about them? Something in me refused to admit the fact that I was in therapy.

"Okay." I steepled my fingers. "On Monday, she came for dinner. I was supposed to make a pot roast, but she ended up cooking the whole thing. She also spent a hundred dollars on groceries. Apparently, I was lacking in condiments."

"You weren't pleased by this?"

"Sure. I mean, I was grateful. But we didn't need groceries. And I was the one who was supposed to cook, remember?"

"Did you want to cook that night?"

"Not particularly. But it's the principle, right?"

"What principle is that?"

He finally blinked. His eyes had swirls of dark amber in them, like small clouds. I tried to pretend that he was just wearing contacts. As far as demonic species went, goblins were fairly similar to humans. Aside from being mostly nocturnal and living 50 percent longer on average, they were closer to humans than vampires. Many of them could pass for people of small stature with surprisingly little effort, provided they wore the right makeup and contacts. There was even a cosmetic procedure to shave their pointed ears, blunting them down to human proportions.

Hinzelmann had chosen not to assimilate. His shaggy blond hair did nothing to conceal his graceful, sweeping ears, which had multiple piercings. In a way, I was almost jealous. He probably had incredible hearing.

"The point," I said, "is that she's a guest in my house. She should just relax and let me take care of her when she comes to visit."

"Old habits die hard, though. Mothers are always mothers, no matter how old we get. Does her behavior surprise you?"

I briefly tried to picture Dr. Hinzelmann's mother, but I had no idea what sort of upbringing a goblin might have. Maybe he was the child of assimilationist parents, and he'd chosen to rebel by keeping his traditional features.

Or maybe he'd come from a well-connected family who worked for the CORE. For some reason, I wanted to think of him as being plucky and working-class.

"Nothing she does really surprises me. But lately, I feel like she's just being really attentive. Like she's constantly worried about something."

"Being attentive and being worried aren't the same thing, even if they go hand in hand." He jotted down something else, then looked up at me. "Is it possible that you're the one who's worried about something, and she's just detecting your anxiety?"

"She wouldn't have to be a very sensitive barometer. I'm basically worried about everything these days."

"Are these domestic worries, or professional ones?"

"Well, they're kind of permanently mixed up. I'm taking care of two orphans, and the CORE is watching me to see how I do. If I screw up, they could take Mia and Patrick away from me."

"But you're Mia's legal guardian. The CORE doesn't have the authority to take away your parental rights."

"They don't need it. We both know that."

He gave me a funny look. "Why do you assume I know that?"

"Because you work for them. You know what they're like."

"We work in very different departments, Tess. I don't engage feral demons in combat. There's a very low mortality rate in this office."

It was weird that he used the word "feral." Like he and I were domesticated demons, not in any way connected to a vampire, or a pureblood. Mages were hybrids, strictly speaking, who'd inherited nothing through their demon DNA except for the ability to detect and control materia. Goblins were a much older species who'd migrated only over the last few centuries from their underground communities. Cities like Vancouver still had dedicated goblin safe houses, well hidden from prying human eyes.

"Sure. My job is stressful. But that hasn't changed for the last ten years. I'm used to it by now."

Hinzelmann consulted his notes for a second. "Last year you engaged in combat with an elder demon, correct?"

"An Iblis."

"You were in the hospital for a week."

"If by hospital you mean a private CORE clinic, then yes. I miss it there sometimes. The Demerol was great."

He didn't smile. "Chemical dependency can also be stressful."

"I didn't say I was dependent. Just that I missed it. And if you're fishing for more information, then the answer is no, I haven't taken any more Hex."

"I wasn't fishing for anything. Just stating a fact."

"Right." I stared at the blank space on his desk. "Dr. Hinzelmann, can I ask you a personal question?"

"Of course. But call me Lori."

"Okay. Lori, do you have a girlfriend?"

I don't know why I was curious. I just was.

His expression didn't change. "We're talking about you right now. That's the point of these sessions: to assess your level of anxiety since the incident last fall."

"Is that what they're calling it? The 'incident'? I think of it more as the fun time I got to have spinal surgery."

"Do you feel like you've recovered physically since then?"

I still had debilitating headaches, nausea, and a bit of memory loss. Other than that, I felt like a trooper.

"I'm fine."

"And emotionally?"

"Depends on your unit of measurement."

He wrote something else down. "How are you sleeping?"

I dreamt about the Iblis once a week. I could still feel

its fingers locked around my throat, crushing my windpipe. I could still see the purple flame rising in vapors from its eyes and mouth.

"Fine," I said.

"And what about Mia? How is she acclimating to the tenth grade?"

"Pretty good. Especially if you consider the fact she's immunosuppressed from all of the antiviral drugs that they're giving her."

"That sort of treatment can definitely have side effects. You should have her see a naturopath as well."

"She's being treated for vampirism, not for a wheat allergy."

He shrugged. "Homeopathic remedies can make a difference. They'd probably help with your headaches as well."

"How do you know I'm having headaches?"

"This is your third visit, and all three times, my receptionist has seen you popping aspirin in the waiting room. Plus, you don't look like you've been sleeping soundly, and your left eye is twitching. Just slightly."

I exhaled. "Is it really that obvious?"

He nodded. "And it's much easier to be honest with me. It's impossible to make any progress if you just tell me whatever you think I want to hear."

"What would you consider 'progress'?"

"That's for you to decide."

"I just want Selena to stop looking at me like I'm a nut job."

"Do you think she's worried about you?"

"She's not saying anything, but yes. I can tell."

"The same way you can tell that your mother is worried?"

I blinked. "Is there a really obvious Freudian explanation for this?"

"Yes. But I wouldn't call it obvious."

"Are you going to tell me what it is?"

"There'd be no point. Also, I'm a Lacanian practitioner."

"What exactly does that mean?"

He glanced at his computer and smiled. "Sorry. Time's up for this session."

"You just don't want to answer any questions about yourself."

"Neither do you, it seems." He was still smiling. If it wasn't for his cat eyes, I'd feel like he had an incredibly soothing presence. The pupils kept distracting me, though.

I wondered if he could see in the dark.

4

The morgue was cold and quiet. The walls were so white that they seemed to glow, and everything smelled of industrial disinfectant with a hint of orange. Beneath that smell was the sour hint of decomposition, which I'd never completely gotten used to. It was an indescribable odor, and no amount of perfume, air freshener, or menthol-rub daubed under my nose could ever eliminate it altogether. It haunted the air, dark and limpid, an invisible organic layer settling softly and entirely over everything.

There was also something peaceful about the place. It wasn't like I wanted to spend a lot of time here, but I appreciated the chill tranquility of the morgue. It was a still space, like a church or a library. I could let my mind wander as I walked down the hallway, and the only sound that followed me was my own footsteps.

The autopsy suite was less tranquil. It was hard to get used to the sounds of various instruments dissecting a body, demonic or otherwise. The bone saw, in particular, made me a bit nauseous, especially when it spread fine dust into the air. It sounded exactly like a dentist's drill.

I stopped in front of the door to the suite. Every time I stood here, I couldn't help thinking about the grim circularity of my profession. Eventually, we all ended up on the steel table, our bodies washed and cleaned, our organs removed, weighed, and replaced in shrink-wrapped plastic bags. How long would it be until Tasha Lieu was cutting into me, trying to determine a cause of death?

Even though I knew it wasn't logical, I was afraid of the prosector's scalpel. I was afraid that I would feel the stainless-steel blade cutting into me, reflecting the skin, fat, and muscle tissue back to reveal my hidden interior. That was my ultimate terror: being cold, blind, and paralyzed on the autopsy table, unable to scream or say a word, as the scalpel bit deep into my body.

Having access to materia didn't tell us anything about the afterlife. Would it be like sleeping? Would I dream? Would I keep coming back until I fulfilled some obscure karmic debt, or was there just nothing after my heart stopped beating?

When a human was turned into a vampire, the biological process was similar to death. Their cells underwent autolysis, decomposing and then transforming into something different as a new genetic blueprint took control of them. But if vampires remembered what it was like to "die," they certainly didn't want to talk about it.

Patrick was probably too young to remember anything about his transformation. For all I knew, he'd been snatched right off the street, then propelled into a dreamless stupor with powerful drugs and magic. Caitlin, the former vampire magnate, had placed her mark on him. But I didn't really know what that meant. It was like the white lily tattoo on Lucian's neck: a cipher.

I swiped my access card, and the door opened with

a loud click. Inside the suite, the temperature was even colder. The walk-in refrigeration unit at the back of the room was closed, and resembled nothing but a harmless freezer. Inside, the bodies were kept on ice, along with tissue samples that would be analyzed later by the histology lab. Scraps and pieces collected for thin-layer chromatography and microwave analysis, which might not even yield anything. Sometimes, death remained unintelligible, leaving no trace on the victim's body.

Tasha was leaning over the steel table with her back to me. I could see the shallow drain underneath the table, where murky water swirled and vanished.

A box of latex gloves was sitting on the counter, and I pulled on a pair, grimacing slightly at the feel of the powder on my skin. I took one of the heavy black aprons hanging on the wall and tied it around my waist, then slipped on a pair of plastic shoe-covers. Even with all of that protection, I always managed to stain my clothes somehow, and the smell never came out. Demon blood wasn't like red wine. It lasted forever.

I cleared my throat to be polite. Tasha turned, and I got a partial glimpse of Luiz Ordeño's body, which she was in the process of sewing up. Coarse thread dangled from the needle in her right hand. It looked like fishing twine.

"Hey Tess. I'm just closing him up."

I could see the stitches from the Y-incision, which stretched from Ordeño's sternum all the way down to the pubis. I tried to remind myself that it wasn't Ordeño anymore; it was just a shell that couldn't feel anything. But somewhere in the pit of my stomach, I could feel a sharp pricking, as if Tasha's needle was threading its way through my insides.

I swallowed. "He looks different without the armor."

"No kidding. It took four technicians over an hour just to undo all those tiny little straps and fasteners. Who knew that something from the Renaissance could be so well made?" Tasha laid the needle and thread on the instrument table. "Cindée's looking at it now in the trace lab. She's got a smile so big, it looks like she just won the lottery."

I chuckled. Then I looked at Ordeño's body, and the pleasant feeling vanished, transforming into coldness. "What about him? Did you find anything interesting?"

She shrugged. "Nothing probative. Liver temp and core temp suggest that he'd been dead anywhere from eight to twelve hours before we found him. The light marbling that I saw on his arms and chest was probably caused by the body lying in an awkward position on the hardwood floor. The breastplate left marks as well, but those are distinctive."

"Probably caused?"

She gave me a slightly irritable look. "I'll tell you the same thing I told Selena. Establishing time of death is an inexact science, and every decedent tells a different story. The only way I could give you an exact number is to travel back in time and record every physical phenomenon that may or may not have influenced the rate of decomposition. Even then, I could be wrong."

"Sorry, Tash. I didn't mean to push you."

She smiled ruefully. "It's fine. I'm just feeling a bit harried. Selena's been calling me every hour, asking for updates. I told her that I'd be working on Ordeño for at least seven hours, but she seems to think that I'm not telling her something."

"She's just under the gun. It's a high-profile case."

"Aren't they all?" Tasha made two swift, sharp movements, making the last stitch in Ordeño's Y-incision. Then she cut off the excess thread, placing the scissors back on the steel-instrument tray. "In this case, the body pretty much speaks for itself. There isn't much I can add to the report."

"You're talking about the wound on his neck?"

She nodded, placing a gloved finger lightly over the mess of sheared tissue and bone that was Ordeño's neck. "There are eight separate, incised wounds to the neck and face. This one"—she pointed to a bloody seam running just below the chin—"transected the internal jugular vein. He would have bled out in three minutes, tops."

"Very *Basic Instinct*."

She shook her head. "No way. Ice picks make distinctive puncture wounds. This was more like a dagger, or a glass shard. Something long and slender, but with uneven edges. That's why the tissue is so abraded." She frowned. "It's strange, though. See this wound on the left cheek?"

I looked closer. It was shaped like a bloody leaf, as if someone had pierced the flesh with an arrowhead. Pink muscle tissue was visible, and, beneath that, small white notches of bone.

"Someone really went to town," I said.

"This wound is different from the others. They aren't exactly clean cuts, but the sharp-force trauma seems more evenly distributed. This looks more like the result of a wild animal attack. Something with talons."

I remembered seeing the body of Mia's aunt, Cassandra, lying on the autopsy table with a similar wound. The vampire Sabine Delacroix had reached into her thoracic cavity and torn it apart with her bare hands, through brute strength alone. I shivered slightly and looked away.

"A vampire could have done it. A powerful one."

"True. But I'm not entirely convinced that it wasn't done with a secondary weapon. Something larger, flatter, but still sharp."

"It's weird."

"Tess, 'weird' is a pretty vague adjective in our line of work."

I returned my gaze to the body. "Ordeño had serious power. He was a skilled necromancer with years of experience, and he had access to destructive and entropic forces that I can barely wrap my head around. How could someone get close enough to tear his face apart like this?"

She shrugged. "Everyone falls eventually, no matter how powerful they are. Maybe it happened too quickly for him to raise an adequate defense."

"Or maybe he trusted his attacker." I let my hand hover an inch above Ordeño's ruined throat. "The first wound could have easily incapacitated him. Adrenaline kicks in, and the blood pumps blood even faster, not realizing that it's all just spilling onto the floor. It was probably over before he even knew what hit him."

"Maybe that's a blessing in disguise." Tasha reached into a cabinet and withdrew a black ALS handscope, which looked like a bulky, industrial-strength flashlight. She switched on the scope, and the 12V cooling fan inside began to hum softly. "You know, they call this thing 'portable,' but it feels like a bowling ball."

I chuckled. "It's better than the previous model, with the big dial that reminded me of my parents' old color TV."

Tasha handed me a pair of protective glasses. Then she hit a switch on the wall next to her, and the autopsy suite went dark, save for the cone of blue light shining from the handscope's xenon lamp. She passed the light slowly over Ordeño's body, from head to toe. Then she switched to an orange filter, and, after that, a red filter.

"Nada." She turned the lights back on. "Not even a stray hair. No biological stains of any kind that I can make out."

"If only we had a filter that measured materia on a body."

Tasha gave me a sly look. "You know—"

I leaned in close. "Lab gossip?"

"Just a rumor. I heard that Miles Sedgwick was working on a pilot project with Ben from DNA and Linus from Ballistics."

"That seems like an odd team."

"I know, right? Supposedly, they're trying to design some kind of crystalline lens for detecting minute traces of materia within tissue samples. It has something to do with Raman spectroscopy, but that's a little beyond my ken."

I wanted to ask her if Raman spectroscopy had anything to do with Ramen noodles, which I found quite tasty. But it seemed like one of those questions that was best left unasked in public.

I also wondered if Derrick knew about this alleged collaboration. Maybe it was the reason why Miles had been looking so tired lately. But Ben and Linus both worked the night shift, and Miles was more of a swing-shift consultant. It seemed like I should have seen them all together in the lab. Unless they were hiding.

"I hope he's not pushing himself too hard," I said. "This year has been a tough transition for him, moving from the Toronto facility, adjusting to our lab. And a lot of dark shit went down last year."

"That's a succinct way of putting it." Tasha gave me a look. "How are you doing, Tess? With the dark shit?"

How am I doing?

Every day, I feel a little bit closer to a complete systems meltdown.

I'm seeing a goblin psychiatrist who knows that I'm full of shit.

I'm trying to raise two teenagers, and both of them have the power to either kill me in my sleep or burn down my house.

And most mornings, I wake up with the feeling of hands on my throat.

I untied the apron, pitched the gloves in the trash, and smiled. "I'm breathing. In and out. Repeatedly. Seems to be working."

"That's really all you can do." She tore a sheet from her clipboard, placed it in a manila envelope, and gave it to me. "We're still waiting for the toxicology report, but here are my notes from the post exam. At least it's something."

"I'll put them on Selena's desk."

Tasha winced. "Try not to make extended eye contact with her. She's especially predatory this morning."

I turned around and walked toward the door, envelope in hand. "I can deal with her. I already live with a predator."

As it turned out, Selena's office was empty. The fax machine was whirring, and a slight breeze from the open window had disturbed the leaning tower of forms next to her computer, but the room's occupant was nowhere to be found.

I started to walk toward the trace lab, then thought better of it. No use disturbing Cindée when she'd probably only just started analyzing the breastplate. It wasn't every day that you got a sixteenth-century suit of armor to play with.

I headed for the break room to look for Derrick, and found it empty as well. Had I missed something? Had everyone gone on a pilgrimage to the Bread Garden across the street? If so, Derrick had better bring me back a cinnamon twist. My blood sugar was starting to dip.

Becka's office door was open. I poked my head in, trying to locate her amidst the slithering blue and red Ethernet cables and blinking routers. Her long black hair had purple tips this week, and she was squinting at a bank of monitors.

"Corrupt boot sector?" She clicked the mouse that was

nearest her, a tad aggressively. "I'll show you a bloody corrupt boot sector, you sack of—"

"Hey, Becka."

She wheeled around her office chair. "Tess. I was just in the middle of fixing the lab's netware."

"I don't really know what that means."

"Actually, neither do I. We just upgraded to something even more complicated than Vista. And I didn't think there was such a thing."

"They're probably not paying you enough."

Her eyes sparkled for a second. "Actually, my paycheck is the one thing I don't complain about around here. The CORE offers some kickass remuneration."

"Wow. Maybe someday I'll see some of that."

"If you become a systems analyst, you definitely will. There's just no money in fieldwork anymore."

I shrugged. "My last application for a line of credit got approved. That's something, at least. And Derrick's pretty good at saving. Unless there's any kind of sales activity at Holt Renfrew."

"I just saw him in the interrogation room with Selena."

I stared at her. "Derrick's getting interrogated? What did he do?"

"I think he's just doing an exercise. Something to do with precognition. Selena had flash cards."

"This I have to see." I waved. "If you're still here in two hours, I'll bring you a coffee. How do you take it?"

"Enormous." She turned back to the screen. "Thank you."

I found Selena and Derrick sitting across from each other in the interrogation chamber. The room was sealed, but I could watch them through the two-way glass. Selena had two decks of cards in front of her, which she kept behind a raised metal partition. Derrick sat with both of his hands palm-downward on the table, staring straight ahead. Selena shuffled the cards.

I concentrated for a moment, channeling a bit of earth materia, which tingled on my fingertips. I let the strand of materia flow into the two-way glass, willing it to change its composition, but only slightly. All I had to do was nudge the atoms in the sheet of glass, convincing them to spread out just a tiny bit in order to allow the sound waves to pass through more efficiently. The air in front of the glass rippled slightly, and then I could hear their voices, which had a slightly a metallic cast. It was like listening to a cell with bad reception, but it worked.

I smiled. Meredith Silver, my old teacher, had taught me that trick. *Just remember,* she'd told me. *Only eavesdrop if you don't mind hearing people say the most beastly things about you. That's the price of listening.*

I missed her. She'd died well before her time.

"Ready?" Selena asked.

Derrick nodded.

She turned over the first card. It bore the picture of a red star.

"Okay. What's on the card? Be as specific as possible."

Derrick kept eye contact with her for a few seconds, unmoving. Then he relaxed slightly and smiled. "Star."

"Good. What color?"

"Red."

"Excellent." She flipped over the next card. It had a yellow square with a purple triangle inside of it. "Okay. This time, I'm going to use a shielding exercise. I'm no telepath, but I have enough training to block out some rudimentary psychic invasions. Let's see if you can break through my defenses."

He nodded.

Selena's eyes hardened. "Okay. Go for it."

Derrick's brow furrowed. Just for a second, I felt something like a tremor pass through the air, disturbing the equilibrium of the materia flows within the room. It raised the hairs on the back of my neck. That was about as close as I ever got to detecting raw dendrite materia, the energy that psychics channeled.

Derrick blinked. "A square?"

"Be more confident. Is that your final answer?"

"Yes. It's a square."

"Good. What color?"

He frowned. "Sort of a buttercream?"

Selena sighed. "We'd also accept yellow. Anything else?"

"There's a triangle inside the square. It's purple."

"You sure it's not mauve?"

He grinned slightly. "I was going to say amethyst."

"Right." She picked up a card from the second pile. "Okay, this is a remote empathy exercise. Each of these cards has an image on it that's designed to elicit a strong affective response. I want you to try to read what I'm feeling. It's different from just picking an image out of my brain. It requires more finesse."

"I've got finesse."

"I'll just bet you do." Selena gave him a small smile. Then she flipped over the card on the top of the deck. There was a picture of a steaming cup of coffee.

I instantly felt content. The test worked.

Derrick frowned. He almost looked like he was on the verge of sneezing. Then he suddenly broke into a wide smile.

"You're happy!"

She nodded. Her expression hadn't changed at all. With Selena, "happy" was a matter of extreme subtlety.

"Right. Next." She flipped it over. There was a picture of a Glock 9mm pistol.

What emotion was this supposed to draw from my supervisor, who carried a gun in a shoulder-holster every day? Irritability? Anger? Maybe it was like showing Becka a picture of a wireless modem.

Her face was set in stone. "What am I feeling?"

Derrick frowned again. His eyes seemed to go distant. I felt that faint charge of dendrite energy in the air again. If I relaxed my vision, I could almost see a current of dim light passing between them.

"Who's Jessica?"

Selena's expression broke. "What?"

Derrick shook his head slightly. "I'm not sure. I just heard the name when I was reading you. Is it important?"

Her features tightened. I saw something like a wall pass before her eyes, and she stood up. "No. I'm sorry, Derrick. I have another appointment. We'll have to continue this exercise tomorrow."

He gave her an odd look. "Is everything okay? Did that name have something to do with the card?"

"It's nothing." Selena opened the door to the interrogation chamber. She couldn't even look at Derrick. "The cards don't always elicit a clear emotional response. Sometimes they can be fuzzy."

"But I did feel something."

She looked at him then. "What did you feel?"

"Fear. I think."

She shrugged slightly, then handed him the card. "When you're dealing with weapons, fear is usually the correct response. You did good, Siegel."

"Thanks. Selena, are you sure—"

"It's nothing. I promise. I've just got somewhere to be."

He nodded slowly. "All right."

She walked into the hallway and saw me. Her eyes softened for just a second, and I saw what the wall was trying to protect. Derrick had been right. I'd never seen Selena Ward scared of anything, but there was fear on her face.

Her mouth tightened again, and the fear receded. Her defenses were nearly impeccable. Far better than mine.

"You've got two visitors," she said. "They're waiting at reception. Make sure they get the proper badges. Probationary clearance only."

"Sure. Of course."

She was already walking in the opposite direction before I could ask her who the visitors were.

Derrick emerged from the interrogation chamber. "Any idea what that was about? I've never seen her that spooked before."

"I've never seen her spooked at all."

He shrugged. "Everyone's entitled to their secrets. At least I got a high score on the precog cards."

"Yeah, you did really well."

He smiled. "Your eavesdropping sucks, by the way. I could sense you coming a mile away. Nice trick with the two-way glass, though."

"Next time I'll tiptoe." I put an arm around him. "Want to escort some visitors into the lab? Maybe they'll faint, or cry."

"Here's hoping."

We headed down the hallway, turned right, and came to the reception area.

Noel, the secretary for this floor, had managed to keep her job for almost three years without going crazy, demanding mental-health leave, or contracting a paranormal illness. She smiled and waved when she saw me, her ponytail bobbing slightly.

"Hey, Tess. There are two guests who need to be signed in." She glanced at her computer. "Mr. Lucian Agrado, and Mrs. . . . um . . . Is it *Duessa*?"

Those names stopped me in my tracks.

I hadn't seen the Lady Duessa since last year, when she agreed to meet with me to talk about the Iblis. Now she was wearing what looked suspiciously like a black silk kimono, and she stood well over six feet in her apple red Manolos.

She smiled at Noel. "Duessa's fine, honey."

Lucian leaned against the counter. He caught my eyes and smiled.

"Miss Corday. Pleasure to see you."

Fuck fuck fuck fuck infinite fuck.

Lucian was here. In my workplace. My place of work, which was entirely separate from my place of play. And we weren't supposed to be playing at all.

"Well," Derrick said, eyeing Lucian and Duessa together. "I have to be somewhere a little less dangerous. Let me know how the visit turns out."

"Thanks," I said flatly.

He winked at me, then escaped down the hallway.

"I've brought in the Lady Duessa as an outside expert," Lucian said, giving me a serene smile that made me want to hit him. "She has a vast knowledge of antiquities."

"You bet your hot little *culo* I do, sweetheart." Duessa beamed at me. "He does have a pretty fine *culo*, doesn't he?"

I swallowed. "I wouldn't know."

"Me neither. Shame." She shrugged. "But that's life. Now. Where's this gorgeous suit of armor I've heard so much about?"

5

Cindée, our head of trace, seemed more than a little surprised at the menagerie of people suddenly occupying her lab. Lucian had agreed to put on a lab coat, but Duessa's cool look told me that her sense of haute couture simply wouldn't allow it. Consequently, she was the sole person in the room wearing black silk and heels. "Tess." Cindée gave me a bemused look. "You've got quite the following today. How can I help y'all?"

"We're here to look at the armor." I gestured to Lucian, who, I had to admit, looked good in a white lab coat. "This is Lucian Agrado, who's consulting with us on the Ordeño case. Lucian, this is Cindée Desroliers, the head of our trace division."

Lucian leaned in and kissed her on both cheeks. *"Enchantée. Mércis pour ta aide, et pour ta indulgence."*

"De rien." She beamed at him. "It's a treat to finally meet you, Mr. Agrado. I've heard so much about you. In a professional capacity, of course."

He returned her smile. "Of course."

"And this is Lady Duessa. I doubt she requires any further introduction."

Cindée extended her hand. "Pleased to meet you. We really appreciate the support you offered us last year, with the Kynan case."

Duessa took her hand. "It was nothing. But thanks."

Something subtle but detectable passed between them, and Duessa held on to Cindée's hand for just a few seconds more. She wasn't testing her, exactly, but sort of nudging her. As far as I knew, Cindée didn't have any specific materia proficiency. But she knew how to handle mages. She didn't break eye contact with Duessa, and kept smiling, but I could tell that she was shielding slightly.

Duessa simply inclined her head, relinquishing her hold on Cindée's hand. She seemed to have passed the test. I looked at Lucian, but he merely shrugged.

"Okay," Cindée said. "If y'all just want to follow me—we're keeping the breastplate in a locked facility."

She led us past the various machines in the trace lab, pausing to check a readout from the mass spectrometer. We came to what looked like a closet in the back of the laboratory with a steel door, except that it had a card reader and a thumbprint panel. Cindée swiped her ID, then placed her thumb lightly on the glass panel. The red light next to it turned green, and I heard the sound of heavy tumblers turning on the other side of the door. Then it opened, and I felt a rush of cold air.

"Wee bit chilly in here, I'm afraid," she said. "But come on in. You'll get used to it in a bit."

The closet was actually a temperature-controlled chamber, large enough for all of us to fit in. There were several pieces on display in Plexiglas holding units—a book that appeared to be made of smoke, a blue glass orb, and a serrated knife—but the armor was the central and most prominent item.

The breastplate was made of steel with a black sheen, probably achieved by heating the iron. That was pretty much the extent of what I knew about metallurgy. It looked slender but heavy, almost like a vest, with two solid plates connected by intricate leather straps. The plate had been fashioned into the likeness of two wings, both covered in scales. Each wing had six eyes, half open, half closed. The open eyes reminded me of Ordeño's. I couldn't tell what animal the wings were supposed to belong to: a bat, maybe, or a dragon? Vancouver had both, frankly, although dragons were difficult to find within the city limits.

Duessa stared at the armor. "*Rayos.* Are you seeing this, Lucito?"

He smiled at the diminutive version of his name. "I actually saw it at the crime scene. But it looks even more impressive under these conditions."

"As far as we can tell," Cindée said, "the steel's been reinforced, or braided, with a kind of materia that we can't identify. Our equipment picks up vestigial traces, but there's no process like carbon dating for materia, so we can't determine exactly what kind of energy was used to forge the breastplate."

I thought of the rumor that Tasha had heard about Miles developing an alternative light source for detecting materia. It would have been pretty useful right about now. Maybe Selena had planned this all along.

Duessa walked in a slow circle around the holding unit, examining the breastplate from every angle. Then she turned to Cindée. "Okay. First, tell me what you think."

Cindée opened up a red folder that she'd been carrying, glancing at her notes. "Well, I'm no expert. But the design resembles a number of types of armor, forged between 1550 and 1590, roughly during the beginning of Spain's

Golden Age. It could have come from Milan, which had an active arms industry at that time."

"It reminds me of something I've seen before," Lucian said, absently scratching at the day's worth of stubble on his cheek. The gesture was unconsciously sexy, and drove me mad. I had to look away.

"In Florence?" Duessa asked.

"Yeah. At the Museo Nazionale. I remember the wings and the eyes. Spooky."

I looked at him. "You've been to Florence?"

"You haven't?" His expression was playful.

"It does resemble an Italian piece—" Cindée continued, flipping through her notes. "A breastplate made for the Duke of Urbino in 1546—"

"By Bartolomeo Campi," Duessa finished for her. "Actually, that piece was made closer to 1549. And this isn't Campi. It's much too fine."

Cindée blinked. "Do you specialize in Renaissance armaments, Lady Duessa?"

She smiled slightly. "I specialize in lots of old things, sweetheart. And I know that what we're looking at is beyond the skill of a natural armorer."

"It looks a lot like Campi's piece, though," Lucian said. "Isn't that strange?"

"Maybe Campi's breastplate was a copy, and this is the real thing."

"Who else could have forged it, then?" I asked. "I mean, if it wasn't this Campi guy. Were there blacksmiths in the Renaissance who had access to materia?"

Duessa turned to me. "Some. Filippo Negroli was the greatest armorer in Milan, and some say that he was a mage. Or maybe he stole dark secrets from someone else in order to create what he did." Her eyes went slightly distant for a moment. "Such beautiful pieces. He made a pageant shield with a gorgon's head on it, and I swear, those eyes could turn you to stone. The gold damascene alone must have taken months. And all so some princely fucking asshat could march in a parade, looking fine."

"You think it should have been used in battle instead?" Lucian asked. "A piece so beautiful?"

"Sometimes beautiful things are killers." She stared at the breastplate. "They have to shed blood like anything else. That shield, and this breastplate, are those kinds of things. They were meant to see blood, death, and carnage. Meant for the field."

Cindée frowned at the armor. "It seems a bit fancy for battle, doesn't it? All those eyes and wings?"

Duessa drew closer to the Plexiglas cube that housed the armor. She approached it as one would inch toward a sleeping lynx in a cage. "These things have a memory. If you want to know more, I'll have to touch her."

Cindée shook her head. "I'm not authorized to let anyone handle the piece. It has to be kept under controlled conditions."

Duessa shrugged. "That's fine. But if you want to know more about where she came from, I'll need to lay my hands on her."

"I didn't know armor had a gender," I said.

Duessa smiled. "There's a lot you don't know, *querida*. There's no real craftsmanship anymore. All the stuff you've got in this lab, it's shiny and it works great, but inside it's just wires and chips. No blood." She returned her attention to the breastplate. "She's got a pulse. She was forged in *el siglo del oro* by a master smith. It's a crime to have something like this under Plexiglas."

Cindée gave her a look. "Is this like an art appreciation thing?"

Lucian interposed himself between Duessa and the armor. "I think what she means is that the breastplate is a sacred artifact. Something that required great skill and intensity to create. That kind of psychic effort leaves a trace, and someone with Duessa's particular skill set can read that kind of trace far more effectively than your mass spectrometer. But only if you let her touch it."

"Her," Duessa corrected him.

He blinked. "Yes. Her."

Cindée looked at me uncertainly.

I shrugged. "Call Selena."

Cindée sighed and picked up her phone. She dialed an extension. "Selena? Hey, this might be a silly question. But I was just—" Her eyes widened. "Really? Are you sure? Well, you can't blame me for wondering. Fine. I will."

She closed her phone.

"She told you to do anything Duessa asks. Right?"

Cindée frowned at me, then nodded. "Basically, yes."

Duessa merely winked at her. "Don't feel bad, sweetheart. It's just one of the privileges of being a senior citizen in this community. Deference is a perk."

I looked at her curiously. "Care to define 'senior citizen'?"

"Don't even try it, Tess." Lucian put his hands in the pockets of the lab coat. "If she won't tell me her age, she's certainly not going to tell you."

Duessa shook her head. *"Una mujer necesita sus secretos."*

He chuckled. *"Tiene secretos peor que este, amiga."*

"And that's how they're going to stay. Secret." Duessa returned her gaze to the armor. "Now. Let's pop this top."

Cindée entered a code into the keypad next to the display case. Then she swung the front open gently. "Please put on a pair of gloves, at least. The amino acids from your hands could do irreparable damage."

I started to hand Duessa a pair of latex gloves, but she shook her head, reaching into her purse. "No worries. I have my own."

She pulled on a pair of gloves and approached the case. We all fell silent. It was like waiting for the armor-whisperer to do something miraculous.

Duessa laid her hand gently on the front of the armor. Her eyes went distant. *"Dímelo tu,"* she murmured.

An arc of white light passed between her fingers and the metal. She leaned in closer. I felt something sharp in the pit of my stomach. Then I heard a strange buzzing in my ears. I turned to Lucian, but his expression was unreadable. If this was a technique for utilizing materia, it was older than anything I knew about. Something close to the way that Miles could "profile" a spatial scene, only deeper and more intuitive.

Curiosity got the better of me. I reached out just for a moment with my senses, trying to brush against whatever power Duessa was channeling. It hit me in the face like a blow, stinging, making my eyes water and my lips ache. There was earth materia bound up in there somewhere, but that was just the surface. Beneath that, there was a layer of roiling dark energies, hungry and incandescent. It took all of my strength not to make a sound.

If Lucian noticed, he said nothing.

Duessa took her hand away. The white light cooled to a glow, then dissipated slowly. Thin vapors curled around her fingers, and I smelled burning plastic. The latex glove was gone.

"You're lucky you didn't set off the sprinklers," Cindée said. "What was that? Some kind of energy-based microscopy?"

"It would take too long to explain." Duessa reached into her purse and withdrew a bottle of hand sanitizer. She sprayed both hands, rubbed them vigorously, then replaced the bottle. "Major magic like that can really dry out your skin."

"Did the armor tell you anything useful?" I asked. "Like where it was made, or born, or whatever?"

She fixed me with a critical look. "Sweetheart, don't take this too personally. But you need to have a little more respect for the powers that you tap into every day. What you call 'materia' is just one property among many that drives the occult universe, and it wasn't put here to make your life easier. You have to honor it. Otherwise, you may call on it one day and find that it's stopped listening to you."

My face went red. "I'm sorry, Duessa. You're completely right."

And she was. I did take the power for granted sometimes. I assumed that it would always answer me, quickly and efficiently, as it had when I was a little girl. But even now, at twenty-six, I found that the magic came just a little bit slower. It didn't always do exactly what I wanted. Basic techniques took more and more concentration to pull off successfully, and the recovery time got longer.

It was the same with drinking. I couldn't pound back two pitchers of beer anymore. Red wine just made me want to go to sleep. Last week, I'd passed out on the couch while watching a Food Network documentary.

Duessa put her hand lightly on my shoulder—the same hand that, moments ago, had burned with frightening light.

"It's okay, honey. We all forget sometimes. But trust me. You have to respect these mysteries, just like you'd respect a loaded gun. Your care and attention is the only thing that keeps them from turning on you. And nobody wants that."

Lucian moved toward me. "Tess had been working really hard—"

Duessa raised a hand. "No excuses. That goes for you as well, Lucito. If any power needs to be respected, it's yours."

Cindée exhaled a tad loudly. "Can I put the cover back on now?"

Duessa nodded. "Of course. She's sleeping now."

"Right." Cindée closed and locked the Plexiglas case. "And what exactly did y'all talk about?"

"It wasn't really a conversation," Duessa said. "More like a silent movie, with all of the scenes played out of order. But I still managed to pick up a few details."

Cindée opened up her red notebook. "Did you find out when the breastplate was forged? Were we close?"

"Well . . ." Duessa raised an eyebrow. "It doesn't quite work that way."

"Of course it doesn't."

"Don't give me sour face. For an artifact like this, determining time of birth can be as tricky as identifying time of death."

Cindée blinked. "Okay. I can see that. How about a blurry estimate?"

"Mid-1570s. I'd guess." She gestured to the armor. "Of course, there are some things you can tell just by looking at her. The cuirass is heat-blackened, with detailed piccadill borders, and overlapping lame-plates. That eliminates anything made in England or France before 1550. It's far closer to Milanese plate."

I nodded. "Right. I knew that."

Cindée was writing things down furiously. "Lame-plates. Got it. What else?"

"There are brass studs on the shoulders and backplates." She gestured to raised gold buttons on the edges of the steel vest. "Post-1550, we might expect these to be Tudor roses, such as the kind you'd see on Henry VIII's famous Montmorency garniture. But these studs are actually solid gold arming nails, meant to reinforce the cuirass against blows from a lance."

"So it's pageant armor," Lucian said. "Meant for show, right?"

"It may have been made to look like pageant armor. But the steel remembers blood and violence. It's definitely been on a field of battle somewhere."

"Time out." Cindée put down her notes. "So far, you aren't really telling us anything that we hadn't already considered. And it doesn't matter if the armor was made for a pageant or a war. We need to figure out where it came from, and why Luiz Ordeño was wearing it the night that he died."

I gave her an admiring look. "Wow. You're starting to sound like a real OSI. Maybe you should transfer to the field."

She sighed. "I've thought about it more than once. There's only so many filament samples you can analyze before you feel like you'll die of boredom."

Duessa was still looking at the armor. "Pieces like this were also national texts. They were meant to encode the values of the empire. When a prince put on a suit of armor like this, he became a Roman hero. The metal tells the story of centuries' worth of bloodshed, warfare, and pain."

I followed her gaze. "So we have to read it like a history book?"

"In this case, you have to read it like a spell-book. Ordeño knew how to read it. Now you have to learn as well."

"Me personally? Because I'm not great with languages. I still don't know how to conjugate *tener* in the simple preterite."

Lucian grinned. "But you're trying. And that's what's important."

"In a way," Duessa said, "you're right. The great metal-smiths, like Negroli, or Diego de Çais . . . they were working with a kind of steel alphabet. The damascene and the acid-etched images form a language, and in this case, the code is meant to conceal an old form of magic. Break the code, and you'll figure out whatever the magic does."

I gave her a look. "Really? That's all you can tell me?"

"Why, Tess. You sound disappointed."

"Come on. This is like when you said that you'd never met the Iblis. You know way more than you're telling me."

"Tess—" Lucian began.

Duessa just smiled. "Some things you have to figure out for yourself, *niña*. I'm not an esoteric GPS. I can't give you directions to everything."

"Of course not. But you can give us something better than 'mid-1570s.' Right? I mean, what would someone like Ordeño even be doing with a fancy breastplate from the Renaissance? What was it supposed to protect him from?"

Duessa returned my look coolly. "To know that, you'd have to think like a necromancer. So maybe you're asking the wrong person."

I turned to Lucian. "Yeah. Maybe I am."

He took a small step backward. "Don't look at me. I don't know anything more than you do about medieval armaments."

"I find that hard to believe. I've seen your library."

"Those books are mostly for show."

"Lucian, come on. Ordeño was a litigator. When we searched his apartment, we didn't find any other bric-a-brac from the Golden Age. Just the armor. So what was he doing with it?"

"I don't know. He was a mentor and an old friend, Tess, but I never knew much about his past. Maybe it was a family heirloom."

"Or maybe he was alive when it was made. A necromancer like that must have been pretty long-lived, right?"

He wasn't looking at me anymore. He seemed to be staring at a patch of space directly above my right shoulder. "It's possible. Skilled practitioners have been known to manipulate necroid materia into slowing the aging process."

"Practitioners. But not necessarily Ordeño. Or you."

He blinked. "Are you asking how old I am, Tess?"

"I'm asking you to give me something that isn't a vague estimate or a cryptic joke. We're working together here, Lucian. If we don't keep the lines of communication open, we're just going to go around in circles."

"There's only so much I'm authorized to tell you."

I gestured to the armor. "We let you into our lab. We've given you access to materials involved in an ongoing investigation. That sounds like trust to me. The least you can do is give us a bit more info on Ordeño."

"What would you like to know?"

I looked at him flatly. "All of his records are sealed. Aside from the bio on his website, we know virtually nothing about him. Date of birth. Family. Attachments. He has no paper trail."

"Most of us don't. You're the ones who value files and archives and standardized tests. Your CORE may collect every scrap of information about its employees, but we're not like that. Necromancers don't have a union. There's no online database that I can pull up for you, with information on all of Ordeño's personal habits."

"Then what do you know about him?"

He seemed to think about it for a moment. "Not a lot. And I'm telling the truth when I say that. I'm guessing that he was anywhere from three to four hundred years old. He was born in Valladolid. I think. No living relatives. He spent most of his time in court, in Trinovantum. He loved his job, and he was very good at it."

"What cases was he working on?"

Lucian made a face. "That's classified."

"Fine. Is there anything you can tell me about his recent caseload? Anything remotely pertaining to this case?"

Lucian looked at Duessa. Something illegible passed

between them. He shrugged, finally, and looked at me again.

"Ordeño was working on a very important piece of litigation. A political agreement of sorts. I can't say much about it, because I don't really know much. But it definitely would have made him a target."

"A target to whom? Other necromancers? Vampires?"

"Both."

"Great. And you have no idea how a sixteenth-century suit of armor ended up in his apartment, or why he'd be wearing it on the night that he died?"

"Honestly—I don't."

I looked at Duessa. "And you have nothing to add?"

"Nothing that I haven't already said." She reached into her purse. "But I might know someone who can tell you a bit more."

She wrote down something on a scrap of paper and handed it to me. I looked at it.

"Are these GPS coordinates?"

Duessa nodded. "In Stanley Park. Follow those coordinates, and you'll find an associate of mine. He's called the Seneschal. Mention my name, and he'll help you."

"What kind of associate?"

"He's a bit of a polymath, and a collector. He knows a little about a lot. But he can be a bit cranky sometimes, so don't piss him off."

I closed my eyes. "Is this associate human or demon?"

"Neither, really. You'll see when you meet him."

"Great. Because I love surprises." I looked at Lucian. "Will you come with me at least? As moral support?"

He managed to look guilty. "I have a meeting. It's sort of important."

"Of course you do." I shook my head. "It's fine. I'll take Derrick. He loves surprises as much as I do."

I walked out of the lab, leaving Cindée to deal with the two of them.

"Tess!" Duessa called after me. "Remember to bring a gift!"

I stopped in the hallway. "What kind of gift?"

Duessa leaned out of the doorway. "Something pretty. He likes things that are bedazzled. At least he used to."

I stared at her. "Are you serious?"

She nodded slowly.

"Perfect." I turned around and walked toward the reception desk. "But if I have to buy something from Forever 21, I'm debiting the department."

6

It was a relief to step through the door of my house. The air was cool, and the smell of coffee drifted from the kitchen. I expected to find Mia studying in the living room, which would have explained the coffee brewing.

I tossed my bag on the table in the hallway. "I hope you're not planning an all-night research fest on the wonders of attending Berkeley. You know, it would be a refreshing change to see you just being lazy for—"

Patrick looked up from where he was sitting on the couch, reading a math textbook. "Mia's not here. She's staying late at school for some yearbook thing."

It was strange to see him home this early in the evening. "That's fine. What are you up to tonight?"

He shrugged. "Nothing really. I might watch a movie later. I made coffee, and there's some left if you want it."

"Thank you. I'd love some."

I walked into the kitchen and rummaged through the

cupboard, looking for my favorite mug. In truth, I was just stalling until I came up with something interesting to say to him. We didn't spend a lot of one-on-one time together, and even though I was the one who'd invited Patrick to live with us, I found myself growing increasingly uncomfortable around him.

Maybe it was because I had no idea what he spent most of his time doing. He was gone most nights. He'd return just before dawn and collapse into bed, then wake up a few hours later for school, looking exhausted. I knew that his constitution allowed him to spend a certain amount of time outside in the sun, without permanent side effects (such as self-immolation), but he wasn't about to join the football team.

Aside from a few mumbled comments, I had no idea how he was fitting in with the rest of his peers in the twelfth grade. Did he have friends? A sweetheart? Maybe he was humping mortals left and right, like a horny vampire rabbit. He certainly wouldn't tell me about it, if that were the case.

I didn't even know what questions to ask. *So, how are those vampire magnate duties coming along? Is it tough to regulate demonic traffic within the city? Do you get competitive health benefits?*

To be honest, I had no idea what a magnate really did. Caitlin had carried an aura of power and glamour about her, like an undead celebrity. But Patrick just looked tired and confused most of the time. He could barely find his iPod every morning. He didn't seem to have the fierce acumen necessary for controlling vampire affairs citywide.

I sat down in the overstuffed armchair next to the couch, which Derrick had rescued from the neighbor's backyard. I thought about sharing the couch with Patrick, but it seemed too intimate somehow. We didn't have that sort of convivial relationship. We kept a polite distance from each other at all times.

"How's school?" It was the most inane question I could think of asking, but it still sprang from my lips. I couldn't help it.

He groaned a little and stared at his textbook, which had colorful geometric shapes on it. "It's killing me. Do you have any idea what molar calculus is?"

I shook my head.

"Me neither. But apparently we have to know it for the AP exam, which Mia is already going to get a hundred percent on. Because she's a mutant."

"I believe she prefers the term 'magical savant.'"

He laughed. "Yeah. I've got weird shit in my blood, too, but it doesn't give me the power to ace these exams. Mostly, it just drives me crazy."

"Yeah?" I tried to sound only vaguely interested. This was the most personal information he'd shared in the last two months, and I didn't want to scare him off. "I know that feeling. Sometimes I wish the earth would just shut up already and stop talking to me. Unless it knows how to get me out of my cell-phone contract."

He smiled. "What does it sound like? When the earth talks, I mean?"

I thought about it, taking another sip of coffee. "Sort of like a vibration that starts somewhere in the back of my head. It gets louder, though. Sometimes the floorboards can sound downright pissed."

"That must be weird."

"Not really. It's just part of my materia sensitivity. I've always heard it. The only thing that freaks me out is when I'm in a brand-new apartment on the thirty-second floor, and I can't hear anything. Just the fridge humming."

"So the earth is like your background noise."

"Basically."

He put down the textbook. "It's different for me."

I held the mug in front of my face, so he wouldn't see

my smile of pleasure. "Different how? Because of your senses, you mean?"

He nodded. "It's crazy. I can smell . . . everything. The neighbor's dog. Mia's hairspray. I know that you had a glazed chocolate doughnut today. Or maybe two."

I lowered my eyes. "You're right. It was two."

He grinned. "If I concentrated, I could probably tell you what you ate for the last week. Except for Miles. I think that guy brushes his teeth, like, four times a day."

"He is superclean."

Patrick nodded. "And everyone's smell is like a signature. I can sense when you're all nearby. I know that Derrick came home for a few minutes today, around three, just to microwave a Sara Lee frozen cupcake."

"Damn him. There was only one left."

Privately, I was more than a little unnerved that Patrick could smell each one of us coming a mile away. But I didn't want to make him feel weird. After all, it was pretty weird that rocks, trees, and crown molding talked to me. Who was I to judge someone for having above-average olfactory senses?

"It must feel overwhelming," I said. This was one of Dr. Hinzelmann's favorite evocative statements. It always seemed to work with me.

Patrick just shrugged. "It's all relative, I guess. I'm really grateful that I have a place like this to come home to. I feel a lot luckier than some people."

I couldn't help myself. "You mean other vampires?"

He avoided my gaze. It wasn't often that I used the "v" word, despite the fact that I was basically raising two of them. But we still considered Mia to be in remission.

"Yeah. It's weird. I mean—" He finally looked up. "Okay, you and Derrick, you're demons. I mean, basically, right?"

I nodded. "We're mixed-race. Part of our DNA is demonic, but the human part is more dominant. It's the recessive genetic material that allows us to channel materia."

"Right. But vampires are different." He managed to look slightly uncomfortable. "They all seem really . . . hungry. All the time. Like they've been forced onto a bad diet, and sharing the world with edible human beings is driving them crazy. You can see it in their eyes. The constant hunger."

Do you feel like that? The question was stuck on the tip of my tongue. I chose to remain silent instead. Patrick just looked at me for a few seconds. Then he sighed.

"It's not the same for me. I do get hungry for blood sometimes, but I can control it. I think it's part of being the magnate. Whatever Caitlin passed along to me, it includes this weird sense of distance. Like, I know I want blood, but I also know that I don't need it all the time. I could just have a V8 instead."

"It is a healthy alternative," I said stupidly.

He laughed. "Don't worry, Tess. I'm not trying to freak you out. The way I feel about blood is probably the same way that you feel about materia. The desire is part of you, inside you, but it doesn't rule you."

Sometimes it does.

I blinked. "Okay. That makes sense."

"Besides. There's this whole subculture of vampires who don't drink nearly as much blood as the others. They're writers, and artists, and teachers. For them, being a vampire is like being a diabetic. They just deal with it, but they don't get sucked into the bullshit hierarchy."

"Do the teachers only work at night?"

Patrick grinned. "Mostly. You'd be surprised how many college instructors are actually undead."

"Maybe I wouldn't."

He finished off his coffee, grimacing as he hit the dregs. There was a spot of coffee on his lip, but it looked like blood. I willed myself not to stare at it.

"There are these safe houses," he continued. "They're called *daegred*, and they're all over the city. You can just chill out there, watch TV, sleep, whatever. It's nice. All the blood-heads kind of keep to themselves, so everyone else can socialize."

"Blood-heads?"

"Those are the vampires who just want to talk about blood. Sort of like jocks who just want to talk about hockey."

I'd never seen the connection before. But I nodded. "It sounds like you're learning a bit more about the scene."

"Yeah. Slowly. They've been letting me set my own pace. The monitors, I mean. They were Caitlin's council before, and now I guess they're mine."

He no longer looked sad at the mention of Caitlin's name. I wasn't sure if this was progress or not. She'd been a compassionate presence in his life, despite the fact that she'd also infected him with the vampiric retrovirus. I knew that he missed her, but he seldom talked about the events of last year, which had led to her death at the hands of the Iblis. In fact, he almost never talked about anything that had happened to him before he was transformed. Lucian had told me that he might not remember. Part of the brain actually died during the siring process, and that could include most of the memories from one's mortal life.

"So . . . they're helping you? These monitors?"

He nodded. "Cyrus especially. He's been showing me a lot of cool stuff, especially how to focus my senses and control my hunger. Modred is a bit more intense. His lessons are more about hunting, and he's kind of a fundamentalist sometimes. But he's still cool."

Hunting. Great.

As if I didn't have enough to keep me awake at night.

I wanted to ask more, but I could see his attention beginning to wander. This was why you couldn't interrogate a teenager. I decided to try a different tactic instead.

"Patrick, can I ask you for a favor?"

He gave me a funny look. "Is this about the gas money? Because I promise—"

I shook my head. "Forget about the gas money. I have to go to Stanley Park and meet a demon. At least, I think he's a demon. I'm a little nervous about going alone. Do you want to come with me?"

He smiled. The pride on his face was unmistakable. "Sure. I mean, if you need protection, or whatever. I can totally come."

"Great. We can grab dinner on the way."

He stood up, looking excited. "Cool. Thanks for inviting me."

"Don't thank me yet. We may just end up wandering around the park looking for a demon hermit."

"That sounds better than calculus."

"Yeah. Most things are."

We crossed the Lion's Gate Bridge, which was oddly empty at this time in the evening, and parked in a pay lot near the edge of Lost Lagoon. I let Patrick drive so I could finish my chicken shawarma. To his credit, he obeyed the speed limit, and only freaked me out once by changing lanes without checking his blind spot.

This side of the park was mostly quiet, save for distant cars and the hum of night bugs. The tall Douglas firs—still recovering from storm damage—made me feel like I was in a primeval church, dark, powerful, and green-scented.

Patrick seemed slightly nervous as we walked along a gravel path. This sort of place seemed like his element, but maybe he was more accustomed to the urban *daegred* of

Vancouver. I wondered if they had pinball machines and Wi-Fi. Probably.

I reached out briefly with my senses, but I couldn't detect any vampires nearby. They had a distinctive genetic trace: rust-colored and salty, like blood itself. Brushing up against one was like sucking on a cut and feeling the blood on your tongue, acrid and always slightly surprising.

"Do you feel anything?" I asked him.

Patrick kept his eyes on the path. "A few kin. But they're pretty far off, and they don't seem interested in us."

"Kin? Is that like peeps?"

He grinned. "Sort of. A lot of the older vampires still speak Anglo-Saxon, and it really alienates the younger crowd. They think we've fallen out of touch with the old ways, that we're all uncultured. But it's not like learning how to read *Beowulf* is going to make me a better vampire."

"Why do they speak Anglo-Saxon?"

He made a disinterested face. "It has something to do with the Norman Conquest. The *alderfolc*, the really old vampires, came over from Germany and Gaul, and they fought with the English vampires. After all the tribes had massacred each other, the only language they could seem to agree on was what they heard all the English villagers speaking. I guess it sounded pretty to them."

"Right." I stared at the formless shadows moving between the trees. "Are there vampire poets as well?"

"Of course. And playwrights. But they're kind of bitchy."

The path opened up slightly, and I consulted Duessa's coordinates. "Okay. I think this is it."

Patrick scanned the grove slowly. Then he pointed to a patch of darkness a few meters away. "That's not supposed to be there."

I looked where he was pointing. If I concentrated, I

could see what looked like a dim, sulfur-colored outline within the shadows. Not quite a materia trace, but more like a paranormal shimmer caused by two realities overlapping. Patrick's description was apt. The lines of space were stretched, and there was a kind of opening or corridor that wasn't supposed to be there.

"Ready?" I asked. "I don't know anything about this Seneschal, except that we're supposed to bring him a present."

"What kind of present?"

I reached into my purse and withdrew a folded T-shirt. The front of the shirt had a kitten's face, made with bedazzled rhinestones.

"Are you serious?"

"Oh, yes. I had to go to three places in Gastown just to find this."

He shook his head. "Demons are so weird sometimes."

We walked over to the patch of shadows. There was a tangle of weeds and briars at the base of a large tree, and the wan yellow light was emanating from somewhere within the undergrowth.

I hesitated. Wasn't this how people got carried off to Tir na nOg? Or did evil fairies eat your face? I could never keep the Celtic legends straight.

"How do we knock?" Patrick asked.

"I'm not sure. Let me try something." I placed my right hand a few inches away from the briar patch, and channeled a weak pulse of materia. It was the closest thing I could think of to ringing the doorbell.

Nothing happened at first. Then I heard something shuffling within the brambles. I was about to ask Patrick if he knew how to fend off a wild coyote, but then the undergrowth slithered open, and a figure wearing a black raincoat appeared.

He was a little over four feet tall, and hunched over. He

carried an oil-burning lantern, which appeared to be the source of the light. The raincoat was so large that it covered most of his body, eclipsing his feet entirely, but I could see that his hands looked more like wrinkled brown talons. He had the face of a dour ostrich, leathery and creased with ancient lines. His eyes were the size of marbles, but they burned blue.

His beak was long and sharp, and when he opened it, I could see a gray tongue moving inside it, like a lump of playdough. Those hard blue eyes fell on me, unblinking, and I was rooted to the spot.

He held the lantern closer, peering at me. *"Vlkl k nnv sk?"*

"Um—" I tried not to stare at his tongue. "I don't speak whatever language that is. How's your English?"

"English," he mumbled, shaking his small, narrow head. "English. Used to be *Anglisch*. So changed. Everything changed."

"Right." I frowned. "I'm sorry if you're feeling a bit disoriented. But we were sent here by the Lady Duessa to speak with you."

The Seneschal made a low, burbling sound deep in his throat, and his gray tongue rippled in the air. I assumed that he was laughing.

"Duessa. *La reina con dos caras.* One laughs while the other slits you *desde cuello a huevos.* She sent you?"

I spoke just enough Spanish to feel slightly queasy. "Yes. We're working on a case involving a suit of armor that may have been forged during Spain's Golden Age. She thought you might know something about it."

The Seneschal looked over my shoulder. "And him?"

Patrick extended his hand. "Hey. I'm Patrick. I'm a vampire. I hope you're cool with that."

Instead of shaking Patrick's hand, the Seneschal grabbed his wrist, holding his hand closer to the light. Patrick looked slightly alarmed, but didn't say anything. The Seneschal turned Patrick's hand palm upward and studied it for a few seconds.

"Old blood," he muttered. "There was a time when yours and mine were nearly the same. Demons of the earth and the air. But nobody remembers."

He shrugged, then beckoned us to follow him.

I exchanged a look with Patrick. There wasn't much else to say.

We stepped into the tangled undergrowth, which gave way to a long passage with a dirt floor. The only light came from the Seneschal's lantern, which cast little warmth, just cloudy vapors that moved across the walls.

Eventually, we came to a heavy wooden door. The Seneschal dug around in the pockets of his raincoat, muttering softly to himself. Then he withdrew a heavy iron key, caked with rust, and slipped it into the lock. The door opened slowly.

Beyond was a surprisingly large chamber, which appeared to have been carved into solid rock. The irregular walls were lined with small alcoves and recesses, holding a perplexity of items. I could see strange baubles, glass figurines, pages ripped out of books, and a pile of what looked suspiciously like Legos.

There was an overstuffed armchair in the middle of the chamber, and the Seneschal collapsed into it, sighing. Then he gestured for me to come closer.

"You have something for my collection?" It wasn't exactly a question.

I handed him the bedazzled shirt. He inspected it, turning it around and examining the writing on the back, which read JUST HANG IN THERE, KITTY.

Finally, he nodded, folded the shirt, and placed it carefully atop a pile of empty picture frames next to the chair.

"Show me the armor."

I reached into my pocket and pulled out a high-quality digital photo, which Becka had printed off for me. "Careful. The paper's glossy."

The Seneschal took the paper in his claws. In the dim light of the cavern, his eyes looked like halogen headlights. I shivered.

"*El alquimista,*" he said.

"Pardon me?"

He handed back the picture. "This *armadura* was made by an *infante* called *el alquimista*. The Alchemist. It is unique. Made with *esencia de sangre*. What your people might call a kind of 'materia.'"

I was writing notes furiously. "Right. We knew that—sort of. But who was this alchemist? Was he looking for the philosopher's stone?"

"Not looking. Didn't need to look anymore."

I blinked. "You're saying this alchemist found something—like, a kind of prime essence, or a fifth element?"

The Seneschal made a dismissive gesture. "Useless literary terms. *El alquimista* was a noble who lived at the Habsburg Court in Madrid. He trafficked with dark elements, and some say he found a way to control the oldest demons who walk the lengths of hell. Others say he was just crazy and talked too much."

"But why would he make a suit of armor?"

The Seneschal shrugged. "Why not?"

I sighed. "Is there anything else you can tell me about this Spanish nobleman? Did he have a real name?"

"Of course."

"And what was it?"

"*El alquimista.*"

"Right." I put the notepad away. "And I imagine you don't know anything about his family connections, or when he died."

He shook his head. "Too many questions. Tired now."

I looked at Patrick. He was examining a collection of stainless-steel tins whose labels had crumbled long ago.

"Of course. We won't trouble you further. Thanks for your help."

I took Patrick by the arm before he could touch anything. He rolled his eyes, but fell into step next to me.

"Lucian knows," the Seneschal called after us.

I turned around, staring at him. "Excuse me?"

His expression was mild, but his eyes burned blue in the dark. "Lucian Eskame Agrado. Ask him. He knows."

Then he closed his eyes and leaned back in the chair.

In less than a minute, he was snoring quietly. The talons of his left hand twitched as he dreamt.

7

We walked silently back to the car. I wasn't sure what Patrick was thinking about, but my mind was fixed on the last words of the Seneschal. *Ask Lucian. He knows.*

But what, precisely, did he know? What wasn't he telling me, and why was he suddenly so unavailable? It took all my willpower not to start furiously texting him, but I wanted to wait until we were home first. I didn't want Patrick to see me in full nervous-breakdown mode. Which was ironic, since up until a few minutes ago the two of us had shared a lovely and mellow evening together.

"That was weird," Patrick said as we crossed the parking lot. "I mean, a little, right? How do you think the bird-demon knows Lucian?"

I shrugged. "Maybe they went to college together or something."

"Did Lucian go to college?"

"I don't really know." I was digging around in my purse for the keys when I felt something. It was barely anything at all. But those were generally the warnings that you had to fear the most. Powerful demons left very soft footprints. I looked up, scanning the parking lot.

"You felt that, too?" Patrick was looking around as well. "It was like something tickled the back of my neck."

"Do you think it's one of your kin?"

He shook his head. "Feels different."

Shit. Different was never good.

I drew my athame from its boot-sheath. It was already warming to my touch, responding to whatever presence was nearby.

"Get in the car." I pushed the keys into his hand. "Lock the doors. If things start to go south, drive home and get Derrick."

"You're not serious." He stared at me. "Tess, I'm not going to piss my pants inside a locked car. I'm staying with you."

"This isn't about being macho, Patrick. You may be strong, but you're also young and inexperienced. I don't want you getting killed."

"I'm already dead."

"That's not the point." I sighed. "Just listen, okay? I may look weak, but I've spent half my life in combat training. I know when to fight, and I know when to run. You don't. You're cocky, and you think you can take down anything because your body's full of hormones."

"Actually, I think your brain stops producing—"

"Get in the car, Patrick!"

He folded his arms. "No."

"Really? You're going to pull a Jimmy Dean on me?"

"I don't know what that is."

"No. Of course you don't." I closed my eyes. "Fine. Stay close to me." I unzipped my jacket so that I could reach my shoulder-holster. Patrick's eyes widened as I removed the

Glock 9mm from its case. I clicked off the safety and held it out, carefully, with the barrel facing him.

"Have you ever fired a gun before?"

He swallowed. "No."

I placed it in his right hand, closing his fingers gently around it. "This is a Glock forty-five semiautomatic. It has ten rounds, and each bullet mushrooms on impact. Aim along the line of sight, like this—"

He pointed the gun at a nearby streetlamp. "What should I aim for?"

"Head and chest. When you fire, try to space your legs apart evenly—" I showed him the best position. "Extend your arm, and keep your target sighted. It takes less than five pounds of pressure to pull the trigger, and if you hold it with your finger, the gun will keep firing. So once you have a shot lined up, just try to keep the gun steady and hope that you hit a vital area."

"You don't sound too confident."

"Demons can be anatomically tricky. And this is your first time using a gun, so I'm not expecting miracles. But any distraction is better than nothing."

I felt the same shiver as before. A figure detached itself from the darkness at the edge of the parking lot. It walked toward us, its pace easy, measured. Not a good sign. Amateurs always hurried, but professionals took their time.

I turned to Patrick. "Look. I made a promise to Caitlin that I'd protect you." It wasn't exactly the truth. I had made an internal promise of sorts, but Caitlin was already dead by then. I didn't think that information was important right now. "It was the last thing I said to her."

He seemed to turn this around in his mind for a few seconds. Then, at last, he nodded. "If things go bad, I'll get in the car and go for help. I swear."

"Good. Thank you."

"But I'm not leaving you if I don't have to."

I held my athame in a defensive posture. With my free hand, I flipped open my cell and dialed home. The answering machine clicked on.

"Derrick," I said after the beep. "Lost Lagoon. Hurry."

I closed the phone, wishing it was a second gun. The thought of introducing Patrick to the world of firearms didn't exactly sit well with me, but I reasoned that his teeth and bare hands were already deadly weapons. In all probability, the Glock was just going to slow him down.

The figure was about twenty meters away now. It looked like a man, but I couldn't tell for sure. It didn't seem to be carrying a weapon, but that wasn't a good sign. Things that didn't need weapons were a lot scarier than gun-toting criminals.

"Should I start shooting?" Patrick whispered.

"Not yet. I'll give you a signal."

"What signal?"

"Mostly likely, it'll be me screaming profanity."

He nodded. "Right. I'll remember that." There was a slight quaver in his voice. The bravado had vanished. "Do you think they'll get your message?"

"Don't know. If *Idol* is on, Derrick's probably screening."

"Guess it's just us, then."

Something clicked in my mind. "Wait. Patrick, you said there were some other vampires nearby. You could sense them."

He nodded. "Yeah. There were two of them." His look went slightly distant. "They're still there. One seems stronger than the other. Maybe closer."

"You can call them."

He blinked. "I can?"

"Yes. I remember." I dimly recalled reading about this ability in higher-tier vampires. I had no idea if Patrick had the kind of mastery over his abilities necessary for such a summoning. But I was willing to gamble. "Just close your eyes and send out an intense thought. Like a mental scream."

"I've never done that before."

"There's a first time for everything."

The figure was ten meters away now. I could see that it was a man wearing dark jeans and a black hooded sweatshirt. There was something wrong with his face.

"Do it now," I hissed. "Just scream on the inside."

Patrick closed his eyes. I felt a wave of power explode from him, sending ripples of seismic disturbance through the night. My athame hummed in a kind of inanimate sympathy with the cascade. Cold claws raked at the edges of my mind, and I tried to shake off the power-shock. He was strong. He had raw energy in spades. Maybe it would actually be enough.

He looked at me, breathless. "Did I do it right?"

"I have no idea. But get ready."

He aimed the Glock, using the sight just as I'd taught him. A quick study, too. Maybe he'd make a good magnate after all.

The figure in black stopped a few meters away from us. His face, which had seemed eerily distorted at first, was actually covered by a metallic mask. The metal was so well polished that it reflected my own face back at me. All I could see were his eyes, dark and still, coldly assessing. Definitely a demon. Humans didn't have that kind of serene, predatory gaze, unless they were sociopathic.

I reached out carefully with my senses, not touching his aura, but just skirting around the edges of it. I felt incredibly dense power, like an iron wall. Not mage potential, exactly, but something else. Something very familiar.

"I'm Tess Corday," I said, keeping my athame level. "I work for the CORE. I'd like to avoid an incident here, if possible."

The figure didn't reply. Instead, he slowly pulled up the sleeve of his black jersey. His right hand was wrapped in a kind of glove, made from intricate leather thongs with gleaming brass buttons. In the palm of the glove was a latticework of golden wire, where three red stones had been set. They looked like carnelians, but there were curious black spots inside of them.

The black spots moved as I stared at them, almost dancing.

I remembered suddenly where I'd seen points of darkness like that before. When the Iblis had murdered Jacob Kynan, it left a tortured imprint on the space of his crime scene. Miles had used his power to make the space remember, and I'd seen those chilling black dots swirling just above his outstretched hand. *Voids*, he'd called them. Points of de-created space, reduced to nothingness.

The spots danced, swirling faster. Red tongues of light gathered around the stones, painting the asphalt bloody. The trace of power I'd felt before grew stronger, clearer. I remembered.

Necroid materia.

"Patrick! Get in the—"

Patrick fired. The gunshot split the silence of the parking lot. Evidently, hearing my scream was enough of a signal for him.

His first shot only grazed the necromancer's shoulder. He squeezed the trigger as I'd told him to, firing a second and a third time. Those bullets made contact, one in the shoulder, the other midthigh.

He wasn't exactly holding the gun steady. But at least he was hitting the target.

The necromancer took a step back, but didn't cry out. The carnelians on his glove were still burning red, like a parody of emergency lights.

"Patrick! Aim for the glove!"

I reached deep underground, searching for a vein of earth materia. We were close to the ocean, which meant that both geothermal and aqueous energies crossed each other nearby. I found a nodal point. It was old and strong, probably part of the structure that kept the entire park in one place.

I pointed my athame at the ground in front of the necromancer. A line of molten green light struck the concrete. The ground shuddered. A ripple passed through the earth, and it went liquid for a moment. It undulated, flashing out like a tongue, veined with granite, plant material, and threads of crystal.

I gestured with the point of the athame, and the ground exploded upward. It swirled around the necromancer, forming a cage.

I turned to Patrick. "Forget what I said about shooting. Get in the car."

"But Tess—"

"Get in the damn car, Patrick! Now!"

But it was already too late.

The necromancer reached out with his gloved hand, wrapping his fingers around the stalagmites that imprisoned him. The lapidary in his glove burned red, points of impossible darkness moving within their core. Something like fire swirled between his fingers, but darker, colder. Threads of light tore across the rock, spooling around it, cutting like taut wire into the sediment.

The threads multiplied. They moved with the speed of a burning vine, covering the rock, seething, like a spreading bloodstain upon the substrate of the rock. It crumbled to powder, shimmering for a few seconds as a haunting red outline. Then the rock was simply gone, as if it had never existed.

The necroid materia felt like a kick to my stomach. I knew that entropic forces could produce molecular disinte-

gration, tearing through cell walls and shattering the va-
lences that created basic life. But this was different. The
materia hadn't destroyed the rock. It had unmade it. The
deadly pattern of light had literally unraveled the bonds
that held both my magic and the rock together, extinguish-
ing them.

De-creation.

I knew that the Iblis could do it, but the Iblis was a pureblood demon. It walked the shores of an immaterial plane,
wielding and ravening the forces that made our world physically coherent. But this wasn't an otherworldly being.

Did Lucian have access to the same power?

Christ. Who was I dating?

Patrick wasn't listening. He fired again, this time aiming
for the head. A Glaser Safety round struck the necromancer between the eyes, resounding with a loud crack against
his steel mask. The mirror image of my face shattered.

He took another step back, shielding his face with his
left hand. Blood and metal fragments glistened all over,
making him unrecognizable. But his eyes were still fixed
on me. I noticed for the first time what looked like three
spots of blood in the corner of his right eye. They gleamed
within the iris, like drops of red paint.

What the hell did that mean?

I extended my athame and concentrated, drawing more
power. The earth was rich in energy here, but channeling it
naked was painful. I was blasting out nerve endings in my
hands and fingers, singeing the hairs on my arms. Holding
on to the materia was like swallowing fire. I gritted my
teeth and kept pulling.

When the power filled my core, I let it flow down the
hilt of the athame, willing the molecular bonds of the blade
to loosen. The metal shimmered and flexed. I kept pushing, and the blade elongated, becoming a line of crackling,
green-tinted light. It was now roughly the size of a katana,

and just as delicately bowed. I wrapped my hand firmly around the hilt, even as it burned me.

"Wanna tussle?" I kept those three bloody drops in my sight, memorizing their precise configuration in case we met again. "Let's do it."

He pointed the glove at me. Electric red vapors blossomed from his palm.

I held the athame extended in front of me, adjusting the wavelength of the intense UV light that was powering it. The field of energy spread outward, molding to the shape of a sphere around me. I drew from the ground one more time. The power moved hungrily through raw channels. I felt a wave of pain, but I stood my ground.

The nebulous red fire washed over my shield, like a toxic cloud. Glowing fissures appeared along the surface of the sphere. Each one was a claw sinking into me. I held on tighter to the athame, staring straight ahead, even as my eyes began to water.

The cloud thinned, then dissipated. I was still alive.

Maybe even for five more minutes.

Patrick yelled something I couldn't understand. Maybe it was in Anglo-Saxon. Then he ran toward the necromancer.

"No! You idiot, get back here!"

His form blurred, and he slammed into the figure in black. They both toppled to the ground. I always forgot how strong he was.

They wrestled with each other. I saw the glove beginning to glow again.

Shit.

If he touched Patrick, the necroid materia would unravel his flesh like a rotten net. Even if he was technically dead already, I didn't think his cells were immune to that kind of annihilating power.

I ran toward the two bodies grappling on the ground,

holding the athame high above my head. If I was going to go out tonight, at least I'd do it in glorious style.

I sliced downward with the blade, aiming for the necromancer's head. As I'd anticipated, he raised his right palm to ward off the blow by reflex. The blade struck one of the glowing gemstones on the glove, cracking it.

Sparks leapt from the glove. The necromancer cried out for the first time as red light crawled up his wrist, searing through the flesh of his hand. I raised my athame for another blow, but something hard and sharp hit me in my solar plexus. The blow knocked my legs out from under me, and I fell.

Both of them were struggling for the gun now. I tried to breathe. My chest burned from whatever offensive power he'd thrown at me. I raised myself to one knee. I was inches away from the car now. It gave me an idea.

I didn't have much strength left to draw on geothermal materia. But the car's engine was an electrical catalyst. I placed my palm against the hood. I could feel the battery inside, dark and asleep.

Wake up!

I pulled with every scrap of willpower that I had left. I didn't have the mastery to draw upon raw electrical power, like lightning from a storm. But I was definitely plucky enough to drain a car battery of its energy reserves.

The stale electricity tore through me, spasming the muscles of my right arm. It hurt even more than I'd thought it would. The pain made everything go white for a second. But I held on to consciousness. I narrowed the snapping electricity down to a small, hot globe of power and intensity.

"Patrick!" He looked at me, struggling to pin the necromancer to the ground. "Get out of the way! Now!"

For the first time ever, Patrick listened.

He rolled away, leaving the necromancer in the open.

I pointed my athame low, aiming for the puddles on the ground, which would amplify the charge. A white-blue ball of electricity exploded from the tip of the blade. It swept over the necromancer's body, and this time, he screamed.

Nice.

I tried to step forward, but my legs were made of rubber. The muscular convulsions brought me to my knees again. I snarled and crawled forward, the asphalt scraping my palms and blackening my jeans.

"Not only," I panted, "have you fucked up my evening . . ." He was trembling on the ground now, smoke rising from his body. "You've fucked up my outfit. And that pisses me off the most."

I managed to stand up. Patrick was approaching me. He wasn't holding the gun anymore. My eyes widened.

"Where's the Gl—"

The necromancer managed to raise himself on one knee. He had the Glock pointed at my chest. His face was a ruin of metal, blood, and acrid smoke.

His eyes were still calm.

I felt a cold emptiness spread through me. The breath left my lungs. I had no more power left. I couldn't stop a bullet.

Patrick's form blurred. He shot toward the necromancer, a dark arrow.

I heard the gun fire. I closed my eyes.

Something hit me in the shoulder. Hard enough to dislocate it. I screamed and tumbled across the ground, opening my eyes.

I was in pain. But I wasn't bleeding. And I was lying against the asphalt, meters away from where I'd been a second ago.

I looked up, and saw a completely unfamiliar person standing between me and the necromancer. All I could see was his back. He was wearing a red Windbreaker and jeans. His hair was blue.

Blue?

He turned around, keeping his left hand extended toward the necromancer, as if he could ward him off through force of will alone. His hair, I realized, was blue only at the tips, almost frosted. He had dark green eyes and a labret piercing. He didn't look a day over sixteen, but his genetic signature was old. Centuries old.

"Stay back," he said simply.

Patrick stared at him. "Modred? What are you doing here?"

Modred reached into his jacket and pulled out a pistol. It looked similar to my Glock, but there was a modified piece attached to the ammo cartridge. He turned and leveled the gun at the necromancer.

"*Hwaet, scathe!* These bullets are hollow-tipped and filled with atrazine. I promise you don't want to see what they'll do to your central nervous system."

The necromancer wavered on one knee for a moment, breathing heavily. Then he closed his gloved hand into a fist. I felt a rush of power, and the two remaining gemstones turned completely black.

A halo of black light enveloped him. The temperature dropped. The cold hit me like a knife, and when I breathed out, the air crystallized in front of my face.

I blinked, and he was gone. A shadow rippled across the ground of the parking lot, coating everything it touched with a mantle of frost.

Patrick limped over to where Modred was standing. He took the vampire's hand, smiling. "Wow. I can't believe you heard my call."

"Corpses heard your call, magnate. You shouted."

"It's what Tess told me to do."

Modred turned to me. "That was quick thinking."

"Yeah. I've been known for it, on occasion." I managed to get to my feet, coming to stand behind Patrick. "Lucky you were close by."

"Yes." His expression was unreadable. "I was in the area."

"Have you got a car?"

He looked at me strangely. "You require a vehicle?"

"My car battery's dead. I killed it."

"Ah. With the electrical blast." He stared at a space a few inches above my shoulder for a second. Then he nodded. "I've called the other monitors. Someone will come to pick us up soon."

"That's some handy telepathy."

"It's closer to sonar, actually."

"Right." I blinked. "Like a vampire dolphin."

Patrick stared at me. Then he burst out laughing.

I laughed, too. But I wasn't quite as relieved as he was. The necromancer was gone, but I knew he'd be back. We'd barely scraped by.

And I didn't trust Modred for a second.

8

I expected a fleet of vampire limousines to pick us up. I was a bit surprised when a lone taxicab pulled into the parking lot. A young guy in a baseball cap leaned his head out of the driver's-side window, smiling. Wavy blond curls spilled out from under the brim of the cap.

"Need a lift?"

Modred glanced at his watch. "You were supposed to be here ten minutes ago."

"Traffic was snarly."

"I don't believe you."

The driver rolled his eyes. "Fine. I stopped for a bite to eat."

I wasn't sure if he was talking about Taco Bell or an actual human buffet. I didn't really want to know, to be honest. Sometimes, with vampires, it was best to just stay ignorant and let them do their business in the dark.

Patrick waved to the driver. "Cyrus. What's up?"

"Not much, magnate. Just finishing my nightly beat."

I frowned. "Do you actually work for a taxi company?"

He looked at me and smiled. "Best way to patrol the city without raising suspicion from normates. Now, I don't believe we've had the pleasure of meeting. I'm Cyrus, the monitor for North and West Vancouver."

"North Vancouver," Modred corrected. "Pilar looks after the West."

"She's on sabbatical."

"That doesn't mean that her duties have been delegated to you. All of us share the responsibility of managing her territory."

"Meh—semantics." He extended his hand out the window. "At any rate, I'm single and employed, if that does anything for you."

I shook his hand. "Tess Corday. And it doesn't."

I flipped open my phone and sent Derrick a brief text. *Safe and coming home. Stay put. Tea + Motrin, plz.*

Cyrus spied the ID badge hanging from the lanyard under my jacket. "Whoa. CORE involvement. Exactly what shit-pile did you fall into, Modred?"

"We can debrief later. We have to get Miss Corday home, and get Patrick back to the *daegred* for a physical examination."

Patrick raised a hand. "I'm fine. Really. Just a few bruises."

"It's policy, magnate. You need to be examined by one of our physicians."

I stepped in front of Patrick reflexively. "Nobody's getting a checkup tonight. I don't care if the doctor has a heartbeat or not. Patrick's coming home with me, and then I'm filing a report with my office in the morning."

Modred gave me a slightly contemptible look. "Your office politics are not our concern, Miss Corday. The magnate is required to submit to a full exam after any sort of combat situation. You have your rules, and we have ours."

"Miss Corday is my mother. Call me Tess." I turned to Patrick. "Look. I don't want to cause a political incident here. If you have to go, then go. But I'd much rather you come home with me."

"Magnate, I really must insist—" Modred began.

Patrick shook his head. "Sorry. I'm going with Tess. You two are my advisors, but she's my guardian."

I tried not to let the satisfaction show on my face.

Modred stared at me for a moment. Not challenging me, per se, but rather trying to assess just how stubborn I was. I met his gaze. He blinked.

"Whatever you think is best, magnate."

"Hop in, folks. Meter's running." Cyrus grinned. "Not really. But we're letting all the heat out of the car."

Modred opened the front door. "*Drihten mödig*, Cyrus! It looks like a fast-food chain exploded in here."

Cyrus managed to look guilty. "Yeah . . . sorry about that, Mo. I was gonna clean it yesterday, but with all my extra administrative work—"

"Never mind. We can all fit in the backseat." His eyes hardened. "And don't call me Mo. We've discussed that."

"Right, right. Forgot." He winked at me.

I could see why Patrick liked Cyrus. He was like the cool skater kid who got you high before fifth-period math class. Nothing bothered him, at least not permanently, and girls dated him solely to infuriate their middle-class dads.

We all slid into the backseat. I thanked whatever powers were listening for my strict jeans preference, since a skirt would have been nightmarish in a situation like this. I ended up squeezed between both vampires, acutely aware of the half inch of space separating my knee from Modred's. He'd seemed taller when he was standing over the necromancer. Now he managed to fold up compactly, hands resting in his lap with perfect gentility.

Everyone was silent for the first few blocks. Patrick

yawned. If I knew anything about teenage boys, he'd be snoring in thirty seconds flat, regardless of the fact that he'd almost been disintegrated tonight.

I examined Modred as discreetly as I could. He had the face of a sixteen-year-old, but his eyes were much older. Until meeting Patrick, it hadn't occurred to me that a vampire could be turned so young and still survive without help. Both Mia and Patrick had the resources of the CORE watching out for them, as well as my own personal brand of fallible parenting. But Modred had obviously gone through the change a long time ago, far from the protective aegis of a magical community.

I imagined him as a boy-knight fighting in the crusades. What had he seen? Who'd sired him, and what had become of his maker and master? Was it a situation of sire-and-run, indiscriminate and cruel? Or had they been close?

I think Selena told me once that 30 percent of vampires kill their sires.

Modred was looking at me now. He'd caught me staring. Now I needed to say something, or he'd think I was some kind of desperate fang-banger.

"I like your piercing."

Really, Corday? That's what you came up with?

Modred blinked. "Thank you."

"Did it hurt?"

"It was surprisingly painful, yes."

"I don't think I've ever met a vampire with a facial piercing before."

"Have you met many vampires?"

I couldn't tell if there was a challenge beneath the question or not. His eyes didn't change. He had that vampiric trait of complete facial immobility that made it impossible to read his feelings. If he felt anything at all.

"Some," I said guardedly.

Cyrus laughed from the front seat. "Yeah. Some of my best friends are mortal, too. The mortal, the merrier, I say."

Patrick had already begun to snore. I envied him. We weren't even across the bridge yet, and already I felt like the conversation was sinking.

"You're correct, though," Modred said. "Most of us choose to avoid body modification, due to the nature of the collagen in our skin. The same elasticity that gives us regenerative powers makes us intolerant to piercings."

"Skin snaps back," Cyrus clarified, "and the piercing pops out. Quickest way to lose fifty bucks."

"Huh. I hadn't thought of that." I frowned. "So how does yours stay in?"

He lightly touched the ring in his lip. "It's made of pure silver, with a very high concentration of argentite."

"But you're allergic—" My eyes widened. "Geez. Doesn't it burn?"

"A little."

"All the time?"

He turned the ring gently. "That's why I like it."

I wasn't sure where to go from there. All I could think about was how useful the power of astral projection would be at this moment.

"So . . . what does CORE stand for again?" Cyrus asked. "I always forget."

"Central Occult Regulation Enterprise."

"Wow. So you guys basically manage every occult thing in the city limits. That sounds stressful."

"It can be."

"How does that work, exactly?" We were stopped at a red light, and Cyrus tapped his fingers against the wheel. "I mean, you must have an enormous staff. Are they invisible or something? Why haven't the normates figured it out?"

I shrugged. "The same reason they haven't discovered your *daegred*. They only see what they want to. Plus, we spend a lot of money on veiling technology."

"Oh, yeah. I heard about that. Like Klingons, right?"

"Yes. Exactly like Klingons."

Modred turned to me. "But surely they must notice. *Some* of them have to suspect something. You can't hide your activities from two million people."

"You seem to pull it off."

"We've had a lot of practice. And we're fewer. We move quietly."

"Not always."

Something flashed for the first time in his eyes. "What do you mean?"

Great. Let's piss off the elder vampire in a confined space, shall we?

I tried to keep my tone politely neutral. "All I'm saying is that some of your kin tend to bite outside the lines. They leave messes for us to clean up. It's not an enormous inconvenience, but it does create extra work."

"Some of your 'kin' do the same thing. I remember an OSI named Marcus Tremblay who butchered a young vampire. A defenseless thrall." His eyes held mine, and I felt a cold heaviness. "That mess was never adequately cleaned up. At least not to my satisfaction."

Marcus Tremblay was a stain that would never fully vanish from my life. Two years ago, he'd nearly killed both Mia and me. He'd always just seemed like a pencil-pushing asshole. I didn't realize that he might actually be a killer until it was nearly too late. The memory of being tied to a chair, drugged and taunted, while Mia looked on in horror, made the bile rise in my throat. I swallowed it down.

"Marcus was sick," I said. "And his accomplice was one of your own kin. Sabine Delacroix. A former monitor, unless I'm mistaken."

"Sabine had her own agenda. We always suspected her of treason."

"Well, now she's exiled. And Marcus is dust. Case closed."

But it wasn't really. Last year, two vampires had come close to killing me at a skytrain station in the downtown core. Sabine had sent them. Obviously, she still had a powerful reach. And Marcus's last will and testament had brought the Iblis to power by giving it a corrupt artifact to play with—Tremblay's own athame. Both of them haunted my life, one dead, the other undead.

"She was exiled by Caitlin," Modred said. "When Caitlin died, her influence died with her. That includes everyone that she ever banished."

I stared at him. "You're saying that Sabine is free?"

"Not precisely. But she has far greater mobility than she did a year ago. Unless the current magnate"—he gestured to Patrick, who was snoring peacefully, his face pressed against the window—"reinforces the ban. And that would require mastery that he doesn't yet possess."

I closed my eyes. "So I'm fucked is what you're saying."

"I wouldn't put it quite so succinctly. But there is cause for concern."

"Don't worry about it," Cyrus said. He smiled at me through the rearview. "We've got your back."

"No. We do not have anyone's back." Modred smoothed his pants, looking irritated. It was an oddly human gesture, making me think that he really was a teenager, all dressed up and on his way to some fancy dinner.

"Come on. Don't be so uptight." Cyrus took a sharp turn, and I found myself pressed against Modred. "Sure, we're not allied with the CORE, but she's also a friend of the magnate. That makes her a friend of ours."

Modred inched away from me. Touching me seemed to

pain him, as if I had some kind of exposed ulcerous sore. "We are not obligated to protect her. The CORE has seldom acted in the interests of our community, and I see no need to do them any favors, friendly or otherwise."

"Are you kidding?" I glared at him. "We clean up after you all the time. You let wild, newly sired vamps roam the city, biting whomever they please. I wouldn't be surprised if a quarter of the most violent, bloody home invasions couldn't be chalked up to hungry vampires. And you call that cooperation?"

His eyes narrowed. "The vast majority of rapists, murderers, and thieves in this city are human, Miss Corday. When we discover a rogue kin who's been feeding 'outside the lines,' as you call it, our discipline is swift and just."

"Right. I wonder if that system ever caught up with the vampires who killed my teacher. Snapped her neck with a choke chain, while I watched."

To my surprise, he looked away. "I wouldn't know anything about that."

"Well, I was fifteen at the time. You could call it a formative moment in my life. I learned that some demons never get what they deserve."

"Is it so easy to make those separations? Demon and mortal?" His eyes lingered on me. "You're part-demon yourself, are you not?"

"Sure. Not practicing, though."

Modred didn't smile. "You have a virus in your blood. Not the same as the one that all three of us share, but still, a virus. Is it true that most humans contract the M+ virus as a result of interspecies sexual assault?"

I'd never heard my power so efficiently described as a pathogen before. *The M+ virus.* It sounded like something from a B-grade horror movie.

"Cool it, Modred," Cyrus snapped. "You're being

a dick. I'm sorry, Tess. He's prejudiced against mages because—"

"You'll shut up now, Cyrus," Modred hissed, "or I'll rip out your tongue. I have no desire to discuss family matters with a member of the CORE."

Cyrus shrugged. "Fine. But you don't have to be so offensive. She practically saved the magnate's life tonight."

Modred folded his arms. "Her role in the battle was peripheral at best. If I hadn't arrived when I did, they both might have been piles of ash."

His posture reminded me of something. I looked at Patrick, then back at Modred again. I smiled. I'd seen Mia strike the exact same pose when she was losing an argument. The *all of you can just go to hell* gesture of crossed arms, narrowed eyes, and scrunched-up face.

I realized that, no matter how old Modred really was, he'd still never completely left adolescence. He may have had the bearing of a centuries-old vampire, but not too far underneath that primeval aura of experience was the soul of a teenager.

Suddenly, I felt bad for him. I wanted to say how sorry I was that his childhood had been stolen. But maybe he didn't even remember it anymore. Maybe all he knew was the inhuman coldness of all those years, pushing down on him. The ineffable sadness of watching every loved thing die, while you persisted.

He was looking at me curiously now. Maybe he sensed my pity. I cleared my throat and changed tactics.

"You're right. You arrived just in time. And I'm grateful for that."

This disarmed him slightly. He blinked. "No thanks are necessary. The magnate called, and I answered. I was merely fulfilling my duty as monitor."

"I was stuck in traffic," Cyrus said. "Otherwise, I'd have been there like a shot."

"You got there just in time," I continued. "I've never seen anything like that strange glove. It had serious magic."

"A Vorpal gauntlet."

"Is that what it's called?"

Modred nodded. "A catalyst that necromancers use to amplify their powers. The gauntlet increases their body's sensitivity to necroid materia. But it comes at a price. Using it can cause permanent physical damage."

"We don't have anything that cool."

"What about your dagger? I find its power impressive."

"Really?" I wasn't sure why that made me feel better.

He almost smiled. "A sophisticated weapon. Much more beautiful than the guns we've been forced to carry lately."

"Modred has lightsaber envy," Cyrus said.

"I do not. I simply hate guns."

"I'm not a big fan of them either," I said. "But sometimes they can be useful as a last resort. Patrick managed to clip the necromancer a few times with my Glock. I was amazed that he held the gun steady."

He looked at me strangely. "The magnate fired a weapon? Successfully?"

"He sure did."

The ghost of a smile returned. "He hasn't been trained in firearms yet. How curious that he would demonstrate an aptitude."

"I'm not sure I'd go that far. But he did manage to make contact."

I could see the pride on his face. Maybe Patrick had been right. Modred really was a good teacher, despite his archaic attitudes.

"Where would a necromancer get one of these gauntlets?" I asked. "They don't seem to be standard-issue equipment."

"Certainly not. The one who attacked you was a baronet. A member of the Dark Parliament, and one of the elite."

"Sort of like the imperial guard?"

"But without the creepy red robes," Cyrus supplied from the front seat.

Modred shook his head. "I don't know what that means. But the assassin came from Trinovantum, the hidden city. Most likely, he was one of the Ruling Nine."

"You must have really pissed them off," Cyrus said. "They're sending the big guns after you."

"They're supposed to be working with us, not trying to kill us." I sighed. "Although, the two often overlap in this job."

"Our sources tell us that there's been dissent lately in the Dark Parliament," Modred said. "The apostate is losing power. I wouldn't be surprised if a rogue faction is trying to strike at you in order to disrupt your investigation."

"Do they know as much about you as you know about them?"

Modred smiled slightly. "We hope not."

I didn't want to get in the middle of vampire power politics. I just wanted to crawl into bed and rub on some tiger balm. I massaged my aching head.

"Nobody ever cooperates. That's the nature of every investigation."

"True. But if you anticipate dissent, you stand the chance of avoiding it."

"You sound like Sun Tzu."

"I'll take that as a compliment."

Cyrus stopped the cab. We'd arrived in front of my house. I hadn't even realized that we were in the same neighborhood.

"Wait." I stared at him. "How did you know my address?"

"Don't question small miracles, Tess. Just accept them." Cyrus smiled. "It was nice to meet you."

Derrick and Mia were both sitting on the steps outside. Derrick saw me, and the tension drained from his face. It was a nice feeling. Being worried about.

I nudged Patrick. "Wake up, magnate. We're home."

"Nnh. Yeah?" He blinked sleepily, looked out the window, and smiled. "Good."

Modred opened the door, helping me out of the backseat. His hand was cold. We stood facing each other in the dark for a few seconds. Then I shrugged.

"Thanks again."

"Of course," he said simply.

"Good night, then."

"Yes. Good night." He placed a hand lightly on Patrick's shoulder. "Be safe, magnate. Get your rest."

"I will. Thanks."

"And you as well, Tess." Modred gave me an uncertain smile.

I followed Patrick to the front door. I could feel the vampires watching me, but I didn't quicken my step.

If I'd learned anything from reading *The Last Unicorn* in high school, it was that you never ran from an immortal.

9

"You look tired, Tess."

Dr. Hinzelmann peered at me from his desk. His small hands were folded politely on top of a green file folder, which, I assumed, held vital details about my life, preferences, neuroses, and failures.

I gently touched the bruise on my left cheek.

"Well, I did eat some pavement last night. I got roughly four hours of sleep, and my painkillers haven't kicked in yet."

"Would you like me to write you a prescription?"

I blinked. "You can do that?"

"Of course." He reached into his desk and pulled out a prescription pad. "What are you currently taking for pain?"

"Motrin and ice cream."

He smiled slightly, then scrawled something on the paper. "I'm giving you seven tablets of Vicodin. Take one at night with food and water." He handed me the paper.

"And don't self-medicate with anything else. It won't mix well."

I put the prescription in my pocket. "Wow. Thank you. Selena just told me to buy a heating blanket."

Hinzelmann shrugged. "Sometimes you need a little something extra. And it's a very small dose. If you come back tomorrow asking for more, I'll know something's wrong. For now, it's mostly just to help you sleep."

"I'd need a clone to help me sleep. There aren't enough hours in the night."

"Is the case taking up most of your time? Or is it something else?"

I settled back into the leather chair. It was almost more comfortable than my bed. I briefly wondered if Hinzelmann would let me have a small nap. I figured he got paid for the session no matter what.

"Things are a bit crazy at home, as usual," I said. "Patrick seems to be accumulating new responsibilities as the vampire magnate. Mia is obsessing over colleges. Derrick is trying to push his psi-proficiency to some crazy new level. I think he feels like he isn't contributing enough to the CORE as a baseline telepath."

"Do you feel that he's contributing enough?"

"Of course. He can pick thoughts out of people's brains. A few days ago, he read Selena's mind like it was a DVD. Perfect accuracy."

"But that isn't quite the same as having a combat proficiency, or being trained as an OSI. He's more of a consultant than a field agent."

I felt myself growing slightly defensive. "He's a great field agent. He's been to as many scenes as I have, and he's learning more each day."

"But there's a limit to Siegel's abilities. He can't start a fire with his telepathy, or channel earth materia like you.

According to his file, he has no telekinetic or elemental materia proficiencies."

"You have his file as well?"

Hinzelmann gave me a bland look "Tess, I have everyone's file. The Department of Psychology and Paranormal Development has files on every employee. We track their physical and mental evolution as agents of the CORE."

"That sounds ominous."

"It's just a database. Nothing to fear."

"Information is power."

"But power is just a word for a vast field of systems that structure our lives from the bottom up. It's not a static entity that bears down on you. It's like breathing."

"Yeah. I've read Foucault, too." I stretched, grimacing. Those Vicodin tablets were going to do a world of good. "It's all well and good to say that power is some magical force field, until someone's ripping out your toenails while they interrogate you. Critical theory doesn't mean a lot in that situation."

"Have you been feeling powerless lately?"

I sighed. "Well, I nearly got shot in the head last night. I had to talk to a bird-demon wearing a raincoat, who told me virtually nothing about the case." Except that my boyfriend is probably a double agent. "And I've discovered that I have almost no aptitude for learning languages."

This seemed to interest him. "Are you trying to acquire a new language?"

"Yeah. I wanted to add something to my CV, so I'm learning Spanish."

"And how is that going?"

"I tried to watch an episode of *DuckTales en español*, but I could barely understand any of it. Did you know that Uncle Scrooge is called Tío Rico? And it's *Patos Aventuras*. Which doesn't even make sense. What are 'duck adventures'? Shouldn't they be 'duck adventurers' instead?"

"I believe that would be *Patos Aventureros*."

I closed my eyes. "Of course you speak Spanish. Everyone does."

"I took a few online courses. But that's not the point." Hinzelmann tapped his fingers on the green file. The secret, sordid history of my life. "People tend to learn languages for one of three reasons. Relocation, post-secondary education, or romantic entanglement. Which category would you say most describes your situation?"

Shit. All I'd wanted to do was distract him with a non sequitur about my life, but now the conversation was taking a dangerous turn. I couldn't let anyone think that I might be involved with Lucian. If Selena suspected that we'd even shared a platonic coffee together, she'd skin me alive.

"I heard there's a pay raise that comes with having a second language."

"Why not learn a demonic dialect, then? Wouldn't it be more useful to read vampiric script?"

"I'd rather watch an Almodóvar film. It would be nice to actually get the jokes instead of just looking at all the hot naked men."

"Learning a language takes years, and it can be incredibly frustrating. Do you feel like you have the patience for that sort of endeavor?"

"I don't know. But it's not like I have any hobbies. It's nice to have an activity that isn't connected with my job in some way."

"You could go to the gym. Some people find that relaxing."

I laughed. "I already have to train several hours a day just to keep in shape. Whenever I'm on a treadmill, all I can think about is how similar it feels to running through a dark alley. The only difference is that we get towel service."

"What about art, or creative writing?"

"Seriously? I don't feel like writing poetry about the viscera that I saw yesterday in the morgue. And the only thing I ever learned to draw as a child was a replica of Garfield with a thought-bubble above his head. I used to spend hours trying to get his whiskers right with the flesh-colored crayon."

"We have some great art therapy programs."

"I think I'm fine with the Vicodin. Thanks."

Hinzelmann got up and walked over to a cabinet in the corner of the room. He opened it to reveal a cherry red Gaggia espresso machine—the precise model that Derrick had been begging me for.

He smiled infuriatingly at me. "Cappuccino?"

"You've had that here the whole time?"

"It's new, actually. I just had it installed."

"Wow. I want your job."

"Don't be too sure of that." He manipulated some complex dials, and the whole thing started to hiss and steam. "I went to Johns Hopkins for six years, and I'm sixty thousand dollars in debt. I also had to do a practicum at the Sagremor Asylum for the Paranormal. It wasn't exactly fun city."

He poured two shots of espresso into a white porcelain cup. Jesus, did he have a whole sideboard in there?

"Isn't Sagremor maximum security?"

"Yes. Designed to hold those with exceptionally violent powers." He handed me the steaming cup. "I met a pixie there who could turn himself into a cloud of mustard gas. Cranky little bastard. Killed thirteen orderlies."

"You're bullshitting me."

"Okay. You're right." He shrugged. "It was only seven orderlies."

I sipped the coffee. "This tastes like everything good in the world. I think I may have underestimated you, Dr. Hinzelmann."

"That's fine. It comes with the height differential." He sat back in the office chair, pumping it up four or five times until we were at eye level again. "Most of my professors thought I had a form of achondroplasia, so they were always trying to enroll me in studies on dwarfism. They just wanted to get another grant."

I didn't really know what to say. "That sucks."

"It wasn't so bad. They always lost sight of me in the lecture hall, which gave me the chance to copy off the people sitting next to me."

My eyes widened. "You cheated?"

"Of course. Everyone cheats a little in medical school."

I frowned. "Wait. Is this some kind of analytical trap?"

"What do you mean?"

"Come on. The espresso—which is fucking divine, by the way—the prescription, the sudden sharing of information. Are you just trying to soften me up so you can dig even deeper into my messed-up psyche?"

"I wasn't aware that your psyche was messed up." Hinzelmann sipped his own coffee, then leaned back in the chair. "I'm not going to say that you're 'normal,' because that's not a word that has much use in my profession. Frankly, neither of us is normal. I'm a kobold, and you're a mage. But we still have many of the same basic psychological investments and concerns."

"Is that like a caste thing, being a kobold?"

He looked at me strangely. "Didn't you take classes in demihuman biology?"

Hmm. Was that the course that I slept through, or the one that I failed?

Maybe it was the one with the professor who always wore high heels and smelled like a Givenchy counter. That was when Derrick was going through his nuclear breakup, so all I remembered was buying fun-size Twix in bulk and watching *The Hours* until I prayed for self-immolation.

"My course work was a long time ago," I said.

Hinzelmann sighed. "Kobolds are the oldest phylogenetic class of the goblin species. We lived in underground cities powered by geothermal energy while most of Europe was killing itself during the Dark Ages."

"Sorry. I didn't mean to offend you. I know more about hostile demon species, since those are the ones I usually deal with."

That was a lie. I barely knew anything about Vailoid demons, and I'd practically been dismembered by one. But there's only so much you can retain from lectures. It's not like Derrick remembered anything from his History of Psychic Phenomena class, except for how great the professor's ass looked in a pair of chinos.

"It's fine." He still looked a bit stung. "I applied to teach a seminar on goblin history, but my unit coordinator told me that there wasn't enough interest in the course. It's just a bit depressing. Ever since *Harry Potter*, people think that all we do is work in a stupid wizard's bank. Most of my kobold friends are grad students."

"Oh—I remember something." I smiled. "You're allergic to eggs, right?"

"Most goblins have a dairy intolerance, yes. But I've been taking Lactaid for a few years now, and it works pretty well."

We fell into an awkward silence. There didn't seem to be much else to say.

I had no idea how we'd gone from talking about my stress at home to discussing paranormal dietary restrictions. But I wasn't complaining. I was actually starting to enjoy these sessions with Hinzelmann. It gave me a break from worrying about what might try to kill me tomorrow. Here, I could just let my mind wander. And if Selena thought I was actually making progress as a human being, so much the better.

"What do you think I'm digging for, Tess?"

I looked up. "Excuse me?"

"Earlier, you were afraid that I was 'softening' you up so that I could dig into your psyche." His yellow eyes regarded me impassively. "What is it you think I'm digging for? Neurotic treasure?"

"Why not? There's a whole El Dorado of crazy in my brain."

"But you seem to be doing just fine. After a series of incredibly traumatic incidents over the past two years, you've shown remarkable resilience. A lot of people in your situation would be asking for more than just a light prescription to help them sleep."

I wasn't sure I liked where this was going. "I manage. I guess."

He opened up the green folder, reading with a veiled expression. I found myself holding my breath. I wasn't sure why.

"It says here," Hinzelmann began, "that you only achieved legal guardianship of Mia Polanski last year. And only after a lengthy court process."

"Yes. I remember the early-morning hearings. They were fun."

"And Patrick Donovan is still completing the legal emancipation process. Which means that his current living situation with you is tenuous at best."

Right. Never trust an analyst. He'd been working me over like a meat tenderizer, and now he was leaning in for the grisly finishing move. I took a deep breath and tried to keep my expression neutral.

"From what I understand," I replied, "Patrick is nearly emancipated. He has no living relatives, and Derrick and I have both petitioned the court for guardianship. My superior has already written a letter of recommendation."

"But Patrick also has strong ties to the vampire community. There's a distinct possibility that they'll issue a counterclaim based on shared cultural values, which could degenerate into a tangled legal battle." He looked at the file, not at me, as he spoke. "The CORE's negotiations with the vampire community have been especially fraught since the murder of Sebastian Escavalon, two years ago. That was the case that prompted you to petition for guardianship of Mia, was it not?"

"It sounds like you already know everything. What's the point in asking me questions if it's all in your file folder?"

He finally looked up. "I have data, but there's also a lot missing. Your memories. Your emotions. I can't tell anything by looking at these reports, except for the fact that you seem to have been very busy for the past two years."

I finished the coffee. Suddenly, it tasted like betrayal. I set down the cup and shifted position in my chair. "Yeah. I'm kind of a magnet for human devastation."

"I'm not bringing up these uncertainties to make you uncomfortable, Tess. I just want you to address the reality of the situation. There is a chance that, despite your best efforts, Patrick may not be living with you forever. And Mia's seropositive status is still in question. Her VR plasmid count is low at the moment, but if it increases, she could be remanded to a CORE clinic."

"So—what—" I glared at him. "I'm supposed to have a eureka moment, where I realize that my life is fragile? I know that already. My life is like one of those towers of crystal wineglasses that you see at a wedding." I chuckled. "Not my wedding, of course. A real *Wedding Story* wedding, without casualties. But the concept's the same. One demon blows on it, and the whole thing shatters. I don't need you to tell me that."

"But acknowledging it and facing it aren't the same thing."

"What do you want me to do? Practice a mantra? Mia's sick. I know that. And Patrick belongs to a world that I'm not a part of. He gets closer to it every day, and there's nothing I can do to stop him, because that's where he comes from. He belongs to a culture that's existed since the dawn of time. Who am I to deprive him of that?"

"You don't know that he wants to be a part of that culture. Maybe he's scared and just wants you to protect him."

I rolled my eyes. "He's seventeen. All he wants to do is watch porn and sneak a few cigarettes when he thinks I'm not looking. But he also has a legacy to think about. Caitlin Siobahn made him the magnate, and he has a responsibility to the city itself."

"You're arguing as an employee of the CORE." He looked at me squarely, and there was something less clinical in his eyes this time. "But what about as a parent? You saved Patrick Donovan from certain death at the hands of an Iblis. You brought him into your family. Now he has an entirely different family, pulling him in another direction. That can't sit easily with you."

I shrugged. "He's almost eighteen. He can do what he wants."

But I could feel my eyes welling up slightly.

I wanted to blame it on the lack of sleep, but I knew that Hinzelmann was more than right. Patrick had lived with me for a year. I'd washed his underwear, vacuumed under his bed, and convinced him to try watercress in a stir-fry (as long as it was smothered in baby corn). As far as I was concerned, he was part of my family. And no Anglo-Saxon-speaking vampire was going to give him a better home than I could.

"I'm not his mother," I said finally. "I understand that. I'm not stupid. He has a million questions about his heritage, and I can't answer them. I can't even help him with his geometry homework, since I was such a spaz at math in high school."

I shook my head. "But I also know that he cares about us. He wants to live with us, but the monitors are pressuring him, trying to make him more vampire than human. Eventually, they're going to win. He has to become fully vampire, or else he'll never be able to rule the city. And who's to say that he won't make an incredible magnate? I don't want to stand in the way of his destiny."

"What if someone had stood in the way of your destiny, years ago?"

I frowned. "What do you mean?"

Hinzelmann rested his chin on his folded hands. It was a strangely intimate posture, as if he was about to tell me a secret. "The CORE found you when you were just twelve years old. They trained you, indoctrinated you, convinced you that the only way to control your powers was to join them. But what if someone had told you the opposite? What if someone had urged you to stay away instead? There are wild talents, after all. Latents. People who can still channel materia, but who do it without sanctioned training or guidance by CORE practitioners."

"What are you getting at?" My face was starting to ache again. The coffee had given me an unpleasantly esoteric feeling, as if I was floating outside of my body, a wired and dry-mouthed psychic projection. "Do you want me to admit that the CORE was wrong in training me? I'm sure my supervisor would love to hear that."

"Everything you say in these sessions is confidential."

"Bullshit."

"You don't have to believe me. But I swear to you, anything you say in this room will remain in confidence. We aren't taping. My notes are sealed."

He had a point. I still hadn't been able to discover a hidden camera anywhere. And Selena didn't seem to have any knowledge of our conversations so far. Not that they were especially probative to begin with.

"So I can say whatever I want."

"Absolutely."

We stared at each other silently for a few seconds. I swallowed. Thoughts warred inside my brain.

I'm terrified.

I'm angry all the time.

I'm surprisingly horny.

I miss my parents.

I have no idea if I'm doing anything right.

I don't know how to raise two kids.

I still feel like a kid. I'm only twenty-six.

I can't figure out how to record anything with my DVD player. It has something to do with the fucking tuner, but every time I hit TV/VIDEO on the remote control, like Derrick told me to, I just get the same black screen.

I never feel smart.

I suck at badminton.

Sometimes I'm so tired of my job, all I can think about is quitting, moving to Mexico, and making beaded jewelry.

Even though I'm not fat anymore, I still feel like I am, especially when I'm standing in an elevator for some reason.

I may be in love with a necromancer.

The alarm on Hinzelmann's desk went off. He pressed the button to make it stop, then closed the green folder.

"Looks like our time's up for this morning."

I rose, straightening my pants even though they weren't wrinkled. "Right. Thanks for the chat."

"It was my pleasure."

I'll bet it was. Asshole.

I smiled and walked out of his office. I couldn't figure out what pissed me off more. Was it the fact that he'd so obviously manipulated me?

Or was it that he'd been right about nearly everything?

10

I met Becka in the AV lab, and was a bit surprised to find her staring at *Las Meninas*, the painting from Ordeño's living room. It was laid across a glass table, and the frame had been carefully removed to expose the borders. A specialized ELMO document camera had been set up around the painting, and it projected a magnified image onto an adjacent monitor. Velázquez looked larger than life on the LCD screen, the Cross of Santiago burning like a brand against his surcoat.

Becka looked up. "Hey. As you can see, we finally managed to acquire most of Ordeño's art collection. The necromancers are being kind of twitchy about it, so we can't keep them for too long."

"They're twitchy about everything." I held out a large coffee. "Are you allowed to drink this near the painting?"

She took the steaming cup from me. "Probably not. But this is a copy, so if I spill on it . . . meh. The original's still safe in the Prado."

"You're sure it's a copy? Ordeño was pretty long-lived after all."

"Cindée used a Fourier-Transform Microscope to analyze the paint, and it's definitely not four hundred years old." She sighed. "We haven't finished looking at everything, though. He may have some originals mixed in with the copies."

I stared at the painting, my gaze divided between the object itself and the projection on the wall. It was a strange tableau. Velázquez the painter was standing next to a canvas, which seemed to be blocking the actual subject of the painting. What the observer ended up looking at was a little girl, blond, wearing a beautiful dress and surrounded by two young female attendants. All three girls had pale, almost blanched skin, and their eyes held the suggestion of melancholy.

Next to them stood two small figures, one of whom was definitely a dwarf, and the other who may have been either a dwarf or a young boy. A sleeping dog lay under the small person's foot, and I couldn't tell if he was stroking it or shaking it awake.

A man and a woman stood behind the girls, seeming to be in the midst of a conversation. The woman looked vaguely like a nun or a lady-in-waiting, and reminded me—although I didn't want to admit it—of one of the female Grail-keepers from the Monty Python film. Zoot, I think her name was. The man was shadowed, resembling an indistinct pillar of darkness and ochre.

The door to the chamber where everyone had been positioned was open, and a male figure stood poised in the doorway. It was impossible to tell whether he was coming or going, but something about him seemed to be in motion. To the right of the glowing doorway was a mirror, hanging from the wall like a silver frame suspended in space. In the mirror, one could barely make out two reflected figures, which may or may not have been the figures that Velázquez himself was painting on the canvas.

"It seems sad," I said. "And pretty. And dark."

Becka nodded. "I think it's all of those things. And what makes it so interesting is that you can't really determine who the 'real' subject of the painting is. Because the observer's perspective and the subject's perspective are the same."

"Right. Like standing in a blind spot." I peered closer. "Are there two dwarves, or is that a child with his foot on the dog?"

She squinted. "Another dwarf, I think. But he does look like a little boy."

"He has such pretty shoes."

I heard footsteps in the hallway. A set of high heels click-clicking against the polished concrete floor. They sounded vaguely familiar. Then I felt the presence attached to the heels, a genetic signature that I would have recognized anywhere. Powerful and stylish at the same time.

Duessa stepped through the doorway. She wore peri-winkle Jimmy Choo heels and a black pencil skirt with a fierce blue top. Her hair was pinned up, and I doubted that anything short of a hailstorm would be able to move it.

She was on her cell. "Right. If he wants it, he'll have to sign it out. No, just—" She smiled indulgently, holding the phone away from her mouth, and whispered: "I'm so sorry. This'll just take a moment."

I nodded. "Of course. Take your time."

You just didn't rush someone like Duessa. She lived in several different worlds, and communicating with mortals seemed difficult for her sometimes. Getting a solid answer from her—about anything—was like winning the meta-physical lottery.

"No." Duessa sighed. "No, it's in the other cupboard. The one with the label that says CONDOMS AND LUBE.

Remember, we bought the label maker, and you—right, right. From Staples. Right."

Becka just stared at me. I shrugged.

"Yes, that's the one. In there. It's way in the back. Behind the dental dams. How many of those do we have, by the way? Do we need more?" She blinked. "We have that many? Jesus, did we get them in bulk?"

"I thought she was an antiquities expert," Becka whispered.

"She is. She also runs a shelter for mage runaways and sex workers."

"Ah."

Duessa was shaking her head. "If it's not there, it must be in one of the plastic totes. Look in the TV room, behind the box of toys. I don't— Well, ask Dukwan; he's the one who had them last. If he's—" She sighed. "*Pobrecito*. Let him sleep, then. Call me when he wakes up. *Sí. Vale. Un besito. Ciao.*"

She closed the phone. "Sorry. Business call."

"No problem at all," I replied. "We appreciate you coming down to the lab again. You must be busy."

"I was born busy. Did you speak with the Seneschal?"

"Yeah. We chatted in his Hobbit-hole. It was very revealing."

Duessa rolled her eyes. "Didn't tell you shit, did he? *¡Hijo de pavo!* That old bird pisses me off. Likes to hoard his secrets like candy."

I wasn't sure if I should mention what he'd said about Lucian or not. It wasn't that I didn't trust Becka. I just didn't want to put him under the microscope. At least not yet.

"Actually, he did give me a name. *El alquimista*. Does that ring a bell?"

She raised an eyebrow. "That's what he said? *El alquimista*?"

"You don't sound convinced."

For the first time since we'd met, Duessa actually looked surprised. "No—I mean, it's possible, but—"

"But what?"

She shrugged. "*El alquimista* is *un riçon*. A fairy tale. He's like that character—how do you call him—the doctor who drinks the potion?"

"You mean Jekyll and Hyde?"

"*¡Claro!* Dr. Jekyll. He was supposed to be an alchemist looking for *la piedra de la filosofía.* The philosopher's stone, or *cincero elementa*. Some say he worked in the court of King Philip IV; others that he was the personal physician to Queen Mariana of Austria." She chuckled. "Whatever the case, he never found what he was looking for. But he did stumble across something else instead: *la manticora*. A manticore."

Becka's eyes widened. "Isn't that the thing with the lion's head and the scorpion's tail? I remember it from the cover of a Piers Anthony novel."

"It's a paradaemon," I said. "Something like a cross between a pureblooded demon and an elemental spirit. They live on the prime elemental planes, where materia exists in its purest form."

"You don't usually see them and live to tell about it," Duessa added.

"And did *el alquimista* survive his encounter?"

"Supposedly, he made a deal with *la manticora*. He did something for her, and she fulfilled one wish in return. But in the end, she turned on him, and *el alquimista* died a horrible death." She smiled. "That's usually where the story gets creative, so that you can scare *los niños*. He gets cooked and eaten; he gets flayed alive; his bones get turned into jelly. Blah, blah, brush your teeth and don't talk back, end of story."

"So you're sure he wasn't a real person?"

"Anything's possible. But I remember *mi abuela* telling

me that story. It's older than this painting. And I never heard anything about a suit of armor being made for him. What would an alchemist need armor for? He was surrounded by potions all day long, and he never left his laboratory."

I sighed. "Awesome. So the bird's yanking my chain."

"Even so," Becka interjected, "it wouldn't hurt to brush up on the legend, would it? Maybe your informant was speaking in some kind of code."

"True. But it's just as possible that he's a crazy old demon living in a hedge."

"Either way, I can pull up more information and e-mail it to you." Becka grinned. "I really do love research."

"Cool. Knock yourself out."

"Now . . ." Duessa walked over to the table. "Speaking of legends, let's take a boo at the Velázquez. Ordeño had good taste."

"Did you know him personally?"

"I wouldn't go that far. But we ran in some of the same circles. Six degrees of undead separation, that sort of thing."

"I understand that he was sort of mentor to Lucian Agrado."

"Oh, you understand, do you?" She smiled at me. "*Preciosa*, don't be so sure that you understand anything about Lucian Agrado. He's a lot like this painting—lovely, confusing, and just the right amount of fucked-up. Don't go jumping to any conclusions about the boy until you've spent more time with him."

Duessa gave me a sly look. She knew full well that I'd spent plenty of time with him, but she was covering for me. A nice favor, and one that I'd probably have to repay someday. Immortals always collected their fees.

I just nodded. "Right. He's an enigma wrapped in a fitted tee. I get it."

"He's hot," Becka said. "For a necromancer, I mean."

"Fire's hot, too, baby. Doesn't mean you should play with it." Duessa returned her attention to the painting. "It's a nice reproduction. Nineteenth century?"

Becka glanced at another computer screen. "According to the microscopy results, it's somewhere between one hundred and one hundred fifty years old. It's tricky to know for sure, since there aren't really any forensic databases for paintings—the closest thing is the FBI database of automobile paint."

"So if Velázquez had spray painted *Las Meninas*, we'd be set." I stood next to Duessa, examining the picture. "Okay, seriously—two dwarves or one?"

Her eyes hardened. "If you're referring to *los enanos de la Reina*, then there are two: Mari-Bárbola and Nicolasito Pertusato. They were both domestic servants within the queen's entourage." Her expression softened, and then she smiled a strange, almost faraway smile, as if recalling something familiar. "They gave Mari-Bárbola four pounds of snow every year. Nobody's sure why. Maybe she used it to cool off in the summer, or slept in it, or ate handfuls of it. But Ponte wrote a poem about her. *Que cada boca suya rumie del invierno.* 'With each mouthful she chews, she ruminates upon the winter.'"

"Did you know her?"

"Nobody really did." She stared at the painting again. I guess that was the best answer I was going to get.

"Okay." I exhaled. "Ordeño's body was found lying underneath this painting. He had other paintings by Velázquez, but none were hung as prominently as this one, in the middle of his living room. Can you think of any reason that it might be significant?"

"The painting itself?" Duessa asked. "Or its placement?"

"Both."

"Well, it's no surprise that any fan of Velázquez would have a nice reproduction of *Las Meninas*. It's a beautiful and puzzling work of art. Maybe he hung it there so his guests could appreciate it."

"But that doesn't explain why he died underneath it."

"Couldn't that be a coincidence?"

I gave her a look. "Do you really think so? He was wearing a suit of armor from the Golden Age, and he died underneath a painting from the same era. Either the guy's just crazy about the Renaissance, or we have a pattern."

Duessa examined the image that was projected on the wall. "It's amazing what we can do with technology. *Las Meninas* didn't even appear in a public museum until the end of the nineteenth century. All an observer could do was stare at it passively, trying to figure out its perspective. Now we can blow it up and study it with algorithms and computer programs. Kind of destroys the mystery."

"Actually," Becka said, "in some ways, it only increases the mystery. If we use a computer program to calculate all of the orthogonals and geometric factors in the painting, we can determine precisely how every subject is placed—their orientation, their depth of field, everything." She pushed up her glasses. "But we still can't figure out why the painter created them that way, or why he used those techniques. So a part of the mystery remains."

Duessa sighed. "I'm just worried that, one of these days, they're going to figure out a computer program that explains all of the magic in the world, down to the last fairy wing. Then everything will just become an endless list of numbers and commands in some government database. And before we know it, they'll start saying who can have access to the data and who can't. Beating Mother Nature at her own game."

Becka shrugged. "It's also just as probable that magic, like any genetic mutation, will eventually be eradicated from our DNA. Or it will become a useless appendage, like the pinkie toe, or the epiglottis."

We both stared at her.

She blinked. "That's the dangly thing in the back of your—"

Duessa cleared her throat. "Anyway. The problem with this painting is that, the more you subject it to analysis, the more it confounds you. It's nearly impossible to say that you *know* who Velázquez is painting, since you can't see what's on the canvas. He could very well be paining *Las Meninas* itself. A painting of a painting of a painting, going on to infinity."

I frowned. "But what about the man and the woman in the mirror? You can see their faces. Aren't they supposed to be the king and queen?"

"Probably. They could be Philip IV and Mariana of Austria. And if the mirror is directly within the observer's line of sight, what would that mean?"

I stared at the painted mirror. A man and a woman stared back at me, but their features were vague and cloudy. I couldn't say for sure what their expressions might be, what they were thinking or feeling, or even if they truly existed at all.

"If the mirror is reflecting what's on the canvas," I said, "and the subjects of the painting are within my line of sight, it would mean that we're actually occupying the same space. The king and queen are standing where I'm standing. That's why I can see their reflection."

Duessa nodded, still smiling. "But that seems impossible. Unless he's trying to suggest that every observer is also Spanish royalty. And what about the Infanta Margarita, and her two *meninas*, Doña María Augustina and Doña Isabel de Velasco? The painting is named after them, but they're only handmaidens. And Margarita isn't the subject of the painting, but she seems to be in the middle of everything. All of the light in the room is falling on her face and her hair."

"She looks sad."

"Maybe she is. Children are allowed to be sad."

I thought about my own childhood. Had I been a melancholy kid? Having the ability to cause an earthquake when you're ten years old can definitely have psychological repercussions. But I didn't feel that my adolescence was particularly sad. I felt like it was normal, which was the strange thing.

Because I wasn't normal. I'd never been normal, and I never would be. I watched my best friend, Eve, die in a fire, and I couldn't save her. The flames hadn't touched me, but they'd reduced her body to ash and calcined bone, crumbling to the touch like a tiny form made of snow and carbon.

You can't see her now, my mother had said. *You don't want to see her.*

Then, I'd trusted everything that my mother said. She was a goddess to me. But after discovering that she'd been a mage all along, that she'd lied to me—just as I'd lied to her—about magic and its place in our family, I found myself revisiting old memories with a sense of anxiety. When had she been telling the truth, and when had she been lying? If magic could spin illusions and cloud thoughts, if it could make you think and feel things against your will, then did I really remember my childhood correctly? Did I know everything I thought I knew?

How much of it was verbatim, and how much had my mother crafted and manipulated in order to provide me with what she thought was a "normal" life? And what made her think that keeping her powers a secret would somehow make us a normal family? She'd always known that I was part of the CORE. She'd even worked with my old teacher, Meredith Silver, to ensure that I was trained. So what had she gained by staying quiet all these years and pretending to be dumb?

It still didn't add up. And my mother wasn't talking about it. Lately, she wasn't talking about anything except recipes, bird-watching, and whatever outfit she'd found on sale at Winners for Mia. I didn't want to hear about any more *supercute* hoodies and skirts that she'd bought two-for-one. I wanted to know why she left the CORE and stopped practicing magic.

Or if she ever really had.

"Maybe it's really a painting of Ordeño," I said.

Duessa looked at me strangely. "Why would you think that?"

"The guy was probably over four hundred, and there's a chance that he knew Velázquez. Maybe the reflection in the mirror is just a trick to cover up the real subject of the painting."

"But why would Velázquez paint a necromancer when he was supposed to be painting the king and queen of Spain?"

"I don't know. Why is there a dog in the picture? Why did he paint so much of the ceiling? We could ask questions forever. All we know is that Ordeño, the painting, and the suit of armor are somehow connected."

Duessa shook her head slowly. "It irks me—the thought of Luiz Ordeño in a suit of armor. He was a lawyer, not a *caballero*. He had enemies, but they weren't the kind that would attack you with a sword."

"Lucian seemed to think that the armor looked more like it was designed for a tournament. Maybe he just liked to dress up."

Becka's eyes brightened. "Like my neighbor!"

Duessa looked at her. "What about your neighbor?"

"He's a member of the Society for Creative Anachronism. He dresses up like a knight, and his boyfriend's a milkmaid, or a wench or something."

She sighed. "That's wonderful for them. But I don't

think Ordeño was into playing dress-up. He had to be wearing the armor for protection."

"But protection from what?" I was still looking at the painting. I couldn't help it. The Infanta Margarita's eyes knew something, and she wasn't telling. I wanted to climb in there and ask her. "You said yourself—his enemies weren't going to come at him with a sword or a crossbow. If they wanted to eliminate him, they'd blow up his apartment or mow him down in the street."

"I never understood the use of that verb," Becka mumbled to herself. "How do you *mow* someone with a car? It's not a lawn mower. If you can mow with your car, does that mean you can speed with your lawn mower?"

Duessa ignored her. "The armor isn't what it seems. I don't know what it is exactly, or what it's capable of. But it's definitely special."

"Couldn't you chat with it again?" I asked. "Maybe oil its hinges, promise it a nice polishing if it gives you more information?"

She smiled. "I wish it worked that way. But it's like talking to a stone. It doesn't precisely tell you anything, does it?"

Duessa was right. Inanimate objects did have their own kind of consciousness, but it was pretty one-sided. When I opened my mind to them, I received a confusing welter of impressions: dark, cold, dampness, layers of earth, immobility, density, and a kind of low, monotonous song composed of a single, unwavering note. They were alive, but not in the same way that even single-celled organisms and amoebae had "life." Their life was ancient, inscrutable, and as opaque to us as our lives were to them.

Still, it was nice to hear their song. I'd be sad if I stopped hearing it.

I tried to refocus on the case. It was growing increasingly more difficult, as of late, to wrap my mind fully around the particulars of my job. Like a dog in an off-leash park, it wanted to wander everywhere, and getting it to return was a bit of a task. I thought about the pills that Hinzelmann had prescribed. Maybe a good night's sleep would help. Maybe the chemicals would kill my dreams. That would be a relief.

"Is it possible," I asked, "that the armor and the painting are two halves of a magical artifact? Maybe we're supposed to put them together somehow."

Becka raised an eyebrow. "Are you suggesting duct tape?"

"Maybe. If the duct tape were magical."

"I think I see what you're getting at," Duessa said, "but it's not that simple. I mean, theoretically, you could create a kind of polymer out of water and earth materia, and use it to bind the two together. But all you'd be left with is an artifact sandwich. It wouldn't produce anything but rust and paint chips."

I frowned. "There's got to be some *Matrix*-y way to handle this. Like, breaking down the armor into its molecular components, and then—"

Duessa raised a hand. "Nobody will be 'breaking down' the priceless *armadura* from the Habsburg Dynasty. Besides—the armor isn't necessarily the heart of the puzzle. There could be other clues hiding in his apartment."

"We've been over it with every piece of detection equipment the lab has access to. If there's something hidden, we should have found it by now."

Her eyes sparkled slightly. "Unless someone else found it first."

"Huh." I gave her a long look. "You think the necromancers are keeping evidence from us? That would be a violation of our agreement."

"Of course. And they'd never, ever violate something written on paper. That would be unthinkable."

Becka looked confused. "I'm not sure what we're talking about anymore. Do we think that Lucian Agrado stole evidence from the scene?"

"Who said anything about Lucian Agrado?" Duessa shrugged. "I'm not suggesting that the necromancers tampered with evidence. I'm just reminding you of the fact that they arrived on the scene first. Or so you tell me."

Once again, I was back to thinking about Lucian. Lucian, who wouldn't return my calls, text messages, or e-mails. Lucian, who seemed to have dropped off the face of the planet without so much as a wave good-bye. Liar. Thief. Illusionist. Bastard. The person who drifted through my thoughts all day long, reclined, indolent, as if he'd taken up residence on some comfortable divan in my psyche.

And why did my psyche have furniture to begin with? Was this something that I should be worried about?

I stared at the Infanta Margarita. "She knows something."

It was better than saying, *He knows something.* At least I could speculate openly about a work of art.

"You mean Margarita?" Duessa looked at the small girl. "See how she receives the cup of water from her *menina*? She's looking at us, but she's also taking the water. It's as if she's saying, *Go ahead, try to figure out anything about my life. You can watch my actions, but you'll never know me.*"

"Did Velázquez know her?"

"He was the *mayordomo del palacio*. He knew the ins and outs of the royal court, and he'd painted the Infanta before. But nobody can say for sure if he really knew her. Even as a child, she seems difficult to read."

"And what about you?"

She looked at me calmly. "What about me, Tess?"

"You know what I mean."

"Are you asking if I knew the Infanta? Or if I knew Velázquez?"

"Both."

Her expression grew thoughtful. "The Infanta? No. Velázquez? You could say we knew each other. But not well."

I smiled suddenly. "Maybe he was painting you on the canvas. Did you ever pose for him?"

Her look soured. *"La perra no cumplió su promesa."*

I blinked. *"¿Perdone?* I don't understand."

She sighed, still looking at the Infanta. *"Yo tampoco.* Me neither."

11

"How many wings were on the armor, dear?"

My mother was washing dishes while I cleared the rest of the table.

Mia and Patrick had already retired to the living room and were watching TV, their bellies full of garlic mashed potatoes and meat loaf. I watched my mother's hands as they slipped into the hot water, passing a cloth swiftly but deliberately over a plate (from the set of dishes that she'd given me last year). Her movements were ordinary and graceful at the same time. She flicked water from the edge of the plate, then set it down to dry on a white towel laid flat across the counter.

"Two," I replied. "Like bat wings. And each wing has six eyes on it, half open, half closed. It's creepy."

For some reason, I was less worried about sharing case-related information with my mother than I was about the possibility of her realizing that my sponges stank, since I didn't wash them often enough. She was a safe. Anything

I told her would remain undisclosed. And really, I had to tell someone with a halfway normal perspective. I already came to her for advice about everything else. Why not armor?

"Like a cherubim," she said. "Remember when I used to read *A Wind in the Door* to you, when you were little? What was the name of that cloud-spirit with all the wings and eyes and flaming tongues?"

"Proginoskes."

"Right!" She shook her head, rinsing a mug. "You cried at the end. But you still made me read it to you three times."

"Four times."

I peered into the living room. Patrick and Mia were deeply engrossed in a shampoo commercial. *Mad Men* would be on soon, and I wasn't allowed to talk for the duration of the episode. Mia's rules.

"When's Derrick coming home?" She'd finished with the dishes, and was gently drying her hands. "I wanted to ask him a question about our satellite dish. Your father can't do much except swear at it."

"It's date night, so he'll be home late. I think he and Miles went to some lounge in Yaletown. One of those places that only serves clear beverages."

"How odd. The lounge, I mean. Not the date." She sat down at the kitchen table, slowly turning her wedding ring back and forth. She always did that when she had something to ask me. "How long have they been together now?"

"Miles and Derrick?" I actually had to think about it. "A year and a month. Or a year and two months, maybe. It depends if you calculate it from the time they first hooked up, or the time they actually—"

She made a face. "I don't really need to know the mechanics, dear. I was just curious how long they'd been dating."

"I like him. And he's good for Derrick."

"As long as Derrick's happy. That's what's important."

I shrugged. "Happiness isn't always the linchpin of a romance. You've got to have your bumps and scrapes as well."

"It sounds like you're describing an unpleasant hike."

"You know what I mean."

"A relationship shouldn't be too painful, Tess. If it is, you're probably doing something wrong."

"What about you and Dad? You've had your rough patches."

"Of course." She got up and started to make tea. There was no sense in reminding her that I drank coffee. My mother would always make me tea, and I would always drink it. Because it was her tea, and nobody else could make it like her. "You don't stay together for twenty-six years without running into a few briar patches."

"Now it sounds like we're talking about Peter Rabbit."

She didn't even bother turning around. Her hands rooted through my cupboards with startling efficiency, finding the loose-leaf tea, spooning it into two mugs, then setting the water to boil. "It makes sense. Relationships are like things that happen in the forest. There's always danger involved, but good stuff, too. Don't medieval stories always involve a forest of some kind?"

"And a dwarf with a cart, usually. I'm not sure why, though."

She smiled as the water came to a boil. For some reason, whenever my mother cooked, the water simply boiled faster. Butter melted with greater alacrity. Meat browned as if it had always wanted to.

On the nights that I cooked, Derrick took the batteries out of the smoke alarm.

"When I was a little girl, I used to read stories about King Arthur," she said. "All of his knights were always feasting and crying and playing tricks on each other. So polite and so violent. I thought magic must be like that. The tinted ermine of Morgan le Fay's cloak; Guinevere's arched eyebrow; the Fisher King with his wound that could never be healed. I thought it was all just a big adventure in the forest."

She returned to the table, setting both mugs down. I inhaled the floral steam. There were wrinkles around my mother's eyes, but she was beautiful. I wanted to know what she knew. I wanted her certainty, and the balletic ease with which she moved through a room.

But mostly, I wanted to know why she'd hid a part of herself from me for nearly twenty-four years. To closet one's magic was sometimes a necessity, but that was for the rest of the world. We were a dyad. Mother/daughter. Our relationship was supposed to be a circuit along which any number of energies could pass, including materia. She'd closed that circuit long ago. I needed to know why.

"It's not always like the stories," I said. "Mostly, magic just hurts you. And it's not even taxable."

She chuckled softly. "It can give you some beautiful moments, though. Listening to a stream argue with itself. Making fire out of a stone." She looked distant. "I can remember lying underneath the stars and trying to hear all of the energy left over from the Big Bang. What's that called again?"

"Microwave background radiation?"

"Yes." She smiled. "It sounded like cicadas. Or sometimes like the crinkly cellophane that you put in Easter baskets."

"You could hear it that clearly?"

"Not every night. But if the sky was clear, and the stars were exceptionally bright, it could be quite loud. Sometimes I fell asleep listening to it."

"That was before you met Dad?"

I tried not to invest too much intensity in the question. But she felt it anyway. She sipped her tea and gave me a look.

"What exactly do you want to know, Tess?"

I let the mug warm my hands. How could I explain that I wanted to crawl into her brain and see everything, like a movie being played in black and white?

But it simply wasn't polite to eavesdrop on other people's memories, no matter how compelling they were. Derrick had told me once that reading minds was almost never worth the trouble that it caused. At best, you got the vague impression of something that you wouldn't have known otherwise, like watching a DVD somewhere in the middle. At worst, you learned something precise and terrible that you'd never be able to forget. That's why the brain was designed to be a closed system.

"Why did you really leave the CORE?" I asked.

She turned her mug slowly, as if feeling the need to turn something more substantial than the wedding ring. "I've told you that. I left because I wanted you to have a normal life. Or as close to normal as possible."

"But I joined the CORE when I was twelve. So in the end, you weren't protecting me from anything. You even worked with Meredith to get me placed as an OSI."

My mother shook her head. "You're wrong. Meredith and I had worked together in the past. When your name came across her desk as a potential, she contacted me. But I didn't pull any strings to get you admitted to the OSI program. That was the last thing I ever wanted for you."

"You'd rather I had a desk job, or a forensic analysis position? At least I have the skills to defend myself when bad things come knocking. And they always do."

"I never wanted you to be defenseless. That's not what I'm saying."

"Then what are you saying?" I stared at her. "Mom, I

know that I lied to you. I don't feel good about it. I looked you right in the face for thirteen years, and I lied to you, over and over. But you lied, too."

"Of course. I did what was needed to protect you."

"How was your silence protecting me? Do you know how many times I needed you—how many times I wanted to come to you for advice, or just so that you could tell me everything was going to be okay? But I couldn't. I thought I was the one protecting you." I felt a bitter knot inside. "All that time, you knew exactly what I was going through, because you'd done it, too. But you didn't say a word."

She sighed. "Sometimes, keeping silent is the harder thing. I never did anything without thinking of you first. If I hurt you, it was for the greater good."

"You sound like a superhero now."

"There was a time when I felt like one. When you're young and powerful, you think you can do anything. You don't think about getting old." Her eyes met mine. They were green and full of secrets. "I used to have mastery over water. I could talk a lake out of being frozen, or make it rain in the middle of summer. If I wanted, I could cook something just by touching it. I didn't need a microwave. I could make the water molecules dance a waltz. It came in handy when I needed to warm your bottles."

My eyes widened. "And can you still do those things?"

She shrugged. "Some of them. But I'm sixty-two now. I can't reach into the heart of the ocean anymore."

"Right. But you can still do—" I peered into the living room again. Mia was staring at the TV screen, and Patrick was already asleep. "I mean, you can still make things happen. The power doesn't just go away. Does it?"

She smiled sadly. "If you're trying to look into your future—don't. Everyone's path to retirement is different. I've lived a fuller life than most people like us, and I don't regret the sacrifices I made. But my days of high magic are over."

"What sort of sacrifices?"

My mother stared into her mug. "Would you like some more tea? I know it's going to keep me awake, but I can't help it."

"Mom, I don't want tea. I want answers."

She laughed. "You sound just like that girl on TV, the one who wears all the different wigs. She's always being interrogated—"

"Mom." I glared at her. "Please. It's time. I need to know."

She seemed to diminish slightly before me. I could see that she was tired. Her face hid all manner of joys and disappointments, and they weighed on her. I felt like I didn't have the right to demand anything. But I could still play my ace. I had to.

I was an only child. When I asked for something, she gave it to me. Was I selfish? Yes. Was it unfair? Probably. But her love was unconditional, and a part of me knew that she would always say yes, even when she said no.

"Please," I said again.

She closed her eyes for a moment. Then she leaned forward. "When you were born, your father"—her voice fell to a whisper—"your *real* father came looking for you. I think you already know that. You saw it in your dreams."

I nodded. "You told him that as long as you lived, he'd never have me."

"Did I say that?" She chuckled. "I was bold then."

"But how did lying to me somehow protect me from my biological father?"

"I wasn't trying to deceive you, Tess. I was trying to deceive him."

"I don't understand."

She touched the handle of her empty mug. "I knew that you'd be born with the power to channel materia. That was unavoidable. But I didn't realize how much power you were going to have. Not until you were a toddler, and it began to manifest."

I stared at her. "When I was a toddler? But I didn't start doing things until I was twelve. That was when Eve—"

"No. What happened with Eve was an unfortunate accident. It traumatized you. It was one of the events that caused your powers to break through. That, and your encounter with those bullies. The ones who were tormenting the smaller boy."

"You knew about that?"

"Of course. Meredith was monitoring you by that point, and she saw it happen. That was when we knew that your powers weren't going to lie dormant any longer."

"Wait—" I swallowed. "Let me wrap my brain around this. If my powers started to manifest when I was two or three years old . . ." My eyes hardened. "Jesus. You were suppressing them?"

"Tess—"

"How could you—" I lowered my voice to a whisper. "I mean—God, Mom—how could you do that to me? It's a psychic violation, for fuck's sake!"

"I'm so sorry."

"Wow. Really? I feel so much better. Now I finally have something to talk about during therapy."

She exhaled. "We were trying to hide you, Tess. Once you started channeling materia, your father would be able to track you. I couldn't let that happen. So Meredith and I put a block on your powers. We couldn't negate them completely, of course. But we slowed them down a great deal."

I rose. Suddenly I had to move. "You're saying that I should have been doing things when I was practically a baby?"

"Your genetic heritage is complex. You had the potential for all sorts of incredible phenomena. But magic like that makes noise. If your father found you, before you were ready to defend yourself—" She sighed. "It had to be done. We both did it for your sake, Tessa."

"So—what? I'm some kind of prodigy?"

She smiled. "You're more than that. You're a miracle."

"I can't hear any more of this." I walked out of the kitchen.

"Honey, wait—"

I grabbed my coat. "Make sure Patrick does his homework, please. And tell Derrick to defrost the chicken in the freezer for tomorrow night. I'll try to be home in a few hours."

"Where are you going?"

I buckled on my shoulder-holster and grabbed my athame. Its weight was cool and reassuring in my hand. The only thing that had never lied to me.

"To break into my boyfriend's apartment."

I wasn't actually going to break into Lucian's apartment. I still had a key, after all—I simply hadn't been using it lately. The last time I'd been alone in his place was more than a year ago, after two vampires beat the tar out of me. We'd slept together without sleeping together that night, and I woke up the next morning alone in his bed. Aside from searching for coffee filters, I hadn't taken the opportunity to investigate his place further. I was afraid that he might come home early and discover me in flagrante with an ALS device and a fuming hood.

Tonight, I'd neglected to bring any equipment with me. I drew the line at borrowing hardware from the lab to scour my boyfriend's apartment. But I still had my athame, and I wasn't above using it for some presumptive testing.

My cell rang. It was Derrick. I flipped it open.

"Hey."

"Your mom just called me."

"What did she say?"

"That you're about to toss Lucian's apartment."

"Did she really say 'toss'?"

"No. I heard it on one of the *Law and Order*s."

"Which one?"

"The one without Chris Noth. Are you seriously breaking and entering?"

"I have keys. I'm unlocking and entering."

"But you're going to snoop."

"Of course."

"And what will that accomplish?"

"I'm not sure. Just a second—I have to cross Pacific and I don't want to die."

Derrick said something incomprehensible. It was raining, and I jogged across the street, trying to avoid the minefield of puddles and potholes. Yaletown residents were walking their dogs, and most of them wore miniature raincoats. The funny thing was that they actually looked pretty sharp in human clothing. I saw an Irish Setter wearing a Windbreaker that made me a little jealous. It had pockets.

"Where are you now?"

"Crossing onto Drake. Oh, my God."

"What?"

"This woman just walked by me, and she was eating a churro. Do you have any idea how much I want a churro right now? Where did she get it?"

"Tess, focus. What happened between you and your mother?"

"We had a fight."

"Did it involve Lucian?"

"No. I don't really want to talk about it."

I could practically feel him rolling his eyes. "Do I have to remind you that you just got your ass kicked by a necromancer? Now you're about to conduct an illegal search of another necromancer's apartment."

"It's not a search. If he asks, I'll just say I stopped by to water his plants."

"In the middle of the night?"

"Yes. I'm a procrastinator. I have to go."

"Please don't do anything stupid."

"Like what? I've been here before. Worst-case scenario is that I knock over one of his scented candles."

"If you see something that looks weird—don't touch it."

"Thanks. Okay, I'm going in."

"Tess—"

"And can you pick up some milk and sandwich bags on your way home? And cream cheese, but not the low-fat kind. I want all the fat. Thank you!"

I hung up before he could protest.

I didn't really have an explanation for my behavior. I was exhausted. I knew that Lucian was lying to me, and I needed to find the smallest scrap of something that would corroborate my suspicions. Or maybe I wanted to find something that would completely exonerate him.

No. I wanted to be right. Even if it meant that Lucian was screwing me over, I wanted to trust my gut.

A lot of things went through my head during the drive over there. I thought about all the times I'd screwed up as an OSI. All the times I'd felt incompetent, weak, or just plain stupid. Every horrible thing that Marcus Tremblay had ever said to me (before I stabbed him, which wasn't as satisfying as it sounds).

But mostly, I thought about magic itself, and how I still didn't understand it. Where did it live? Was it breathing somewhere inside me? Was it hidden in some node of my central nervous system, impossible to detect? And if so, did it exist as a beneficent cluster of cells, or was it more like a cancer?

I'd never felt powerful. I'd always feared that I was getting by on a mixture of charm and tenacity. Nobody had ever described me as an impressive or fearful mage before. I was nearly an OSI-3, but when (or if) I made that rank, it wouldn't be because I was some kind of prodigy. Hell, I threw everything I had at that necromancer in the park, and it barely fazed him. A vampire had to bail me out. I wasn't going to win any contests for firepower, and I couldn't read minds.

But according to my mother, none of that was true. I had power. So much power that two gifted mages had to put a block on it, so that I wouldn't burn like a crazy flare for my father to see. I'd been muzzled.

I had so many questions for her. Was the block gone now? Would I catch up to the other superstars, or would I always be in the remedial class? Was I going to go through some kind of second magical puberty? At twenty-six, the prospect seemed both terrifying and slightly attractive.

Maybe that was why I'd recognized the latent power so early in Mia. Her magic had been suppressed as well, in order to transform her into a kind of weapon. Maybe we were both bullets in the same gun.

I crossed Drake and approached Lucian's apartment. I could hear jazz and laughter coming from Aqua, the upscale restaurant on the corner that celebrities favored when they were filming in Vancouver. Neon made the asphalt look gold, like an ominous version of the Yellow Brick Road. Suddenly, I wished that I could sync up my whole life to *Dark Side of the Moon*. The last time I'd tried it, I'd been in no real condition to operate a turntable. But maybe it would work now. It must have worked for someone, right?

The key fit perfectly. I exhaled. Now or never.

I opened the door, and cool air washed over me. My boots clicked against the polished concrete floor. I could smell detergent, and something else. Maybe a hint of bachelor suppers past. The man loved Thai food.

I walked upstairs to his loft bedroom. The bed was made neatly. It didn't look as if it had been slept in for a few days, but Lucian was also very adept at tucking in hospital corners. For all I knew, he'd made it just a few hours ago. I wanted to think that I'd be able to sense his presence, but it didn't work quite so easily. Necroid materia didn't resonate on the same frequency as the elemental materias that mages worked with. Trying to detect it was like fiddling with an unfamiliar radio in the hopes of landing on a coherent station.

All I felt was anxiety. If Lucian had a detectable essence, I couldn't distinguish it from the ambient sounds and smells of the apartment.

I opened up the top drawer in his dresser. Socks in various shades. Assorted underwear, including the plaid boxers that he'd worn a year ago when we first had sex. I smiled when I saw them.

What was I looking for? I didn't really know. But all signs pointed to the fact that he was hiding something from me. Duessa hadn't called him out specifically, but she didn't trust the necromancers, and neither did I. Ordeño had been one of their own, and it was in their best interest to protect his secrets. Lucian may have been ostensibly cooperating with our investigation, but he was also holding something back. If he had something to hide, it was going to be here.

I opened every drawer. No false bottoms. No secret compartments. But he did have several pairs of neatly folded jeans, eight black collared shirts, and a collection of cuff links that I'd never seen before.

I took out my athame. The concrete floors were dampening my senses, but I could still detect a few pockets of air and liquid materia. I remembered the stairs to the loft, which he'd only recently built. They were made of clean, unvarnished pine, smooth to the touch. I drew energy from the wood and let it flow into the athame. The handle warmed to my touch.

I flicked the athame, and a cone of infrared light shone from its tip. Not as powerful as an IR camera with treated film, but it could still penetrate through most substrates. I scanned the walls and floor, going over every inch. Nothing but a few scuff marks and one badly installed piece of drywall.

The bed looked so comfortable. I was suddenly aware of my aching muscles and latent headache, which was about to blossom. I thought about the Vicodin in my purse. It would be so nice to pop a few pills and fall asleep in Lucian's bed. Maybe I'd wake up next to him in the morning, and he wouldn't even ask how I got there. He'd just kiss me and ask what I wanted for breakfast.

Right. That always happened.

I went downstairs. The coffee table had a few scattered magazines—*Discovery*, *Popular Mechanics*, and the *Walrus*. The couch was tidy, and the remote control had been placed neatly on one arm. Ours was usually buried underneath the cushions, and you had to practically go spelunking just to find it every night.

I walked down the hallway. Some people hid things in their bathroom, but Lucian didn't strike me as the type. Besides, I'd looked through his medicine cabinet the last time I was here, and he didn't even have so much as an aspirin bottle. Just Q-tips, nail clippers, and rubbing alcohol.

His laptop was humming quietly in the office. As I crossed the threshold of the doorway, I felt the first pang of real guilt. Up until this moment, I could have pretended that I was just a neurotic girlfriend. Now I was actually invading his workplace. There were locked filing cabinets in here, and removable hard drives, and all sorts of digital caches of treasure. Things meant for his eyes only.

The desk had an accordion file on it I looked through it briefly, but didn't find anything but tax receipts and old bank statements. I didn't look at the balance. But for some reason, I was surprised that he used a credit union.

Twenty minutes later, I found myself staring at the two locked filing cabinets. I didn't sense any materia coming from them. If I really wanted to, I could probably pick the locks with a bobby pin.

Christ.

What was happening to me?

"This is stupid," I said. "If he's hiding something, you're not going to find it. The guy spends half of his time in a hidden city."

I wasn't about to get a bus ticket to Trinovantum. Nobody in the CORE knew where it was, or how to get there. All we understood was that, sometimes, stillborn infants were brought to the hidden city by nurses who weren't what they seemed. The babies were swaddled and cared for and—somehow—brought back to life. Or brought into unlife. We didn't understand how it worked. Lucian had told me only bits and pieces about his past, and when I pushed for more information, he just shut down.

I flicked on the light switch. I was going to leave him a nice note: *Miss you, watered your plants, hope all is well, besos.*

That was when I noticed the picture for the first time.

It was hanging above the desk. I didn't remember seeing it before, but I'd never really spent a lot of time in Lucian's office. Maybe it had been there all along. Or maybe he'd just put it up recently. It was definitely a Picasso. The lines and shadows were all askew, but the room in the painting seemed eerily familiar. I stared at it. There was what looked like a figure standing in an open doorway. Another figure was kneeling, and above its head was a swirl of white, like a flashbulb.

It wasn't the figures themselves, but rather their positioning, that made me realize what I was looking at. *Las Meninas*.

Only, it wasn't. It was Picasso's version of *Las Meninas*. The Infanta Margarita was a perplexity of geometric shapes, her head a large octagon, her torso a narrow rectangle. Her dress was still spread out on the floor, but now it looked more like a fat scalene triangle. The man standing in the open doorway resembled a tall lamp, or possibly a distended umbrella. Velázquez the painter was a cluster of forms draped loosely over the Cross of Santiago, which in Picasso's version resembled a coatrack with body parts hanging from it. Vaguely threatening triangles and half shapes floated around Margarita's head in shades of vivid blue, yellow, and red.

Come to think if it, I'd read somewhere Picasso had made abstract copies of *Las Meninas*. He'd been nearly obsessed with the original.

But why did Lucian have a copy of this particular painting? It seemed like too much of a coincidence. Two necromancers. Two versions of the same painting. And Ordeño had been Lucian's mentor.

What knowledge had he passed on to his pupil? Was Lucian working to ensure that his secrets would remain hidden?

It made sense. Necromancers were marginalized, misunderstood, cryptic. They kept to themselves, protected one another. But Lucian's sense of loyalty was now squarely in the way of my investigation.

I used my cell to snap a picture of the Picasso. Then I turned the light off and returned to the living room. Everything looked exactly as it had when I'd first opened the door. I closed my eyes, grounded myself, and concentrated.

The earth materia responded to me, even from beneath the concrete floor. I thought about white things: snow; the fur on the underbelly of my childhood cat, whom I'd named Opal for reasons known only to my six-year-old self; clean foolscap; freshly washed sheets; primed walls; and polished bone. It was an old trick that Meredith Silver had taught me for erasing one's presence.

The materia settled itself into a neutral field, which then sank into the walls and floor. It was like metaphysical air freshener. Unless Lucian could smell me, he'd probably sense nothing untoward when he returned home.

I closed and locked the door. I was already dialing as I crossed the street.

"Hey. I'm fine. What can you tell me about Picasso?"

12

My father the demon was painting me.

Like Velázquez, he wore a black surcoat, but instead of the Cross of Santiago it was embroidered with three drops of blood. As I watched them, the drops danced, forming first a triangle and then a slowly spinning circle. Sometimes the blood looked real, and sometimes it was just thread.

He was tall. Maybe six-two or six-three even. His hands and face were nearly translucent, the same color as glazed porcelain. Veins flared underneath the surface of his flesh, and the blood that coursed through them was multicolored. Looking at them reminded me of the abalone that coated the inside of shells. Was his blood really different colors, or was it just a trick of the light streaming through the windows?

"Tess. You should really hold still. He can't capture you otherwise."

I turned at the sound of the familiar voice. Mia was standing to my right, wearing a voluminous yellow gown and holding a silver chalice. As I stared at her dress, the flowers on it moved before my eyes. I thought of the glasses that our data technician, Esther, always wore, with their shifting reflections. The flowers bloomed and then shriveled as I watched them, crumbling to red and yellow powder.

Two young girls knelt beside Mia, fussing with her dress and shoes. The girl on her right was Eve, my childhood best friend, who'd perished in a fire. Seeing her again was like a blow to the stomach. Years ago, she'd run away from me, terrified when I channeled a bit of fire materia to make my hands glow. She was supposed to think it was pretty, but she fled from me instead, like I was a monster.

She died that same day. I'd crawled through the smoke and the flames, searching for her, but all I'd found was a blackened body, flaking away even as I stared at it.

In my dream, she was whole and beautiful. The last time I'd seen her like this was when Marcus Tremblay tried to kill Mia. I'd tapped into Mia's reserve of power, and for a brief moment, my connection to the elemental planes where materia came from—the secret chambers of the visible universe—allowed me to see Eve one last time. She'd forgiven me, even if I couldn't forgive myself.

Now she smiled at me. *"¿Qué pasa, amiga?"*

"What are you doing in my dreams again?"

"What are you doing in *our* dreams?" The girl on Mia's left spoke to me. I'd never seen her before. She was dark-skinned and had beautiful green eyes. She couldn't have been more than twelve—the same age as Eve.

"I don't know you," I said.

She smiled. "That's not really the point."

A dog slept at Mia's feet, and I realized that it was Baron, who belonged to Miles. He opened one eye and stared lazily at me.

I looked past him, and saw both Derrick and Miles

standing behind the girls. Derrick was wearing a beautiful black suit with a white silk tie, and Miles wore a pristine white suit with a black tie. A white hand-shape had been sewn into his tie, and I recognized it as the ASL sign for *reverse*.

Reverse of what?

Miles leaned close to Derrick, whispering something in his ear. Derrick grinned. He signed something rapidly to Miles, but the only word I recognized was *tell.*

Then they kissed. It was a slow, deliberate kiss. Miles laid his hand on the back of Derrick's neck. Derrick pulled him in closer, still smiling. He opened his eyes, then bit Miles gently on the bottom lip. Miles chuckled.

"A kiss to build a dream on," he said.

But it was my father's voice that I heard. A growl lingered just below its surface. A drop of blood appeared on Miles's lip, hovering, tensile.

"Oh. Hold still. I can get that." Mia left her *meninas.* Both looked disappointed, but neither said a word. Mia was nearly as tall as Miles, so she didn't have to strain to reach him. She dabbed at his mouth with the sleeve of her dress. The blood soaked through the fabric, spreading across it, until the gown was entirely red.

"I think it looks better this way," Mia said.

I gestured to her cup. "What are you drinking?"

"Memories, mostly." She smiled. "And some ginger ale, for my stomach. Derrick made it for me. It's called a *desmemória.*"

"It comes in pill form, too," Derrick said, holding out his hand. Three Vicodin tablets lay in his palm.

I heard a knocking. My father let out an exasperated sigh, still holding his paintbrush. It was dripping on the floor.

"Somebody's come late. Please let them in, Tessa."

I looked at the open entrance. The necromancer from

the park was standing there. His steel mask was broken in places, revealing patches of skin crusted with dried blood. He no longer had the Vorpal gauntlet. His eyes were fixed on me.

"Take your mask off," I said.

He passed a hand over his face. The mask disappeared. It was Lucian. He stared at me impassively.

"No," I said. "It wasn't you. Those weren't your eyes." I shook my head. "I would have recognized you. This is wrong."

But was it? Would I really have recognized him in the heat of the moment? What had I ever really known about him?

"Was it you?" I asked.

He looked bemused. "I'm not sure I understand the question."

"In the park. Was it you, Lucian?"

He put a hand over his heart. *"Tu eres mi espejo, preciosa."*

I glared at him. "I'm your mirror? What's that supposed to mean?"

"Tessa! Come see it!" My father was gesturing maniacally with his paintbrush. "It's nearly done!"

I walked over to where he was standing. He turned the canvas. He'd painted Luiz Ordeño, dead, his neck lacerated and covered in blood.

"It looks just like you," he said.

I woke up with that image fresh in my mind.

It was hot in my bedroom. The digital clock on the nightstand read 6:35. No time for a shower. Fantastic.

My subconscious is either trying to kill me or get me fired. Maybe both.

I walked unsteadily into the en-suite bathroom. There was a dirty towel on the floor, and I could smell a patina of styling products, their various scents mingling into something nebulous and sweet. I washed my hair in the sink. The blow-dryer was so hot that it burned, but I kept it on the highest setting. Pain meant that I was awake.

I pulled on a pair of jeans that were only slightly wrinkled. I needed to wash my bra, but that wasn't about to happen in the next five minutes. Selena probably had twenty bras, all fitted and always freshly laundered. I felt like a barbarian.

Fifteen minutes of indecision later I emerged from the bedroom, still groggy, but now at least wearing a sharp tan sweater. Mostly its purpose was to hide the semi-clean blouse underneath. I'd been planning to do a load of laundry last night, but my detour to Lucian's apartment had changed things. Instead of washing whites, I'd ended up talking to Derrick about Picasso and Velázquez until three in the morning. He had the day off, but I wasn't so lucky.

I walked past his bedroom and saw that the door was partially open. The room was immaculate, as always. His OSI textbooks were lined up on shelves, along with other novels and works of criticism. Derrick had always been a voracious reader. His DVDs were stacked neatly by the small television set. Probably alphabetized. Sometimes I had no idea why Derrick and Lucian weren't good friends. They definitely shared a love for organizing.

I didn't mean to look at the bed, but it was sort of impossible not to. Miles and Derrick lay in each other's arms, only partially covered by the blanket. Derrick's legs were wrapped around Miles's, their feet touching. They both snored in unison.

I thought of how they'd appeared in my dream, wearing polarized suits. I almost wanted to look and see if Miles had blood on his mouth. But I didn't dare.

My life would be a lot simpler if I could sleep like that.

I closed Derrick's door lightly. Then I made my way into the kitchen. Mia was sitting at the table, studying. I couldn't tell if it was the same textbook or not, but some-times all of her textbooks looked the same to me, with their bright colors and strange geometric designs. Kind of like Picasso's *Las Meninas*.

She didn't look up. "There's fresh coffee in the thing."

"And by 'thing,' you mean coffeemaker?"

"Well, it's not really a coffee*maker*, is it? I'm the one that makes the coffee."

"I see your point."

She underlined something in her notebook. "Derrick came home last night with the half-and-half, but I told him that you only liked the real coffee cream. So he had to go back." She sipped from her mug. "He didn't even argue."

For a second, all I could do was stare at her. When I first saw Mia, she was short and skinny, with unruly brown hair and eyes that never missed a beat. She favored oversized painter jeans and etnies.

It had been only two years, but suddenly she seemed impossibly older. Her hair fell in soft curls across her face, and I'd wager that she'd actually combed some anti-frizz product into it. She wore jeans that fit and stylish black boots. Her red sweater had a neckline that, although not technically sloping, was definitely low enough to expose her neck and a bit of her shoulders. She wasn't thirteen anymore. Strictly speaking, she wasn't entirely human anymore, since the vampiric retrovirus was swimming through her bloodstream. But nobody else living here was 100 percent human either, so at least she was in like-minded company.

"Did you take your meds yet?" I asked.

Mia made a face. "I was going to after I finished this quiz. I hate doing it in the school bathroom. It's like a Turkish prison in there."

"I can do it. They changed your dosage, and I want to make sure it's okay."

"Sure." She sounded resigned. No teenager wanted to take daily injections. But, to her credit, she rarely complained. Derrick and I had explained to her that she may have to inject the antiviral medication for the rest of her life, or at least until they refined it into a transdermal patch.

I opened the fridge and withdrew a vial of the medication, which needed to be chilled so that the plasmid inhibitors didn't separate. It was clear, like water.

"Where's your pen?"

"In my bag." She gestured to the chair. "Under my spare shoes, I think."

I reached into the depths of her bag, rummaging around until I found the hard black case with the pen. It resembled a similar hypodermic pen for injecting insulin, and included separate ports for mixing two different chemicals.

"They just changed the short-acting antivirals," I told her, refilling the pen. "The long-acting are still the same." I turned the knob on the end of the pen, adjusting the dosage to two units of antiplasmid. "Okay, lift up your shirt."

"Wow. Just what every girl my age longs to hear."

"I know you. The only words you long to hear right now are 'early acceptance' from Stanford and Brown."

She chuckled, lifting up her blouse to expose her abdomen. "That's true."

"You're whiter than me. Maybe we need to do some fake-and-bake tanning."

"Ooh, and can we read *Hello* while we're doing it?" She glared at me. "I don't care how white I am. Nothing's going to get me into one of those cancer-pods just so I can look like I spent my weekend at Jericho Beach."

"Fine. You don't have to give me stink-eye."

"That wasn't stink-eye."

"Oh, yeah?" I pinched her belly and swiftly injected the needle. She didn't even have time to grimace. "Looked like stink-eye to me." I counted to five silently, then withdrew the needle. "There. Done. Make sure to keep using this setting, and if you feel any side effects, let me know so that I can adjust it."

Mia smiled. "It never hurts as much when you do it."

I replaced the pen and put the case back in her bag. "I've got magic."

"We all do. That's kind of the problem."

I filled my coffee mug and sat down across from her. "Shouldn't Patrick be getting ready as well?"

"It's like seven. He won't be awake for another half hour at least."

"And when did you wake up?"

She sipped her coffee. "I've barely slept. I had two essays to finish, plus a photo assignment for yearbook. Most of the girls don't actually know how to use their cameras, so only a few of us are actually doing any real work."

"Does it have a theme? Our yearbooks always had a theme."

"Mediocrity."

"Ouch."

She shrugged. "It's not like I'm trying to be a bitch. It's just—most of the kids I know aren't exactly gunning for grad school."

"You're fifteen. I don't think you should be gunning for grad school either."

"But I have plans. They don't."

"I'm sure that's not true."

"You don't go to school with these kids. I do."

"But I went to school with kids just like them. And that was only ten years ago. No. Eleven." I blinked. "Man. I guess eleven years is a long time. Does everyone still listen to Pearl Jam?"

She stared at me as if I'd just grown a second head. "Not really."

I heard a thump on the floor above me, like a bowling ball or a dead body hitting the ground.

"Sounds like he's awake."

Mia shook her head, returning to the textbook. "He's just getting up to go to the bathroom. He'll go back to sleep for another twenty minutes at least."

"As long as he gets to his classes on time."

She rolled her eyes. "Right. Like it matters."

"What do you mean?"

"Nothing."

"I'm pretty sure you mean something."

"I'm pretty sure I don't."

"Mia."

"Tess."

"Don't say my name like that."

"Like what?"

"You know like what."

Mia sighed, finally looking up from her book. "If you want to be a parent, then be a parent. Ask me whatever you're going to ask me. But don't try to be all friendly about it, like, stealth-parenting or something. Just ask."

And . . . now we'd returned to our regularly scheduled teen programming. I was the bitch monster from hell, and she was the hapless victim, forced to put up with me. Had I really done this to my mother for eighteen years?

Of course, my mother had also performed psychic surgery on me without asking. So maybe we were even.

I exhaled. "Fine. What did you mean earlier, when you said it didn't matter if Patrick made it to his classes on time?"

"It doesn't."

"Why not?"

She looked at me as if I were impenetrably stupid. "Because he's failing."

"Failing what?"

"Everything, as far as I can tell. Except for PE. He's so strong and fast that the teacher's probably scared to give him a bad mark."

"But he's flunking his other classes?" I suddenly felt like the mother who learns that her kid is doing drugs. *How could this have happened?* The truth was that Patrick could have been moonlighting as the school mascot, and I still wouldn't have known anything about it. I couldn't watch him 24/7. I couldn't even watch him 7.

"He stopped trying, like, three months ago," she said. "He goes to that creepy vampire club every night, where they teach him, like, how to smell humans from a mile away or something. It's way more interesting to him than calculus."

"But he can't possibly be failing everything."

She shrugged. "I don't know. But it's not like he's studying."

"I saw him studying math the other day."

"Yeah? Did you see him writing anything down?"

My stomach sank. "No."

She nodded. "Uh-huh."

I stared at my coffee cup. There was no online forum with tips on how to raise paranormal teenagers. I needed help. Derrick did everything he could, but we were both working long hours. My mom stopped by often, but she was mostly focused on Mia. Patrick often fell beneath her radar. Maybe intentionally. I suspected that, like me, she felt a bit uneasy around him.

"I don't know what to do," I said simply.

To my surprise, Mia looked directly at me, and her expression was one of sympathy rather than irritation. "Tess. You're doing fine. It's not like we're the easiest kids to deal with. We've both got issues. But you're doing the best you can, and we totally understand that."

"If I was doing my best, I would have realized that Patrick was failing." I shook my head. "He's gone most of the night, and when he comes back, he looks like—"

"Like a vampire?"

We both stared at each other for a second.

"Yes," I said. "Exactly like that."

"And it's scary."

"Yeah. It is."

Mia stared at her hands. "He's kind of like my big brother. So it freaks me out, too. Because I don't want him to change."

"Me neither."

"But there's nothing we can do, right? I mean—it's who he is. And, like—" Her voice fell slightly. "I mean, it's sort of who I am, too, right? On some level. I'm just a version of him that's all doped up and medicated."

I didn't like where this was going.

"You're not doped up," I said. "You're managing an illness."

"But to him, it's not an illness. It's everything."

"Is that what you want? To be just like him?"

She sighed. "Not really."

"Being a vampire isn't the easiest thing in the world. You need blood to survive. You can't go out in the sunlight—"

"But he can. I mean, he stays in the shade, and he doesn't sit next to the window, but he can manage during the day."

"That's because he's the magnate. He has abilities that other vampires don't."

"Maybe I do, too."

I didn't know what to say. My cell rang.

"One second." I flipped it open. "Hello?"

It was Selena. "They're here."

"Who?"

"The necromancers. They're in the lab."

My stomach flipped again. I wanted to ask her if Lucian was one of "them," but I couldn't risk sounding too interested.

"Why are they here?"

"Because of you. They said that they're very concerned about your incident in the park." She didn't sound entirely convinced. "They want to reassure us that we're working together, not in opposition. And they want to talk to you personally."

I swallowed. "Really?"

"Yes. Get here as soon as you can. They brought something for you to look at."

"What did they—"

But she'd already hung up.

"Urgent business at the lab?" Mia asked.

I nodded. "I have to brave a shitstorm."

"Sounds like a weekday."

"Lately. Yeah." I gave her a look. "Let's chat when I get home."

"That sounds ominous."

"It's not. I just want to play catch-up."

"Do you want me to spy on Patrick for you?"

"Would you if I asked?"

"Probably not."

"So is this a trick question?"

"Possibly."

I got up and placed my mug in the sink. "Then my answer is maybe. But don't get caught."

"Do you think I'm an amateur?"

"No. Just don't follow him anywhere."

"That's no fun."

"Seriously. Don't."

"Okay, fine."

"Fine means you won't follow him?"

"Fine means fine."

I grabbed my jacket. "You're both going to drive me crazy."

She'd already returned to her textbook. "That's the plan. Then we can force Derrick to do whatever we want."

"Never going to happen."

"Whatever. Bye."

"Bye."

I closed the door behind me. Even this early in the morning, the sun was bright and clear. The air chilled me. For a moment, all I could do was stand there, breathing in and out slowly.

Sometimes, I loved them so much that it paralyzed me. They weren't even my kids. All that bound them to me was a stack of papers. But they still felt like a part of my own body. A breath that I was always taking in. I didn't want to let it go. I wanted to hold it in my lungs forever.

And then I got scared.

What if they got hurt or broken? What if they needed me and couldn't reach me? Or what if the opposite was true? Maybe I was doing irreparable damage to them. Maybe I was a pathetic guardian, a monstrous parent doing everything wrong, and someday they'd talk about me with a goblin therapist.

Chances are, my brain said, *you'll be dead before that happens.*

With that thought turning itself over and over in my mind, until it was polished smooth, I headed off to meet the necromancers.

13

Selena was giving the necromancers a tour of the lab facilities when I arrived. My stomach seized a little when I saw Lucian, accompanied by a young man and a middle-aged woman. At least that was what they looked like on the outside. Who knew how old they really were? Lucian caught sight of me, but didn't smile or acknowledge my presence, aside from a brief second of eye contact.

After spending nearly a week wondering where the hell he'd disappeared to, I felt like I was entitled to at least a nod. But in truth, I already knew—or at least suspected— where he'd been the whole time. Trinovantum, the hidden city. That was where he always vanished to. It was like a necromancer time-share.

Selena gave me a look as I approached. I couldn't tell if it was a *shut up and let me do the talking* look, or a *help me because I'm exhausted and overwhelmed* look. I decided to play it safe and take her lead.

"Sorry I'm late." I extended my hand to the necromancers. "Tess Corday. I'm the senior officer assigned to the Ordeño case."

The older woman took my hand. Her grip was firm and cold. "Deonara Valesco. Third Solium of the Dark Parliament, and tactical advisor to Lord Nightingale."

She had graying black hair and blue eyes that seemed only mildly interested in my presence. The rest of her attention was occupied by the lab itself. I, in turn, was fascinated by a kind of black shawl that she wore, which had delicate silver stitching around the edges. If I looked at the embroidery for more than a few seconds, I swore that it moved a little. But maybe it was just me.

"Thanks for meeting us here," I said. "We appreciate your cooperation."

"Not at all." She was staring at a mass spectrometer. "This place is fascinating. I've always wanted to visit, but never had the opportunity until now."

"There's plenty to look at," Selena said. "Hopefully we can learn a bit about each other's analytical methods."

"Yes." Deonara tore herself away from staring at the equipment with some difficulty. "Of course."

I didn't buy it, though. She wasn't interested in sharing information. She'd learn as much about our resources as possible without actually telling us anything useful about her side of the investigation. Then she'd have plenty of information to take back to Lord Nightingale, whoever he was, and we'd be left with nothing. If we wanted to learn anything about her world, we'd have to pull it forcefully out of Deonara's brain. And Derrick was nowhere to be found.

Luckily, we had Selena, who was excellent at gleaning information from uncooperative sources.

The young man took my hand. His touch was actually warm. "Braxton Tel. Fourth Solium of the Dark Parliament. It's a pleasure to meet you, Tess. You come highly recommended to us by your supervisor, Detective Ward."

He had glasses and short brown hair. Kind of cute, actually.

I shook his hand. "Nice to meet you, Braxton. What exactly does a Fourth Solium do for the Dark Parliament?"

"Mostly dull things. I wouldn't want to bore you with an explanation. Deonara gets most of the fun jobs."

"Of course. If you call delicate treaty negotiations 'fun.'" She was staring at one of the scanning electron microscopes. "Are any of these tools powered by what you call 'materia'? Or are they strictly electronic?"

"Most of them are just sophisticated devices for microscopy," Selena said. "We're working on engineering a few hybrid tools. But that's far into the future."

Actually, we already had hybrid tools, like the Nerve simulation chamber. But she wasn't going to tell them that.

I suddenly realized that I was still shaking Braxton's hand. It was surprisingly soft. I let go of it, smiling awkwardly. "Sorry."

"Not a problem." He smiled back.

Lucian was staring at both of us. I couldn't tell if he was jealous, or simply annoyed. At this point, I didn't really care. There wasn't even much to be jealous of anymore. We barely saw each other, and when we did, things were awkward at best. We were supposed to be working on the same case, but he'd frozen me out practically from the beginning.

I held out my hand. "Lucian. It's nice to see you again."

Confusion flashed across his eyes. But he took my hand all the same.

"Likewise. Thank you for lending us your expertise."

He searched my face briefly to see what I was feeling, but I kept the mask on. It seemed like the most appropriate thing to do.

Deonara turned to me. "It was brought to our attention that someone attacked you and your ward. Are you all right?"

"Just some bruises and scrapes. Could have been worse, though."

"Indeed. The individual in question broke protocol by transporting a Vorpal gauntlet out of the city. Military tools such as those are strictly regulated. We're quite disappointed by the situation."

I wasn't entirely sure what that meant. Were they actually going to do something about it, or did they simply plan on shaking their finger at someone?

"It's sad that someone felt the need to endanger your safety in this manner," Braxton added. "But we do have some dangerous factions within the Parliament. Rogue cells and whatnot. There's little we can do to control them."

I chose my next words carefully. "Do you see any chance of apprehending a suspect? Or is it going to be a hit-and-run?"

"Well," Deonara said, "that will depend on how sophisticated your detection equipment is. We don't have the means of identifying a suspect, but you might."

"I'm not sure I follow you. We weren't able to recover any trace from the scene, and it's been days since the attack."

"They found the Vorpal gauntlet," Lucian explained. "It's here."

"Yes. Someone disposed of it on the outskirts of Trinovantum." Deonara seemed to have lost interest in me again. Her eyes were elsewhere. "In the interest of political harmony, we thought it best to bring the evidence to you."

Ah. This was what Selena had meant by a surprise.

"Cindée has the fume hood ready," Selena said. "She's waiting for us."

The five of us walked down the hallway and entered the trace lab. Cindée looked up and smiled at me. "Hey, Tess. Good to see you're still in one piece."

"That's me. Hard to kill."

I looked at the hood, which was actually more of a steel cupboard with an industrial exhaust fan on the top. It was set against the wall and had a movable fiberglass partition, attached to an aircraft-grade stainless-steel cable which was used to raise and lower the sash. The fiberglass was lined with both cement and a special epoxy resin, to protect the operator from toxic cyanoacrylate fumes.

The gauntlet was sitting inside the cupboard. It looked innocuous, even defeated, with one of its red crystals shattered. But a chill passed through me as I remembered what it had been capable of. Its power had literally ripped my magic to pieces, dissolving and de-creating it, as if it had never existed.

"Should we be wearing some kind of protective gear?" Braxton asked. "I don't want my lungs filled with deadly chemicals."

It sounded strange for a necromancer to refer to anything as "deadly." Weren't deadly chemicals like catnip to them?

"No need to worry," Cindée assured him. "The blast shield is heavy-duty, and all the fumes get sucked through a charcoal filter at the top. You'll be fine."

Cindée lifted the sash, exposing the gauntlet. Pulling on a pair of plastic gloves, she dropped a tablet of cyanoacrylate, or superglue, onto the burner. Then she replaced the sash and turned the burner on low. White vapors rose from the tablet. I watched in fascination as they coated the gauntlet, like a dusting of snow. The glue worked its way into every contour, crack, and crevice within the glove, as well as the irregular surface of its red crystals.

After letting the fumes settle for a few moments, Cindée switched on the exhaust fan, which got rid of the excess vapors. Then she gently raised the sash.

"Y'all are sure this thing's dormant?" she asked. "I don't feel like getting disintegrated today."

"The gauntlet's been completely vitiated," Braxton confirmed. "When the catalytic gem was broken, its power vanished."

Cindée grabbed a pair of forceps, using them to gently manipulate the surface of the gauntlet. She turned it to the side, then smiled.

"There it is, folks."

A single print had crystallized on the intricate leather straps of the gauntlet. It was slightly distended because of the textile substrate, but it still looked beautiful, pristine and white from the superglue.

"Fascinating," Deonara said simply.

Braxton frowned. "How accurate is this type of test? Isn't it what you call 'presumptive' in nature?"

"No," Selena said. "Spraying a surface in search of hidden blood is a presumptive test, because the luminol can detect all sorts of things. These results are far more probative, as you can see for yourself. The fingerprint is right before our eyes."

"Care to do the honors, Tess?" Cindée asked. "After all, you nearly got killed by this pretty little thing."

"Gladly." I walked across the room and opened a cupboard, retrieving a professional SLR camera with a special diffusion lens for the lab's poorly lit conditions. I snapped two shots of the white print, then plugged the camera's memory card into a nearby computer. I tinkered with a few filters to the best of my ability, until the resolution of the print seemed acceptable. Then I fed the digital file into the CORE's fingerprint database, which recognized both human and demonic prints.

"This will take a few minutes," Selena told them. "It's not like on television. Why don't we sit down in the conference room in the meantime?"

Braxton looked at the screen curiously. "How many fingerprints do you have in your database?"

"A few hundred thousand. We're still entering a lot of the older prints that were recorded on ten-cards. The software's always being updated, and we have covert access to the FBI's IAFIS print bank, as well as our own encrypted database."

I waved good-bye to Cindée as we followed Selena to the conference room, which was a slightly plusher version of the interrogation chamber. Everyone took a seat. Selena had called ahead to order refreshments from the cafeteria, and we all helped ourselves to coffee and shortbread. She'd thought of everything.

Lucian was the first to speak. "I know that this investigation has been a bit awkward. Perhaps we haven't shared as much information as we could have. But we're committed to helping you in any way that we can."

"Within reason," Deonara added. "Obviously, there is sensitive information that can't be divulged. Ordeño was working on a number of political projects before his death. We're still going through his records to determine the extent of his involvement with the vampiric community, among others."

"I don't suppose you'd reconsider releasing those to us."

Selena flashed her best smile. I had to hand it to her. She was really keeping her emotions under wraps. If this had been a regular informant who refused to share information, she'd be slamming his head into a steel table by now.

"It's simply not possible," Deonara said. "As you know,

Ordeño was the chief litigator involved in drafting an updated treaty between the Vampire Nation and the Dark Parliament. He'd been working on this for nearly half a century, and he made extremely detailed notations pertaining to nearly every aspect of our city's political organization. Much of that information needs to remain classified."

"That doesn't mean," Lucian added, "that we can't give you some idea of the direction of Ordeño's work. As Prime Solium of the Dark Parliament, he was Lord Nightingale's principle advisor, and one step away from governance of the hidden city itself. That position gave him considerable power to direct toward drafting a peaceful accord between necromancers and vampires."

"What would this treaty entail, exactly?" I asked. "Was it a military agreement? A human rights accord?"

"It covered several different categories." Lucian didn't look at me directly when he spoke, but I could feel his aura touching me, like a shadow. I was on his mind. As always, I had no idea what that meant. "On the surface, it was a military document that would ensure mutual harmony between our nations. But it also addressed a number of social issues: citizenship rights, intermarriages, fostering arrangements, and even questions of inheritance."

"What do you mean by citizenship rights?"

"As it stands," Deonara said, "no vampire is allowed to set foot in Trinovantum without a diplomatic passport issued by Lord Nightingale himself. The revised treaty would open the border, allowing vampires with community ties to live and work within the hidden city. It's quite a radical shift in Trinovantum's foreign policy."

"There must be opposition to this," I said. "Ordeño probably earned himself a lot of enemies from the conservative end of your parliament."

Lucian chuckled. "It's all conservative. Ordeño was probably the most liberal Solium at the table."

"Don't sell yourself short, Lucian," Deonara chided. "You've certainly done your part to maintain a democratic voice. You are Seventh Solium after all."

"Seventh—" I felt my stomach sink as the information sank in. "You're a member of the Dark Parliament?"

This time, he managed to meet my gaze. "Yes. My position is nowhere near as important as Ordeño's was. But I do sit at the table."

Great. Now I was dating an MP. An MP who lied to me, then disappeared whenever it was convenient. I couldn't believe that he'd neglected to mention this until now. What else was he keeping from me?

"Ordeño was very concerned with ensuring civil liberties for vampires who might decide to live in Trinovantum," Braxton said. "He also wanted to make it legal for necromancers to participate in the governance of the Vampire Nation. If his changes to the treaty were to go into effect, citizens of Trinovantum would be allowed residence within vampire safe houses across your city. And that would just be the start."

"So it's a paranormal NAFTA." I tapped my fingers on the table. "Would that be so bad? Free trade between Trinovantum and the *daegred*?"

"There are several schools of thought on that matter," Deonara replied. "Ordeño believed that social parity was essential for the survival of both our communities. Otherwise, we'd continue depleting our resources by fighting with each other. As minorities, we can't afford that."

"If you're minorities, does that make us the majority?"

"Technically, mortals—I believe you call them *pedestrians*—are the majority. But there are still more of your kind—mages—than either necromancers or vampires."

"Most of the Dark Parliament opposes the idea of cultural integration," Braxton added. "The same goes for the Vampire Nation. Your city's magnate holds what you might call a 'swing vote' in this particular case. But since he's too inexperienced to make a decision, his counselors are trying to decide for him."

"Modred and Cyrus," I said. "The monitors. Do they have the power to ratify the treaty in Patrick's name?"

It was Lucian who answered. "We're not sure. Only Ordeño knew the finer points of vampiric clan law. That's why we're searching through his records. We need to find out what steps are necessary in order to make the treaty go forward."

"If it's capable of going forward at all." Braxton's posture was stiff. He was obviously uncomfortable with the discussion. "It needs to receive a majority vote from both sides. And very few members of the Dark Parliament are willing to endorse an incomplete document."

"Where do you stand on the treaty?" I asked him.

Braxton blinked. "What do you mean?"

"I mean what's your political position?"

Deonara rolled her eyes. "Braxton is a permanent fence-sitter."

"Like a graveyard Republican?"

They all stared at me.

I didn't know why I even bothered anymore.

Braxton shifted his position. "I'm not fully comfortable with every aspect of Ordeño's design. But on the whole, I support integration."

Deonara shrugged. "It's in the spirit of capitalism. Once we lower the border, both communities can profit from each other."

Selena leaned forward slightly. "I think what we're all curious about is where this treaty leaves us, exactly. And by 'us,' I mean the CORE."

"We have a long-standing pact of nonaggression with your organization," Deonara replied. "That wouldn't change."

"But a pact isn't the same as a treaty."

"Does anyone know what a détente is?" I asked. "I remember it from my twelfth-grade history class, and nobody could ever explain it to me."

Selena ignored the question. "A treaty between Trinovantum and the Vampire Nation is also a consolidation of power. Should we be worried?"

Deonara kept her expression neutral. "That depends on your definition of 'worried.' It's not as if we're launching an offensive against the CORE. That would be nearly a logistical impossibility at this time."

"At this time, yes. But maybe it would be feasible in the near future."

"The Vampire Nation has a pact with your people as well. I see no reason for them to violate that agreement."

"Up until the murder of Ordeño, we saw no reason for vampires and necromancers to join forces. But now they are."

"Nobody's joining forces quite yet," Braxton stressed. "All we have is an incomplete treaty, whose finer points are buried within pages of nearly indecipherable legal notes. There isn't going to be a quick resolution to this."

I could see what Selena was doing now. By switching from docile to aggressive, she was trying to throw the necromancers a little off guard. If they couldn't figure out where she stood as the CORE's representative, they were more likely to let slip something by accident. Plus, if they were focused on placating her, that left me a bit of maneuvering room to ask questions while they were distracted. I could play good cop.

"Have you had the chance to look over Ordeño's autopsy report?" I directed the question at Braxton. Deonara had a poker face, but Braxton seemed to fluster a bit more easily. I could tell that he was more conservative than he wanted to admit. His lip curled slightly whenever he used the words "culture" and "integration."

"I read it briefly," he replied. "You concluded that he died from a wound to the neck. Sharp-force trauma."

"He seemed to have faced his attacker head-on. Who do you think would be powerful enough to kill someone like Luiz Ordeño with a knife?"

Braxton shrugged. "You're asking for speculation."

"By all means. Speculate. That's what we've been doing."

He looked slightly uncomfortable. "A lot of things could have killed him. A pureblood demon. Or even a mage. Don't you carry daggers?"

"Yes. But an athame is a ritual tool. And the wound-track doesn't match the serrated pattern of an athame blade."

"That seems overly convenient."

"How so?"

"You've managed to rule out your own weapon, with your own equipment. One might accuse you of analytical bias."

"Come on, Braxton." Deonara put a hand lightly on his arm. "You've seen what an athame looks like. It's certainly not what killed Ordeño."

Braxton looked at me, and I saw something different in his eyes. "Maybe it was an Iblis. Didn't you tangle with one of those recently, Miss Corday?"

I started to say something, but Lucian raised his hand. "I don't think these questions are getting us anywhere. We need to get back to—"

There was a knock at the door. Cindée appeared.

"The program finished its search," she said.

"Was there a match?" Selena asked.

"You'll have to come see for yourself."

We all followed her back to the trace lab. I saw the white print flashing on the computer screen. The whorls and tented arches of the fingerprint looked like patterns drawn in snow. Three points on the dermal surface had been highlighted by the program, but that wasn't normally enough to make a match.

"There's insufficient data for a confirmation," Cindée said. "But the print does share some characteristics with a few that we have on file. They're definitely humanoid, and there are traces of materia on some of the epithelial tissue. But the pattern's too degraded for us to match it to anything."

"It would help if we had even one genetic profile from your community," Selena said. "Simply for purposes of elimination."

Deonara sighed. "I suppose you're right."

Braxton glared at her. "What do you propose? Is the Third Solium going to have herself fingerprinted?"

"Of course not. There's no need for that." She sat down in front of the computer. "I can give them temporary access to our records."

"Deonara!"

"Don't have a stroke, Braxton. The uplink is encrypted."

"You need majority approval from the Parliament—"

"I'm the chief tactical advisor. I can approve it myself." She gave him a cold look. "If you want to lodge a grievance, you're more than welcome to."

Braxton made no reply.

Deonara rebooted the system. As the computer began to perform its start-up checks, she quickly pressed a sequence of keys. A blue screen appeared. She typed in a long string of unfamiliar characters, then pressed the enter key.

"Tricky," Cindée said. "Becka's going to have a fit when she reads the security logs at the end of the day."

"Not to worry. They'll be wiped clean as soon as I exit the system." Deonara typed something else. A new menu appeared, with the fingerprint saved in a frame. She clicked on it, and the word SEARCHING appeared.

"Our local area network is a lot smaller than yours," she said. "This should only take a few seconds."

A new window popped up:

/ERROR CODE 901/

SHADOW SECTOR: GLOBAL OVERRIDE REQUIRED

"What's a shadow sector?" I asked.

Deonara shook her head slowly. "Very strange. A shadow sector is a part of the database that's been triply encrypted. Only the Prime Solium, or Lord Nightingale himself, would be able to access this."

"Prime Solium. That's Ordeño, right?"

"It was Ordeño," Lucian clarified. "The seat is currently vacant."

"So who has his access code?"

"Nobody," Braxton said. "It was disposed of when he died. The only person who could decrypt this file now is Lord Nightingale."

"But what does that mean? Is the print a match to someone from the Dark Parliament? Is that why the information's being protected?"

"I'm not entirely sure," Deonara said. "Without a higher security clearance, we can't know for sure."

"Maybe we can ask Lord Nightingale to decrypt the file."

She rebooted the computer again. "You'd have better luck reversing gravity. He's in the middle of locating a suitable replacement for Ordeño. He's not about to give you access to a protected piece of government information, simply because of a print that you found on a smashed Vorpal gauntlet."

"Even if that gauntlet was attached to a necromancer who tried to kill me?"

She shrugged. "I suspect you'll need more than that. I'm sorry."

"I think we've shared enough already," Braxton said coldly.

I studied his face again. His eyes seemed to be changing from moment to moment. They'd seemed warm at first, but now there was a metallic edge to them. His cheeks were angular and hard, his mouth compressed. The light from the computer screen threw odd shadows across the lenses of his glasses. Colors danced across them, reminding me of something. I blinked.

"Braxton, can you do me a favor?"

He looked at me. "Possibly."

"Can you let me see your glasses for a second?"

"Why?"

"They remind me of a pair I used to own. I just want to see if you have the same frames as I did."

The question seemed to disarm him. But he took off the glasses and handed them to me. "They need to be cleaned."

"Yes." I studied the lenses. More important, I studied the reflection of his eyes in the lenses. "You have to use a special cleaner. Otherwise, they get spotty."

Now I remembered those eyes. Cold and still. Detached.

I looked at Braxton's right hand. The skin of his palm was slightly lighter than the skin surrounding the rest of his hand. That was why it was so smooth. Part of the dermal layer was still growing back. That was what happened when you suffered a second-degree burn. He was a fast healer, but not fast enough.

Still looking at the reflection in the lenses, I scanned his face. No damage. Except for a small mark underneath his left eye, nearly invisible. It could have been anything, but I knew exactly what it was. A piece of shrapnel from a metallic mask had cut his eye, drawing blood. Everything else had healed already, but a few physical marks from our altercation were still there, written on his body.

Braxton was the necromancer who had attacked me in the park.

14

I waited for Braxton and Deonara to leave before saying anything. I didn't want to cause some sort of cultural incident by accusing a Fifth Solium, or whatever he was, of attempted murder. After Lucian left to escort them out of the building, I turned to Selena, and the fake smile vanished from my face.

"It was Braxton."

She was in the middle of refilling her coffee. "What was Braxton?"

"He was the one who attacked me in the park."

She paused with her fingers on the stir stick. "Are you sure?"

"Positive."

"On what basis?"

"His eyes."

Selena sipped her coffee. "His eyes. Care to explain?"

"I recognize them. I didn't at first, because he was wearing glasses. But now I'm completely certain."

"Anything else?"

"The skin on his right hand is slightly pink. It's from the burn that he sustained when Modred destroyed the Vorpal gauntlet."

"I thought you said his face was cut as well."

"Yeah. It was. But necromancers heal fast, and if we don't act soon, even that tiny burn is going to disappear. Then we'll have nothing."

"We already have nothing. There's no such thing as an eye database. You can't finger him for attempted murder without any concrete evidence."

"And what about the fingerprint?"

"What about it?"

I rolled my eyes. "Come on. You know it's his. Somehow, he's managed to seal his own record. But if we could gain access to that file, I know that his name and photo would pop up in a second."

"You may know that, but there's no way to prove it."

"Prove what?" Lucian came striding down the hallway.

Selena looked at me. "Do you want to share your theory?"

"Not especially."

"Come on, Tess. Share." He grinned.

"You first."

"What's that supposed to mean?"

I sighed. "Fine. I'll tell you. But don't freak out."

Selena chuckled into her coffee cup.

"When have I ever freaked out?"

"There's a first time for everything."

"Just tell me. We're sharing information, remember?"

"Okay." I swallowed. "I think Braxton was the one who attacked us in the park. I recognize him. But I can't prove it."

He frowned. "Braxton's a bureaucrat. Even if he wanted to attack you, he'd never do it himself. He'd send someone."

"I know it was him. There's a recently healed burn on his hand."

"That could be from anything."

"There's also a small cut beneath his right eye. It's from the mask shattering."

Lucian shook his head. "That's not enough to launch an investigation."

"No. That's why we need to find out who the fingerprint belongs to."

"If Deonara couldn't access the file, I can't think of anyone else who'd be able to. It's locked up tight."

"I think Braxton stole Ordeño's access code. That's how he was able to encrypt the information. Now he's the only one who can get to it."

"Lord Nightingale could, but Deonara's right—he's too busy to deal with something like this. He doesn't trust the CORE as it is."

"Maybe you can convince him."

"I don't have that kind of power."

"Oh, yeah? A few minutes ago, I didn't even know you were a politician. Maybe you've got another ace up your sleeve."

Selena sighed. "I'll be in my office. If you think of anything that might impel a search warrant, just let me know."

She walked away. Lucian and I stood in silence for a while, not looking at each other. Finally, he moved to touch me, but I flinched.

"No."

"You're suddenly concerned with propriety?"

I glared at him. "You've been AWOL for most of this investigation. When you do show up, you can barely look me in the eye. I'm not going to pretend that everything's okay here."

He exhaled. "When is everything ever okay? We take

what we can get, right? The least we can do is try to help each other."

"That's the problem. You're not helping. You're hindering."

"I'm hindering? How am I hindering?"

"You're keeping things from me. From Selena and me."

"Who is it? You, or you and Selena?"

"Don't be cute."

"I don't know how not to be." He smirked.

"Follow me outside, at least. I don't want to have this conversation in the hallway."

We went through the fire exit that led to the parking lot. This concrete space had witnessed several nervous breakdowns on my part. It was also the first place where Lucian revealed his power to me. I remembered watching the necroid materia shimmering between his fingertips, revolving like a deadly red flower.

"Okay. We're outside now. Explain to me—"

"Why do you have a Picasso painting in your office?"

He blinked. "Excuse me?"

"You heard the question."

"Because I like Picasso?"

"Nice try. The painting's a reinterpretation of *Las Meninas*."

"Yes. I believe it is." He frowned. "When were you in my office? You never go in that room."

"That's not important."

"I think it is. Have you been to my apartment recently?"

Shit.

"Yes."

"When?"

"A few nights ago."

"That's news to me. What were you doing there?"

"I was looking for you. I let myself in with the key."

"And then you decided to explore my office?"

"I wasn't exploring anything. The painting's hanging on the wall. I saw it, and I was curious. Why do you have it?"

"I told you."

"¡No seas denso!"

He smiled. "Hey, that was pretty good."

"I'm serious. You know that Luiz Ordeño had a reproduction of *Las Meninas*, and you have an abstract version of the same painting. It's not a coincidence."

"It sounds like one to me."

"Those paintings have power. They're a key to something."

"To art appreciation?"

"Lucian, come on."

He raised his hands. "I don't know what to tell you, Tess. A painting's a painting. Luiz and I have the same taste. I'm a fan of Velázquez, too. So what?"

"What do the paintings do?"

"They sit on the wall."

"Is there necroid materia in them? Are they catalysts?"

"Catalysts for what?"

"Please don't do this."

"I don't understand what I'm doing."

"You're fucking lying to me. And you know it."

"All I know is that you're suspicious of some paintings for no reason. I'm sure you have some nice prints at home. Do they do anything?"

I shook my head. "Do you even believe me? About Braxton? Or do you think that I'm crazy?"

"A little of both, to be honest. Braxton's a prick, but he's not a murderer. Even if he stole a Vorpal gauntlet and came after you, it doesn't make sense that he'd confront you later. Why risk it?"

"Because he knows that we can't do anything. The print is locked behind a firewall, or shadow wall, or whatever it's called."

"Shadow sector."

"Whatever. He knows that we're humped. And if he shows up at the lab, it only gives him more credibility. He gets to waltz right into our territory like he owns the place, and nobody raises an eyebrow, because he's got his fancy necromancer passport. The only one who doesn't trust him is Tess the lunatic."

"Your story does sound a bit lunatic."

"No. I'm the lunatic, not the story."

"'Lunatic' is both an adjective and a noun. So your story can be lunatic, and so can you. Everybody wins grammatically."

I glared at him. "Is that it? You're just going to crack some jokes and then disappear to the hidden city again? That's our song and dance now?"

"I never thought of it in Vaudeville terms. But maybe."

"Fuck off and answer the question."

He sighed. "I have loyalties to my community, Tess. I can't play double agent. I'm cooperating with the CORE, but I also have to do what's in the best interest of my people. And some lines can't be crossed."

"Then why are you even letting us investigate Ordeño's murder? Why not just freeze us out entirely?"

"Because you have access to resources that we don't, just like we have access to information that you don't."

"But it's only going one way. We're giving you our resources, but you haven't given us a scrap of real information. At least not yet."

"Maybe you haven't asked the right questions."

"Really? You're going to play that game?"

"I'm not playing at anything."

"You're always playing at something."

"Yeah? You think you know me that well?"

He raised an eyebrow. I wanted to do a lot of things to

him, right now, in the parking lot. Most of them were illegal. I let out a breath.

"Tell me honestly. What's up with the painting?"

"Nothing's up. It's a painting. There's nothing more I can tell you about it, Tess. Look it up on Wikipedia if you're curious about Picasso."

That was what his mouth said. But his hands said something very different. They danced through a series of rapid-fire signs. Normally, I wouldn't have caught them all, but I'd been practicing with Miles lately.

His fingers said: *Ask Modred.*

I looked him in the eyes. "Guess that's your final answer."

"It's all I can say on the subject."

If somebody was watching us, I wanted to give them something interesting to look at. I leaned in and kissed him lightly on the cheek.

"Call me if you think of anything else," I said.

"I will." He smiled. *"¡Suerte!"*

"Yeah. You, too." I turned to walk away.

"No pare buscando, tormentita."

That was what he'd started calling me a while ago. His little storm. Maybe it meant that a real storm was coming. The rest was more literal.

Don't stop searching.

Hah.

I never did. That was my problem.

"I don't know about this," Patrick said. It was about the fifth time he'd said it in as many minutes.

"It'll be fine."

We stood outside the vampire safe house on Granville Street, which was below a shop that sold skater clothes.

You could blink and miss it. But if I looked closely, I was able to make out the small character in vampiric script that had been painted above the door, announcing that this was a *daegred*.

"Some of them really don't like humans."

"Well, I really don't like them. So it all evens out."

"Just try not to piss anyone off too much. And if someone insults you, don't stab them. Just ignore them."

"Right. It'll be like high school all over again."

We walked down a narrow flight of stairs, which ended in a reinforced steel door. Patrick knocked twice. A few seconds later, the door opened, and a young vampire wearing dirty jeans and a ripped T-shirt opened the door.

"Magnate. Welcome back."

"Thanks, Trev."

Trev ushered us into what sort of resembled a vampire community center. There were couches along the walls, with demons of various ages and persuasions lounging on them. Some slept; some read; some watched TV. Two young vamps were making out in a corner. Definitely like high school, except everyone here was undead.

I recognized Cyrus playing a vintage arcade game, which someone must have "liberated" from the business above. He saw me and waved.

"Hey. What are you doing here?"

"I came to talk to Modred."

"He's in the kitchen. I'll go get him for you."

Cyrus vanished through a doorway. I stood next to Patrick awkwardly for a few moments. One old vampire was glaring at me. He muttered something under his breath. Probably in Anglo-Saxon. I smiled at him.

I heard a familiar voice coming from the kitchen. "She's *here*?"

The door opened, and Modred emerged. I had to say, he looked pretty good in a pair of pressed khakis and a nicely fitted T-shirt. But I only glanced at him for a second. The girl standing next to him occupied my immediate attention.

"Mia?"

She smiled nervously. "Hey, Tess. What's up?"

"What the hell are you doing here?"

"Don't freak out. I just came to look around, you know? See what the place is like. After Patrick told me about it, I was curious."

I turned to him. "And you knew about this." It wasn't a question.

He nodded. "Sorry. But she had lots of questions. And I didn't have even half of the answers. It seemed easiest to just bring her here."

"Right. Because that's a safe plan."

"She's in no danger," Modred said. "Mia has the magnate's beneficence. Nobody will quarrel with her while she's here."

I gave Patrick a long look. "What exactly is your 'beneficence'? Is that some kind of euphemism?"

He had the decency to blush. "It just means that she's under my protection. Like she has a little piece of my aura that others can sense. Modred taught me how to do it. He wanted to make sure that she'd be safe."

"I've got pepper spray, too," Mia added. "You know, in case the aura thing decides to crap out at the wrong moment."

I sighed. "Fine. I guess I can't control your every move."

"Please. You can barely keep up with my homework."

I decided to ignore that jab. Instead, I turned to Modred. "Look. Is there someplace private we can talk?"

"Of course. But the magnate should be present."

"That's fine."

"What about me?" Mia gave me a slightly petulant look.

"Must I remain ignorant yet again? You know that only causes problems down the road."

"I'm willing to risk that," I said. "Stay with Cyrus. We'll be back in a few minutes, and then we're all going home."

"But we're playing bingo later."

"Home. No bingo."

Mia rolled her eyes and sat down on the couch. "You suck."

"I know. And I'm comfortable with that designation."

We followed Modred through the kitchen, then up a flight of stairs, until we came to a room full of disused equipment: old chairs, broken shelves, an empty fridge, and what looked like a ping-pong table that was missing three of its legs.

"Take a seat if you can find one," Modred said.

"It's fine. I'll stand."

I automatically checked the room for escape routes. It was a habit of working with vampires. Just the one door, and Modred was blocking it. Maybe not on purpose, but you never knew. If he decided to go medieval on me, I probably didn't stand a chance, even if Patrick intervened. He was young and strong, but Modred was old and cunning. That usually won out.

"What do you know about necromancy?" I asked him.

He blinked. "Are you looking for a dictionary definition?"

"No. I need to know what a necromancer might do with a painting."

"Sell it on eBay?" Patrick suggested.

I ignored him. "Luiz Ordeño had a reproduction of the painting *Las Meninas* in his apartment. Are you familiar with it?"

"Yes. It's by Velázquez."

"Right. What if another necromancer had a similar painting? Could that be more than a coincidence?"

"It depends. Are we talking about Lucian Agrado?"

"We are."

"And did he send you here to ask these questions?"

"He did."

Modred nodded. "I thought as much."

"Do you and Lucian know each other?" Patrick asked.

"We know of each other." He grew thoughtful for a moment. "It's possible that the painting is a speculum."

"What's that?"

"A kind of passageway between worlds. A necromancer could use one to travel between here and Trinovantum. But, as magical artifacts go, they're quite rare. Only someone with a great deal of power could fashion one."

"Someone like Ordeño?"

He nodded slowly. "It's possible. He may have created two—one for himself, and a second for Agrado. He was Ordeño's protégé, correct?"

"You probably know more than I do about that."

"I heard that Ordeño was training Lucian to be his replacement someday. Eventually, he could take the place of Prime Solium. A powerful position."

"Well, he's always been full of surprises. But I'm not here to talk about him. How would a necromancer go about using one of these speculum things?"

"The portrait would emit necroid materia at a specific frequency. All the necromancer has to do is match the tone of the power, and that would be enough to activate the speculum. Then they'd just walk through it like a door."

Maybe that was why Ordeño died underneath the portrait. He was trying to escape to Trinovantum, but something got to him first. That still didn't explain why he was wearing the armor, though.

"Maybe he wore it to bed every night," I muttered to myself.

Modred frowned. "What was that?"

"Nothing. Sorry. Just speculating." I shook my head. "So there's no way that someone could activate the speculum without having access to necroid energy?"

"No. It's a necromantic artifact. You'd need a necromancer to take you across the border between worlds."

"Great. They either attack me or lie to me."

"Have you recovered fully from your altercation?"

"More or less." I considered not mentioning Braxton Tel. But Modred had no love for necromancers. Maybe he knew something about Tel that Lucian didn't. "We have a suspect, but there isn't enough evidence to prove anything yet."

That wasn't entirely true. I had a suspect, but nobody believed me. Still—I didn't have anything to lose at this point.

"Who are you considering?"

"Braxton Tel."

His eyes narrowed. "I wouldn't put it past him. Tel is young, but he's gotten a reputation for being an archconservative. He may very well have attacked you and the magnate in order to silence you."

"We think that he left a fingerprint on the Vorpal gauntlet. But when we ran it through Trinovantum's print database, it came up as something called a shadow sector. The information was encrypted."

Modred smiled slowly. "I may be able to help you with that. Come back downstairs with me, and I'll introduce you to someone."

Patrick and I followed him back to the common room. Mia was texting someone on her phone, and didn't even look up.

"Kit." Modred waved to a boy who was sitting on one of the couches, glued to his laptop. "Come over here for a second."

Kit approached us, looking a bit wary. He couldn't have

been older than sixteen. The thought of a boy that young being turned into a vampire made me heartsick. But Patrick hadn't been much older than him.

"Magnate." He inclined his head.

"Hey, Kit. What are you working on?"

"Something for Computer Science." He pushed long black hair out of his eyes. "The teacher wants us to design this supersimple animation using some outdated programming language. So I'm doing something cool instead."

Modred laid a hand on Kit's shoulder. "This is Tess Corday. She works for the CORE, and she needs your help. She needs you to argue with a computer."

"Argue?" I smiled. "Like how my dad yells at the remote?"

"Not quite." Modred smiled, watching the boy as he began typing something rapidly. "You talk to the earth. Kit talks to—" He frowned. "What do you call them again? Servants?"

"Servers." Kit rolled his eyes.

I looked at him in surprise. "You're a forge?"

"I don't know what that means."

"A forge is someone who can channel materia to manipulate electronics and airborne networks. It's an incredibly rare proficiency. Only a few people who work for us can do what you do."

He shrugged. "I just tell computers what they like to hear."

He kept typing rapidly. The screen went blue, and then the words REMOTE CONNECTION appeared. Kit stared at the screen, but didn't say anything. A window popped up, and a series of characters typed themselves into the text box. Then the window closed, and the screen went black.

"So what am I looking for?"

I handed him a flash drive. "There's a fingerprint on this. I need you to run it against the necromancers' database."

He smiled. "That's all?"

Kit plugged the flash drive into the computer and loaded the JPEG of the fingerprint. Then he typed another string of characters. The screen turned blue, and the word SEARCH-ING appeared.

"Need anyone's address or phone number?" he asked.

"Just match the print," Modred said firmly.

Kit sighed. "Boring."

A few seconds later, the fingerprint appeared on the screen again. Six points of comparison lit up on the dermal surface. MATCH > COMPLIANCE.

"What's compliance?" Patrick asked.

It was my turn to smile. "Just watch."

A second window appeared, and with it, a familiar image. Braxton Tel's face stared out at me from the screen, looking as annoyed as he did in person.

"Who's this guy?" Kit asked.

"A bad person," I said simply.

"You can't show this to anyone but Agrado," Modred said. "If another Solium discovers that we've hacked into their network, it could jeopardize the treaty process even further. I can't risk that happening."

"It's invisible evidence," I said. "Like something obtained without a proper search warrant. We know it's there, but we have to proceed as if it isn't."

"How will you proceed, then?"

I smiled. "Hard to say, Modred. I never really know until I'm in the middle of it. And by then, it's too late to get out."

"Sounds like war."

I put my arm around Patrick. "Family is war. This is just overtime."

15

I arrived home to the smell of something amazing. Derrick must have been cooking again, even though it wasn't his night. God bless him. Mia kicked her shoes off in the entryway, still muttering about the tragedy of missing vampire bingo. Patrick was up the stairs and heading for his room before I could even ask him what his plans for the rest of the night were. Not that he would have told me to begin with.

"Mmm." Mia inhaled deeply. "Whatever it is, I want it."

I could hear voices coming from the kitchen. Maybe it was Miles doing the cooking. I hadn't seen him for a few days, and I still wanted to know more about the possibility of developing a new spectroscopy method using his spatial profiling abilities. It wasn't strictly dinner conversation, but in this house, you could talk about pretty much anything over the table.

We walked into the kitchen. Derrick was standing at the

stove, his hand poised over a frying pan, like a domestic Greek statue.

Lucian was standing behind him.

Great.

"Okay," he was saying. "Now, the trick is to turn the pancake with your fingers. Do it quickly, but gently, so you don't break it."

"But the pan's really hot."

"Don't be scared of it. You won't get burnt. Just get right in there and rotate the whole thing clockwise."

"Should I spit on my fingers first?"

"No. That's gross. Just do it quickly, and you'll be fine."

Derrick reached into the pan. "Hey, you're right. It actually feels neat."

"Perfect! Now do that for a few more seconds, and it'll be ready."

"Hey," I said, dropping my purse on the kitchen table. "Did you stop by to give some cooking lessons?"

Lucian turned and smiled at me. It was one of those warm, inviting smiles that almost made me forget how little I'd trusted him lately. It's tough to be mad at someone who looks so happy to see you.

"Hey. I thought you might be a bit bogged down at work, so I decided to solve the food crisis for one night. We're making *panqueques con dulce de leche*. They're going to change your life."

"Lucian's making them," Derrick clarified. "I'm mostly burning them."

"No, you're doing great. Now scoop that one onto the plate, and we can put the filling in. Not too much. You want it to ooze out the pores of the *panqueque*, but you don't want the whole thing to explode."

"Oozing, but not exploding. Got it."

"We have to talk," I told Lucian.

"Try one first." He handed me what looked like a hot, rolled-up crepe. "Seriously. It's going to change everything."

"Fine. But you can't just solve everything with—" My eyes widened as I tasted the *panqueque*. "Sweet baby Jesus, why haven't I been eating these every single day of my life? Have you always known how to make them?"

"Of course."

"Wow. It's all I can say. It tastes like the universe loves me."

"You've got a bit of *dulce de leche* on your mouth."

"Where?"

"Okay, I lied. It's not a bit. It's all over." He wiped my mouth gently with the sleeve of his shirt. "There. Got it. Sorry if you were saving it for later."

I smiled. "Thanks."

"No problem."

Mia was already stuffing two of the *panqueques* into her mouth. "Tess, can you wash my plaid shirt?"

"You have a plaid shirt?"

"Yeah, the green and red one."

"I thought that was a Christmas blanket."

"Ha-ha. Seriously, can you wash it? I have, like, nothing to wear."

"You have, like, a whole closet full of clothes to wear."

"Half of them are dirty!"

"You do know how to operate the washing machine. I distinctly remember giving you a tutorial when we moved in here."

"I have homework to do. And the basement has spiders."

I sighed. "Fine. Lucian, come with me."

"Sure. I'm great at folding."

"I'll bet you are," Derrick murmured.

I gave him a look. "What was that?"

"Nothing. Just mixing the batter."

"Right."

Lucian followed me down the stairs. The laundry room was cool and slightly cavernous. It was one of the only places where neither Patrick nor Mia usually followed me, so I could actually get some peace here. The bathroom used to be my sanctuary, but lately, Mia seemed incapable of actually knocking before she barged in.

I stared at the laundry in the hamper. One of Patrick's socks was on the top, and it was filthy. How did boys get their socks so dirty? Were they actually playing in the mud and just not telling anyone about it? Maybe there was some secret game of shoeless rugby that broke out at every workplace, precisely at two p.m.

"Tess?"

For a moment, I'd forgotten that he was in the laundry room with me. He was standing there in his blue jeans and his black collared shirt, and I suddenly pictured him in front of the mirror every morning, flicking his collar to give it that chic-messy look. I felt an irrational cloud of annoyance rising somewhere within me. Asshole. With his perfect clothes and hair and breath that always smells like the same gum. Standing in my laundry room, looking at me like I'm some kind of crazy domestic.

He blinked. "Where did you go? You were just staring at the clothes. I thought it was some kind of divination."

"It was nothing." I started shoving clothes into the washer. Jesus, where had Derrick found black socks with an argyle pattern? Who did he think he was? A Harvard professor? I felt the intense desire to make them disappear.

"It obviously wasn't."

"Yeah?" I stared at the clothes piling up in the agitator.

"Is that a question?"

"I don't know; is it?" I closed the door. No sense in slamming it.

Still, a secret part of me hoped that the fight we were about to have would progress to those kinds of epic proportions. Slamming of washer doors, the laundry basket upended, blood on the Downy drier sheets.

Maybe I'd been working as an OSI too long.

"Hey. *¿Qué pasa?*"

I turned around and glared at him. I could feel something heating up inside now, slow and red and slightly dangerous, like a wire coil.

"*¡Estoy super enojado para ti! ¡Quiero tener un choque en tu boca!*"

He gave me an odd look. "You just said you're very angry for me, and you want to have a car accident on my mouth."

"Fuck." I rubbed my forehead. "My Spanish sucks."

"No it doesn't. You conjugated *querer* exactly right." He walked over to me and put his hands on my shoulders. "What is it? Tell me."

"It doesn't work that way." I got out from under his hands. "You can't just be like, *What's wrong*, and then have this eloquent explanation flow out of me like a logic fountain, then everything gets to be okay for you again."

"What's a logic fountain?"

"I don't know!" I really did want to have a car accident on his mouth. Whatever that meant. "I don't know how to talk to you anymore. First you disappear. Then you show up and act all nonchalant, like we're not both involved in this case. Then you slip me some vital information in code, telling me to talk to a vampire who isn't even supposed to know you, but he does—"

"We don't really know each other, but—"

"You know *of* each other; yeah, I got that from Modred." I shook my head. "Why couldn't you just tell me about the painting?"

"Because I wasn't sure who was listening. What did Modred say?"

"That it's a speculum. Both of them are. That Ordeño probably made one for you, since you're supposed to take his place as Prime Solium."

Lucian blinked. "Is that what the vampires think?"

"That's what Modred thinks."

"I have no intention of taking Luiz's seat. I don't want that kind of responsibility. If anyone's going to get the seat, it'll be Deonara."

"I don't care about Deonara. We're talking about you."

"What about me?"

I wasn't going to let him start with the circular questions again. "Don't be coy. It's not cute anymore, and you know it."

He sighed. "Fine."

"You're not present anymore, Lucian. You're in another world most of the time. You refuse to engage, and you don't want to answer any questions."

"Is this about us, or about the Ordeño case?"

"Both. We're in both of those places. We don't get to come home each night and pretend that we have regular jobs."

He shrugged. "I don't have a job, Tess. I mean, not in the strictest sense. I have certain obligations to different communities, but I'm not going to work from nine to five and collecting a paycheck for it."

I scowled at him. "I don't know what sucks worse. The tone you use when you talk about me 'collecting a paycheck,' or the fact that you actually believe I only work eight hours a day."

"I don't think either of those—" He shook his head. "No. I'm not doing this. I'm not getting sucked in."

"Oh, by all means, don't get sucked into anything. Don't bother yourself with it. The smartest choice is to just deflect everything."

"Did you learn that in therapy?"

I stared at him. "How did you know I was in therapy?"

"I guessed. Now it's confirmed."

"You guessed? What's that supposed to mean?"

"It doesn't mean anything."

"Right. You don't think I'm some lonely crackpot who can't deal with her stress, so she needs some therapist to tell her everything's going to be fine."

"No. I don't think that at all."

"I don't believe you."

"Well, you don't know me, then."

I folded my arms. "No. I don't know you, Lucian. I met you more than two years ago, and last year we started having sex. But I don't really know anything about you. And that's not my fault."

"So it's my fault?" He was actually getting angry. I felt weirdly vindicated.

"Kind of. I mean, I'm not exactly the greatest girlfriend. Maybe there's things I'm supposed to be doing. To be honest, this is the first real relationship I've had since I was a teenager, when I stopped believing in relationships."

"Is that what we're having? A relationship?"

Really? We were going in this direction now?

"Well, what would you call it, Lucian?" I turned on the washer, and its low, dry hum filled my ears. "Be precise."

"We've got something complicated."

"Define 'complicated.'"

"I'm not sure I want to."

"Of course. You don't want to do anything. Why would you? It's so much easier to just sit on the fence and jerk off, watching your future fly by."

"That's kind of an upsetting image."

"Lucian!" My face was red. I wanted to cry or decapitate something. Maybe both. "What do you want? Just tell me. Precisely."

He gave me a funny look. I remembered that look from

a dream I'd had about him two years ago. He was stripped to the waist, and the lily tattoo on his shoulder blade looked like it was made of glass, or transparent fire.

"I'm in love with you."

I blinked. I didn't say anything. My tongue was made of cotton.

He took a step toward me. "Tess."

"You're bullshitting me."

He frowned. "Why would you say that?"

"Because it's ridiculous. Why would you love me?"

Now he looked confused. "I don't understand the question."

"Come on, Lucian. You're you. I'm me."

"Are we back to grammar?" He smiled and put his hands on my shoulders again. "Yes, you're you, I'm me. We're us. And I like us."

"Don't be cute."

"What do you want me to say?" One hand moved up my neck. His touch was always light. "*Te amo.* I love you, Tessa. You make me happy."

"But—" I wanted to scream in frustration. But his hand on my neck was also making me excited. *No. Focus. You are in control of this conversation.* "Where have you been lately? If you love me so much, why do you act like you don't care?"

"Because caring freaks me out. It's dangerous. I could lose you, and I don't want to. Just thinking about it makes me terrified."

"What's happening to me? Where am I going?"

"You know what I mean."

"Actually, I don't. Are you worried that I'll leave you, or that I'll get killed because of you?"

"Both."

"The probability of those things happening simultaneously is pretty low. Unless the roof falls on me while I'm breaking up with you."

His hand was moving down my neck. I was losing focus. Shit.

"I'm afraid of everything," he said. "That you'll break up with me. That you'll die. That I'll put you in danger."

"I shot you in the chest last year. Who's putting who in danger?"

"You did what I told you. And I knew I'd come back."

"You said you weren't sure."

"I was. I always do."

I looked at his eyes. They were exactly the color of brown eyes. I was starting to feel warmer. Everywhere. This did not bode well for argumentation.

"Are you immortal?" I asked him.

"Kind of."

"What does that mean?"

"I don't know. Can you explain materia?"

"Yes. I had to study a textbook on it."

"But do you believe everything you read?"

"No. Especially not the footnotes."

He held his left hand a few inches away from my face. His right hand was still touching my neck. I felt a surge of power. A lily appeared, hovering above his palm. The petals were liquid glass, and at the core of the flower there was a mineral structure, humming with light. The flower revolved slowly before my eyes.

"Does this mean that you're a flower?" I teased.

"Sort of." He smiled. "It means that I'm different. My cells are more plantlike than human. That's what allows me to regenerate."

I just stared at him.

"Say something."

I reached my fingers through the image of the flower. It

trembled and vanished, leaving a faint impression of smoke behind. I touched his face.

"So you're a plant."

"That's a simplified explanation. But sort of. Yes."

"Wow."

"Does that freak you out?"

I smiled. "Not at all."

I kissed him. His lips were dry, but he responded immediately. His tongue flicked the edge of my mouth. I put my hand on the back of his neck. I loved the soft hairs there. Sometimes I dreamt about them.

"Take me to Trinovantum," I said.

"What?"

"You heard me."

"Tess. It's not that simple."

"It is." I kept my hand on his neck. "I know that Braxton tried to kill me. He probably tried to kill Ordeño, too, so that he wouldn't be able to complete the treaty. But I can't put all of the pieces together until I visit the hidden city. I think that's where the murder weapon came from. And it's where Ordeño was trying to escape to, just before he was killed. That's why we found him underneath *Las Meninas*."

Lucian stared at me for a long moment, considering this. "What do you propose to do once you get there?"

"Get me an audience with Lord Nightingale. All I want to do is talk to him. He's the wild card in all of this."

"That won't be easy."

"But I know you can do it."

His face was close to mine. His breath smelled like *dulce de leche*. "Did they teach you this in your interrogation classes?"

"Maybe."

I reversed our positions, so that he was standing in front

of the washing machine. I pressed him lightly against it. He gave me a questioning look.

"Really?"

I stared at him. "Really."

Instead of arguing, he pulled off his shirt.

"Sit on top of the machine."

"Is this some private fantasy of yours?"

"Yes."

He pulled himself on top of the washer. "It's a good one."

"I don't need you to talk anymore."

Lucian grinned and smiled, but didn't reply. That was one of the things that I loved about him. Such a good listener.

I undid his belt and pulled down his jeans. He was wearing blue underwear that I didn't recognize, but they had the right effect. I slid them down. He was already half-hard. I rubbed his legs, and I could feel the muscles twitching slightly beneath my touch. He was shivering.

I took him in my mouth. He groaned and put his fingers in my hair. Everything vanished into heat and momentum. I felt his feet knocking slightly against the washing machine. I jerked him off with my right hand, while letting my left linger on his legs, just brushing them lightly.

I was thinking of cold water and the color orange. I don't know why. For a second, I imagined that his whole body was a liquid with something gold and luminous at its core, like a perfect weapon.

He started breathing quicker, and his muscles tightened. I took it out of my mouth, but kept moving my hand.

"Fuck," he whispered. "Don't. I'm going to come."

"Then come."

"I don't want to." His eyes were clenched shut. "What about you?"

"Who said we're finished when you come?" I kept moving my hand. "We've got thirty minutes left in the spin cycle. That's enough time to deal with me."

"Are you sure?"

"Lucian." I pressed my mouth against his. *"¡Cállate!"*

His knees buckled. I kissed him harder. He said something with his tongue still in my mouth, but I couldn't understand him.

I wasn't listening anyway.

16

We stood in front of the Picasso. I took a deep breath.

"Ready? This could get a bit hairy."

"I think so. What's it like to travel by speculum?"

"You're about to find out."

"Okay." I closed my eyes. "Now what?"

"Just take my hand and step forward."

"Does the magic require physical contact?"

"No. I just like holding your hand."

I smiled. Then I felt his fingers in mine.

We stepped forward.

I felt nothing. Then a blow to the back of the head. Then cold.

I opened my eyes, shaking the dizziness off.

It was night. We were standing at an iron gate. I had no idea how we'd gotten there. I had felt a pinching sensation, then nothing, and now: an iron gate.

At first I thought it was overgrown with vines, but as I

looked at them more closely, I realized they were packed too densely to be weeds. They were actually different plants growing on trellises. One had silver-edged leaves, like chervil. Another had pendulous flowers that were wine-colored. It resembled hanging fuchsia but probably wasn't.

"Are we in Trinovantum?" I asked.

Lucian stood beside me. "This is the entrance to the Conclusus."

"What exactly is that?"

"The garden that encloses Trinovantum."

I looked at the sky, which was alive with stars. "Did we go through some kind of temporal shift?"

"It's always night here."

"How do the plants survive? Even night-flowering plants require sunlight."

"These don't. They've been grafted and bred for centuries. They're all adapted strains of nocturnal fauna."

"Oh." I could see what looked like colored lights dancing past the gate. "Are those lamps?"

"Sort of." Lucian placed his hand on the gates. They opened silently, revealing an even stone path. "Follow me. Stay close, and don't touch anything."

"Thanks, Mom."

He gave me a look. "I'm serious. You aren't supposed to be here, and you can't stay here for too long. Don't touch anything, and especially don't eat anything."

"Is it like a Persephone thing?"

"You don't want to find out." He stepped through the gate. "Let's go."

"Is it dangerous?"

"Of course. Gardens always are."

The path was shaded by trees. After a short space, it divided into a crossroads. A stone basin had been placed at the center of the junction. Flame burned inside of the basin, coming from the stone itself. That was a tough trick. The flame cast no heat, and had a slightly violet cast to it.

We turned to the left, and some of the trees gave way to stone enclosures. Night flora bloomed within them: trumpet-shaped moonflowers, which clung to sculpted iron trellises; evening primrose with wan pink petals; evening iris the color of sherry; and vesper iris, magenta with white spots, which I recognized from my mother's garden. The iris blooms were surrounded by light green leaves that exuded a sweet, familiar smell. I realized that they were nicotine plants. Instantly, my fingers reached for a cigarette that wasn't there. I'd left my emergency pack on the kitchen counter.

I pointed to a vivid white flower edged with purple. "What's that?"

"Datura. It's quite poisonous. The leaves are sometimes called thorn apple, or Devil's apple, and they contain a neurotoxin."

"I can see why you didn't want me to touch anything."

"Only about half the plants here are poisonous. I think."

I spotted white gaura and yucca flowers as well, the former resembling a spray of icicles, the latter so thickly clustered they looked more like coral, or bone.

The trees began to thicken again as we continued.

A small shadow crossed my feet. I looked down, and was surprised to see a black-and-white cat sitting at my feet. The cat regarded me with bright eyes the color of spearmint. Two other cats, one entirely black, the other calico, sat a few feet away from the first one. All of them appeared to be watching us.

"What's with the cats?" I whispered.

Lucian smiled. "Don't worry. They're harmless. We have a lot of them here."

"Why?"

He shrugged. "It's one of the places they go whenever you can't find them. Cats can move between worlds fairly easily."

"And they come here?"

"Often. Probably because of all the birds."

I looked up for the first time, scanning the boughs of the trees that shaded either side of the path. The branches were thick with birds. Some perched silently, while others preened their feathers. A few appeared to be sleeping. There were numerous types of owls, but the only ones I could recognize were the spotted and the great-horned variety. The others came in varying shapes: compact and gray, oblong and white, masked, variegated, and pygmy-sized. Some had amber eyes, while others had eyes that resembled bottomless pools of black liquid.

The owls occupied the highest branches, and smaller nocturnal birds, like nighthawks and frogmouths, clung to the lower branches. The nighthawks shook their white-banded tail feathers at me. I felt chastised.

"Should we be asking their permission to be here?"

"It wouldn't hurt," Lucian replied.

"I was kidding."

"The Striga have their own court here, along with the other fowls. They watch over the gardens and hunt prey."

"Like mice? Or humans?"

"Sometimes both."

"Right." I gave them what I hoped was a polite smile. "Well, I'm sure they're doing a fabulous job."

"Wait until you see the night bugs. They work twice as hard."

"I'm not sure I want to know exactly what that means."

Lucian chuckled. "Just follow me. You'll see."

We came to a walled-in grove with a fountain at its center. The fountain was made of a glossy black material that could have been hematite, but I wasn't sure. It almost looked like polished obsidian. It was shaped like a giant lotus. Night lilies floated within it, their petals so narrow and sharp that they looked like porcelain knives. They drifted with the movement of the dark water.

Seeing the flowers made me think of Lucian's tattoo, and I was struck once again by how closely it resembled a real flower.

"How many different types of lily are there?" I asked.

He smiled slightly. "*Lilium* belongs to a large family. There are red Martagon lilies, Tiger lilies, yellow Bosnian lilies—" He frowned. "Some of them I only know by their names in Spanish. *Llilácea. Azucena. Lirio mariposa.* Those are the kind that butterflies like best. And *ninfea.*" He gestured to the fountain. "This is the night-blooming water lily, or *lirio de agua.* That's my family's flower."

I looked at him strangely. "Family? Do you mean like uncles and cousins who live in Trinovantum?"

I'd thought his family was long dead. The idea that I might have to attend a necromantic family reunion made me start sweating immediately, despite the moist, chill air that pervaded gardens.

"More like *antepasades.* Ancestors. But they're connected by tradition rather than strict heredity. Certain families have cultivated certain powers, and that includes particular styles and secrets for using necromancy."

"What's yours like?"

"My family? Or my style?"

"Both."

He gently touched one of the floating lilies. It may have been a trick of the dim light, but I thought I saw a strand of white vapor move between his finger and the flower. I could feel a subtle type of energy connecting them, not precisely what I would have recognized as necroid materia. Although we could barely even recognize that. It was as different from elemental materia as dark matter was from the regular variety.

"Lilium is an old family," he said. "Proud, but not impervious. We've nearly been wiped out on more than one occasion, but we always seem to survive."

"And what sorts of things do you specialize in?"

"That's a trade secret."

"Come on."

He shrugged. "I can't tell you everything, Tess. You're not even supposed to be here. If Lord Nightingale hadn't granted his permission, you wouldn't have made it through the front gates."

"Is he like the head gardener?"

"You could say that. He rules the Dark Parliament."

"Does that make him one of your cousins?"

"No. He's Vespertine. All of the flowers in his family are poisonous, and that includes datura."

"So I shouldn't shake his hand."

He actually looked startled. "Absolutely not. Don't touch him, even if he invites you to. And don't eat anything he gives you."

"This is starting to sound like a fairy tale."

"Trinovantum is an old city, with old politics and traditions. You may find it easier to be here than most mages, because you have an affinity for earth materia. But what you call necroid materia is very different. It's toxic, unless you know how to use it. And you don't."

I nodded. "Sure. I don't really want strange men touching me anyway."

"It's not that you *can't* touch him. You just probably shouldn't." His expression was curious. "Lord Nightingale exerts a certain influence over people. Physical contact only makes that influence more powerful. It's best to keep your distance."

"I thought nightingales were sweet little birds that liked to sing."

"They are. But they're also very determined. In medieval legends, the nightingale sang most sweetly when her heart was pierced by a thorn. She was willing to sacrifice herself in order to sing a perfect note."

"That's beautiful. And scary."

"You've just described Trinovantum. It's both of those things."

"But I haven't actually seen a city yet. Just gardens."

"You will. They're both connected."

We came to a thick hedge that was spotted with white blooms. Lucian gestured, and I felt a subtle wave of necroid materia stir around him, almost like a breeze. Shadows flickered along the surface of the hedge, and the leaves drew back, forming a narrow entrance. Lucian stepped through it, and I followed.

On the other side of the hedge was a small square of dark soil, enclosed by a glass wall. The wall was only about four feet high, but the threads of glowing necroid materia that coursed along its surface were warning enough to anyone: Don't touch.

The flowers planted in the soil were white and brittle. As I looked closer, I realized that they weren't flowers at all, but rather skeletons of flowers. The petals were made of bone, and the leaves were a kind of ash-colored tendon, a black tissue that must have terminated in unimaginable roots. The flowers remained still despite the wind, their stiff, osseous petals looking more like spiked cactuses.

"They look like fossils," I said.

"They are. Each of those flowers is extinct. All that's left are the bones, but even they have a trace of power left in them."

"Like undead perennials?"

"Basically. Some of them you might recognize. Those Hawaiian lobelias have been extinct since the nineteenth century." He pointed to a group of extremely delicate floral skeletons in the back of the row. "Those are from the Palaeozoic Era. The stringy ones that look like algae are Cambrian flora. Next to them, with the sphenophyte bulbs on each branch, are Cooksonia."

"So this is where flowers go when they die?"

"These have been collected over time. Most extinct flowers are simply gone, but we've managed to preserve some of them in fossilized form. We call this place the Bone Garden. As long as the plants stay in this soil, they can't ever decompose completely."

I shook my head. "You know, I always thought that necromancy was about destroying cellular structures and tearing apart systems. Like chaos theory. But this place is full of life. It's like an ecologist's wet dream."

"Necromancy is a natural force," Lucian said, "like entropy. When a system expands, it loses heat. The same goes for the universe. On a planetary level, death makes room for new life."

"Does that make you like a Venus flytrap?" I grinned. "A killer plant?"

He smiled as well. "Maybe. Our power is linked to the earth, like yours. Only, your earth materia functions as a result of photosynthesis, mytosis, convection, and other biological forces that make life possible. Necroid materia comes from things that are already dead: compost, cadaverine, putrescine, necrotic tissue, and decay. Even the heat produced by maggots invading a dead body can be converted into necroid power."

"Romantic."

"Isn't it?" He placed a hand lightly on the small of my back. "Keep walking. These are the suburbs. We're about to reach Trinovantum proper."

I noticed that the cats had mostly disappeared. "What happened to our feline entourage?" I asked.

"They tend to stay in the outer gardens. Most of these plants are toxic to them, and the birds roost close to the entrance. That's their primary entertainment."

We came abruptly to a body of water. It wasn't exactly a lake, but it was large and dark, receding into shadows. Water lilies drifted across its surface. The stone path terminated at the edge of the water.

"This is the Flood," Lucian said. "It's like a moat that encircles the city. Living things aren't supposed to be able to cross it, but you've been given Lord Nightingale's dispensation. So you should be fine."

I glared at him. "Should be?"

Lucian winked. "*No seas preocupada*. Just let me summon the ferry."

He held his hand over the surface of the water. I felt another wave of necroid materia, and red vapor swirled between his fingers. The water lily nearest him began to tremble. Then it swelled in size, growing until it resembled a floral vessel. The petals shimmered and turned translucent, becoming like glass, or ice. The flower was now just large enough to hold both of us.

"Hop on," he said.

"Is it seaworthy?"

"Of course."

We both stepped onto the surface of the flower, which trembled slightly beneath our weight, but was still surprisingly firm. It began to drift along the surface of the water, moving at stately pace.

"This is my first time traveling by flower," I said.

"And how do you like it?"

"Better than the skytrain, so far."

I could see lights and indistinct shapes along the edges of the lake. As we drew closer, I realized that the lights were coming from massive trees. Each tree had a structure nestled within its roots, a building made of glass, iron, and polished stone. Some of them looked like temples, while others more closely resembled greenhouses.

The trees themselves were enormous. Points of colored light moved within their leaves, winking in the darkness. Once we were close enough to them, I saw that the lights were actually gemstones, which hung from the boughs like pendulous fruit.

There were diamond trees, sapphire trees, amethyst trees, and other gems that weren't immediately familiar. Some were black with green veins—chrysoberyl, maybe? Others were striated or multicolored. A cluster of bejeweled apples, much darker than rubies, had to be carbuncles. We passed by what looked like a topaz tree, and I watched in fascination as the glow of the gemstones struck the glass surface of the structure beneath them, making it seem to burn with amber light from within.

"This is the Grove of Souls," Lucian said, his voice hushed. "Each tree belongs to a different family, and yields a unique gemstone."

"Where's your family tree?"

"Right there." He pointed to an emerald tree, whose gems were bright and oblong, almost pear-shaped. "The gemstones are the souls of my ancestors. They hold the collective memory of Lilium."

"Are the souls—" I frowned. "I mean—"

"They're alive, in a sense," he said. "But they're more like memories. We learn from them, but they don't communicate in any kind of straightforward manner."

"What are those buildings underneath?"

"Family arboretums. Sort of like a cross between a mausoleum and a conservatory. You can go there to be alone, or to pay respect to your ancestors. They're full of family history."

We passed the final row of trees. For a while, it was impossible to tell if we were moving at all, since the water was so dark and still. It felt like we were penetrating into the heart of some uncreated universe, something dormant and immense.

Then I started to hear sounds. Metal striking metal, voices, and a low buzzing whose source I couldn't identify. We seemed to pass through a nebulous wall of shadow, which felt like spiderwebs against my face and hands. Beyond the outer layer of darkness, a high wall emerged from the water. It was white and smooth.

I realized that it was made of bone.

A portal was set into the wall—two massive doors, also made of bone. The surface was so smooth and burnished that I could see a distorted version of my reflection within it. Stone embrasures had been set into notches within the bone at regular intervals, casting shaky firelight. The wall seemed uncomfortably alive.

"We're here," Lucian said. "Are you ready?"

"No."

"Is there anything I can say to reassure you?"

"I doubt it."

He smiled. "All right, then. Welcome to Trinovantum."

The gates began to open. I took a deep breath.

Suddenly, the Bone Garden, with its haunted fossils, seemed comforting.

We walked through the gates and stepped into the middle of a crowded square. Kiosks and tables had been set up everywhere, and I could smell a hundred different things. Some of them smelled amazing, and others worried me slightly, but I couldn't exactly say why. Most of the customers browsing the tables wore black, but some wore gray, and a few didn't seem to be dressed at all. Sometimes it's hard to tell with paranormal species, though.

"This is the Night Market," Lucian said. "Really, just the market, since it's always night here."

"Wow. It's bigger than the one in Richmond."

"You can get almost anything here, but whatever you buy is native to the city. It can only leave Trinovantum for a short time before it vanishes."

"Like the Vorpal gauntlet?"

He nodded. "Even in your lab, under controlled conditions, it won't last for more than a few days. No amount of magic can slow down its deterioration."

I saw too many things to even mentally absorb, let alone describe. Black woven tapestries hanging from steel racks, with silver thread that trembled and rewove itself every second, as if playing a film. A produce stand filled with black watermelons, tomatoes, and gourds. They were so shiny, they looked like beetle shells. I wondered if their seeds were white instead of black. What did their juice look like? Congealed blood, maybe, or tinted sangría.

One kiosk was arrayed with books, but only a few of them were made from paper. There were volumes bound in stained glass, polished steel, jet, and bone. One book, separated from the others, was just a formless outline made of smoke. Seeing it made me remember the smoke volume from Ordeño's apartment. I pointed to it.

"What's that? Ordeño had one."

Lucian followed my gaze. "A Polybius Book."

"I thought you said nothing lasts long outside the city."

"If you kept it in a special container, it might be able to survive a bit longer. Maybe he took it back and forth with him."

"It was on a stand when we found it. Almost like a work of art."

"They have to be kept away from most other books. Artifacts that powerful don't tend to get along well with their social inferiors."

"What kind of power are we talking about exactly?"

"Gravitation. Entropic tampering. Curses one-oh-one."

"Like cursing for laymen?"

"No. Curses that last for one hundred and one years."

"Wow." I stared at the book in fascination. I couldn't see any images within the smoke. It was all just black and gray vapor. "How do you read it?"

"Very carefully."

"Can you do it?"

He made a face, almost like a grimace. "To an extent. I'm not nearly as competent in that language as Ordeño was."

"Smoke language?"

"Polybius, yes. The oldest form of long-distance communication in the world."

"Like a Dark Ages tweet."

He frowned. "Do you have to make fun of everything?"

"Have we met?" When he continued to look annoyed, I sighed. "No. I don't have to make fun of everything. It's really just whistling in the dark. It keeps me from being scared out of my mind most days."

"I can relate to that."

"Do you think Ordeño would have gotten his book here?"

He shook his head. "They shouldn't really be sold. This one could be a fake. It doesn't seem that way, though."

"Let's ask."

We approached the table, which was partially obscured by a red velvet curtain. When I was about a foot away from the Polybius Book, the curtain was yanked open, and a creature emerged.

It resembled a cross between an insect and a worm. It was about four feet long, and its thin legs moved rapidly as it slithered forward. Its body was divided into ten segments, black and plated like a beetle, but also covered in fine white hairs that quivered. Its tail was bulbous and glowed a pale blue-green, making its body appear all the more spectral.

The giant glowworm swiveled its head toward me. Its antennae drifted in my direction, and its small black eyes regarded me. They were hooded by chitinous plates that resembled a helm, tinted rust red, like the rest of its body.

"Sshh crrcr h scr kk hss 's?" it asked.

"She's a Lampyrid," Lucian whispered. "They keep the gardens in working order. Just speak to her in English. Neither of us have the soft palate necessary to duplicate colloquial Lampyr."

"I'm sorry," I said, trying unsuccessfully to meet her eyes. They kept moving in their sockets, like black ball bearings. "I only speak English."

"Sss's hh. Is fine, is fine." She gestured to the book with her antennae. "Polybius Book. You're looking, *sssh*?"

I assumed that her *"sssh?"* had to be something like *hmm?* But I wasn't entirely sure. I tried to keep my tone neutral.

"Do you sell a lot of these?"

She made a strange sound, halfway between a hiss and rattling that emerged deep within her carapace. Her tail flickered blue, then green, then blue again. Maybe this was how a Lampyrid laughed.

"No. No. Not many. Got this one from the Hamakei."

I gave Lucian a blank look.

"They're avian demons," he said. "Kind of like vultures."

"Like the Seneschal."

His eyes widened. "You've visited him?"

I wasn't sure what to make of his surprise. Did he suspect that the Seneschal had mentioned him? Or was he just impressed that I'd known where to find him?

"Sure. We had a chat."

The Lampyrid made a slight movement of its head in Lucian's direction. *"Buenas tardes, hechicero. ¡Suerte a Cámara de Llilácea!"*

The glowworm had a much better accent than I did.

"Igualmente," Lucian replied, also inclining his head. *"¡Suerte a Madriguera de los Luciérnagas!"*

"My *shhshr'r'ii'p* worked in the arboretum of Lilium," she continued. "Always good things to say. Fine family. Fine."

Maybe a *shhshr'r'ii'p* was like a maternal grandmother. I tried to imagine what her tasks might be within the garden. Perhaps the Lampyridae were the ones who provided most of the lighting with their tails.

"We were lucky to have her," Lucian said. "May I ask your surname?"

"Of course. It's Rr'ssshhs'srl: sshl'k h ullssh. But I'd be delighted if you called me by my familiar name, which is hnnnh'S."

To his credit, Lucian didn't miss a beat. "Thank you, hnnnh'S. You say that the Hamakei sold you this Polybius Book?"

"Yes. Yes. Two nights ago."

I tried to imagine precisely what unit of measurement the glowworm was using. If it was always night, then how did you ever know which night you were in? And how did you discern the "middle" of the night?

"Did the Hamakei say where he got it?"

hnnnh'S made a clicking noise. "Said it came from a Dark Parliament fellow. Stolen, most likely. Don't know how he would have done it, though. Like stealing air and darkness. Hard to hold."

"You seem to be holding it," I observed. "It's part of your display."

"Of course. Came with a reliquary of holding. Very safe."

I looked at the book again. As my eyes adjusted to the shifting vapors, I saw that they seemed to be contained within an invisible square. The smoke teased the edges of the square, but ventured no farther.

"Reliquary comes with book," she added. "No cost."

"How much did the Hamakei sell it for?" Lucian asked.

"Crate full of moon-grubs. Seemed to want to get rid of it."

I looked at Lucian. "With the reliquary thing, would the book survive long enough to reach the lab for some tests?"

hnnnh'S reared her head back, as if startled. "Taking it offworld? Where?"

"Vancouver," I replied.

"Where's that?"

"Earth," Lucian clarified.

She shook her head vigorously. "Not a good idea. Polybius Book is fragile, fragile. Even with the reliquary, transit will be too hard."

I turned to Lucian. "How did Ordeño do it, then? He had the same vessel. At least it looked the same."

"I'm not sure. I'm no expert in transporting goods out of Trinovantum."

"Ask the Hamakei," hnnnh'S said. "He's *shr'L'ehhs*. Very handy."

Lucian frowned. "I'm not familiar with that word in Lampyr."

"Don't know in English. Is like—" Her head wove back and forth slowly for a few seconds as she pondered the translation. *"¿El contrabandista?"*

"¡Sí, claro! A smuggler."

"If you find the proper container, I can sell it. Otherwise"—her antennae made a shruglike gesture—"no sale. Too precious."

"Can we take it out of the reliquary first?" Lucian asked. "Just for a second?"

hnnnh'S considered this, her head swaying. Finally she nodded. She half crawled, half slithered over to the book, her small legs moving surprisingly fast across the ground. She brushed the air next to the book with her antennae, and I felt a brief shiver of power as the mystical enclosure that was holding it vanished. Instantly, the "pages" began to swirl and smoke with greater zeal.

"Careful. Has a temper."

I was pretty sure I didn't want to know exactly what that meant, or what an angry Polybius Book was capable of.

Lucian examined the book, frowning slightly. His fingers hovered near the edges of the smoke, but he didn't touch it. Finally, he reached into his jacket and withdrew a black silk pouch, tied with a drawstring. He untied the pouch and removed a small, slender pipe made of bone. It was carved into the shape of a calla lily.

"Is now really an appropriate time for that?" I asked.

"Just watch. Not all books are read the same way." He turned to hnnnh'S. "Could I trouble you for a pinch of *tabaco de pipa*? I seem to be out."

"Of course." She reached into some unfathomable space behind the counter with one of her small legs. Or was it an arm? The appendage reappeared a second later holding a twist of paper, like a chemist's bag. The tobacco inside was even more fragrant than the night-blooming plants from the garden.

Lucian sprinkled a pinch of brown herb into the pipe. Then he lit it with a small Zippo, which had also come from the pouch. Did he carry this around all the time? I suppose you never knew when you were going to encounter a Polybius Book. Or maybe he just enjoyed a relaxing after-lunch smoke. I was reminded once again of how little I knew about him.

As soon as the pipe was lit, the smoke of the Polybius Book began to tremble and swirl. Lucian inhaled, and the tobacco flared orange. He inhaled again, more strongly this time, and a tendril of smoke from the book was sucked into the pipe. It mingled with the tobacco smoke, and the orange glow suddenly turned green.

He blew out a long peal of green smoke, sighing as he did so. The smoke rippled in the air for a moment, and then, to my amazement, flickering characters began to appear within its depths. They looked like serpentine tails and mysterious paint strokes to me, but Lucian could obviously read them. He scanned the characters closely, which had already begun to fade. He had the same expression that I got on my face while reading an arcane credit card statement.

He smiled suddenly, pointing to a small character hovering near the tail end of the green smoke. It actually looked like two serpentine letters that had been drawn on top of each other, wriggling slightly in the air.

"Ordeño's signature," he said. "LO. This book belonged to him. But it's impossible to read because half the pages are missing."

My eyes widened. "He must have separated the books. We have one half in the lab, and this is the other half."

Lucian snuffed out the pipe and replaced it. The Polybius Book returned to its normal "shape." The glowing characters were now nothing but smoke again.

"It won't last long, even under your lab's conditions," he said. "We have to combine the two books, before the first one fades out altogether." He turned to hnnnh'S, who didn't seem unnerved by anything that had just happened.

"Can you hold this behind the counter while we talk to the Hamakei? We're very interested."

"Of course. Of course." Her antennae waved in accordance. "He has a stall next to the Night Hob. Close by."

"Thank you, hnnnh'S. *¡Mucho gusto!*"

"*¡Igualmente!*" If a glowworm could be said to smile, then she did.

We made our way through the crowd. Mostly, I just followed Lucian, since I had no idea what a Night Hob was or where I should be looking for one. We passed a stall that seemed to be selling nothing but small stones stacked in pyramids. Each pyramid was composed of about twenty multicolored pebbles.

"Are those paperweights?" I asked.

Lucian glanced at the table. "Personalized cairns. If you're willing to pay, you can make them project an image of someone who's died. You put it on their grave so that you can look at the picture."

"I thought the souls of necromancers went into those giant trees."

"Not everyone who lives in Trinovantum is a necromancer. And not all souls get the same treatment. There are catacombs underneath the city full of unmarked bones."

"Like Paris. Neat."

We passed another kiosk from which a variety of amazing smells issued. A goblin was pouring steaming batter into fantastic steel molds: tropical fish, wolves, great horned owls, and even castle battlements. A giant bat was yelling at the goblin while he cooked. The bat hung upside down from a gilded wooden perch, its leathery wings crossed over each other. The louder it screeched, the more it swung, back and forth, like a perpetual-shrieking machine. The goblin tried to cook faster.

"Can we get an owl pancake?"

"No. You're not allowed to eat anything."

"But they smell incredible."

"Everything does. But it's not worth the price."

"I think I should be able to decide that for myself," I muttered, keeping my eyes on the stacks of savory fish and wolves.

"Just follow me."

"Is everyone only allowed to wear two colors in this city?"

"Black fruit tends to produce naturally black dyes. So black clothes are in fashion. But you saw the tapestries—there are other colors as well."

"And what about the people wearing gray?"

"Subcastes. They're mostly domestic servants."

"Wow. It's like an undead version of Monaco."

"Class lines run deeply in Trinovantum."

"What class are you?"

He smiled slightly. "Lilium has old and powerful roots."

"So you're bourgeoisie."

"We're stable. We used to have more resources, but for the last few decades, the Vespertine family has been on the ascendancy. They're the center of power. At least for the present moment."

We eventually reached two kiosks that had been set up close to a stone wall. The first table was presided over by a slightly stooped vulture wearing glasses. I had no idea how the glasses managed to stay on his beak, but somehow they remained in place. He was selling a variety of instruments—fountain pens, bone knives, magnifying glasses, crystals, and plants with star-shaped black berries.

The vendor next to him was small enough that he could actually stand on the table rather than behind it. He measured about two feet tall, and was completely covered in velvety black fur. I couldn't even see his mouth. Only his eyes were visible, and they were a luminescent green. They reminded me of the Lampyrid's tail.

Lucian approached the Hamakei, who was whistling softly as he (or she) dusted and rearranged the sundry items on the table. "I was speaking with a Lampyrid vendor, and she said that you sold her a Polybius Book. Can you tell me where you found it?"

The Hamakei frowned at Lucian—if a bird could be said to frown. "Why is it any business of yours?"

He gestured to me. "She's from offworld, and she's investigating the murder of a citizen. A member of the Dark Parliament, in fact. The Polybius Book may have belonged to him."

The Hamakei gave me a long look. "What's she doing here?"

"I just explained—"

"I know *why* she's here." His small eyes narrowed even further. They looked like black peach pits behind the lenses. "I want to know *how* she's here."

I sensed that it was best to stay quiet. It was one of the rare moments when I actually stopped talking and just let someone else do the verbal acrobatics for a while. The hidden city had that effect on me. Once you see someone smoke a book, you kind of realize that you may be out of your element.

"She has an audience with Lord Nightingale," Lucian said.

"Oh, does she? How fancy." The Hamakei snorted. "I had an audience with him once. He was supposed to grant me a license to move my kiosk closer to the entrance. I waited for three hours without ever seeing him."

"That must have been frustrating."

"It was. And my table hasn't moved an inch. I'm still stuck with the Night Hob and his fake silverware."

At this, the Night Hob stamped his foot on the table and

hissed something. His eyes burned an even deeper green. I realized that he looked like a very small Wookie, but I didn't think it would do any good to tell him that.

"Maybe we could get you that license," Lucian continued. His voice was suddenly smooth. "We're meeting with him momentarily. If you tell us where you got the book from, we could make it worth your while."

The Hamakei clicked his beak. I was surprised to see that his tongue was bright pink. The Seneschal's tongue had been like a gray lump. Maybe it was an age thing. How could you determine if a bird was middle-aged?

"I don't want any trouble. I don't always work through the regular channels, and the penalty for illegal trading is—prohibitive."

I could only imagine. In a city where death was enshrined and transformed into a kind of art, punishments had to be pretty lavish. There must have been a gallows tree somewhere, and it wasn't souls that hung from it.

"We have no interest in exposing or interrupting your channels," Lucian assured him, "be they legitimate or otherwise. We just want to know where you found the Polybius Book."

The Hamakei's long neck swayed back and forth. Then he made a sound halfway between a hiss and a chirp.

"I got it from a Thanatar," he said at last. "As part of an estate sale."

"Whose estate?"

"Some fellow of the Dark Parliament."

"Which fellow? There are seven."

The Hamakei's eyes narrowed to small black slits as he considered the question. Then his pink tongue darted out again, tasting the air. "What's your house?"

Lucian's smile vanished. His hand lashed out, grabbing the Hamakei's skinny neck. The bird squawked. Lucian drew him closer.

"*¡Escúchame, hijo de gallinazo!*" he whispered. "My family history is none of your business. Tell us where you got the book from, and how we can transport it offworld—then we'll get you the license to move your wares. Keep trying to extort us, and you'll get nothing."

He let go of the Hamakei's neck. The bird shook itself, looking visibly distressed.

"Fine, fine. You don't have to get violent." He blinked. "You'll need a crucible to hold the book if you're taking it offworld. Your precious Lord Nightingale may be able help you with that, if he's feeling so inclined."

Lucian nodded slowly. "And?"

The Hamakei sighed. "The one who gave me the book didn't tell me his name. He was a Thanatar—who was I to argue? But supposedly it belonged to another Dark Parliament fellow who died. Ordeño was the name."

I couldn't stay quiet any longer. "Luiz Ordeño?"

The Hamakei seemed to notice me for the first time. "Yes. After he died, his estate was sold off in pieces. I had my ear close to the ground—which meant that I got most of the pieces. The book wouldn't sell, though. Too dangerous. Only one willing to take it off my hands was the Lampyrid, but she just loves to collect things."

"When did you meet with this—what's he called again?"

"A Thanatar," Lucian said. "One of Lord Nightingale's guards."

"Right. When did he give you the book?"

"A week ago. The Lampyrid's had it since then, but it's never going to sell." He looked darkly satisfied. "She gave me forty moon-grubs for it. Excellent deal."

Apparently, to a bird, grubs were worth more than books. But I wasn't thinking too much about the particulars of the exchange. One week ago, Ordeño had still been alive. As alive as any necromancer could be, strictly speaking. But this Thanatar had said that he was already dead, and that his estate was being sold.

I turned to Lucian. "Someone's lying. I don't know who yet, but maybe this Lord Nightingale can clear some things up."

"Doubtful," the Hamakei said. "He never says anything that makes sense."

Lucian ignored him. "We'll have to take transit to Nightingale's court. It's not too far, but I'd rather not walk."

"Is there a subway?"

"Not exactly. You'll see."

The Hamakei gave Lucian a hopeful look. "About that license—"

But he was already walking away.

"We'll try," I said. "Thanks for your cooperation."

But he'd already returned to polishing his wares, mumbling to himself in some impenetrable dialect. It seemed to be the only activity that he genuinely enjoyed.

17

"**This place is like an acid trip,**" **I said, once I'd** caught up to Lucian.

"Wait until we get to Spidergate."

"I don't know what that means."

"Don't worry." He put an arm lightly on my shoulder. "There are three gates that lead to Lord Nightingale's court. This one is by far the least bad."

"What are the others like?"

"It's probably better not to know. First we have to find some transportation."

We made our way through the market crowds, which gradually thinned out the farther we got from the main entrance. The square branched off into a number of narrow streets, like spokes on a wheel.

"Try not to look back once we take this road," Lucian said.

"Look back at what? The market?"

He nodded. "Just keep your eyes on the road ahead of you. Sometimes the streets have a mind of their own."

We walked for a few minutes, passing only a few scattered buildings that I couldn't identify. They may have been houses, or stores, or banks, for all I knew. Everything was made from the same pale stone, with leaded glass windows and heavily reinforced doors. Some of the buildings had massive stone balconies, but they were all empty and choked with leaves.

Despite Lucian's advice, I looked back, just for a second. Instead of seeing the market in the distance, I saw white fog. The fog obscured everything. Confused, I turned back to the path, but it was gone.

"Lucian?" I tried to keep the panic out of my voice. "Lucian, I looked back! I didn't mean to, but now—"

I felt a warm hand close around mine. He stepped out of the fog. I don't think I'd ever been more relieved to see him.

"I warned you," he said. But his tone was more playful than anything else. He squeezed my hand. "Stay close."

"Where did the fog come from?"

"It was always there. You just didn't see it."

I decided not to puzzle out that particular statement.

The fog thinned, and we emerged into a small square lined with hedges. Silver flowers grew within the hedges, their thorns glistening. In the center of the square was round structure made of stone.

"Is that a well?"

"More like a pool. Come see."

I could hear something splashing as we approached. *Please let it be fish,* I thought. *Just fish. No monsters.*

I peered over the rim of the stone pool. At first, all I could see were indistinct shapes moving in the water. Then a pair of red eyes appeared, followed by a snout. I heard something clicking against the surface of the stone.

The creature rose to the surface, revealing a long, muscular neck with a matted green mane that looked like tangled seaweed. Its glowing eyes gave the water a reddish cast, and I could see other creatures swimming around it. They seemed to be made partly of liquid, their dark shapes swelling and shrinking in waves as they circled one another.

"They're Nightmares," Lucian said. "They'll take us to the court."

"Are they made of water?"

"Among other things." He extended his hand, and I saw that he'd taken a black apple from one of the kiosks. The Nightmare breathed cautiously for a few seconds, eyeing the apple with some skepticism. Then it reached forward, lowering its snout. Lucian extended his open palm a bit farther, and the Nightmare snapped the apple up in its jaws, eating it in one bite.

"There's another apple in my pocket," he said. "Go for it."

"I don't want to lose a finger."

"Don't worry. They're herbivores."

I took the apple and approached the stone pool. Three more sets of red eyes regarded me, waiting for my next move.

I held the apple over the edge. After a few seconds, another Nightmare reared up from the water. It leaned in closer, until its head was a few inches away from my hand. Part of its body was still submerged, and I couldn't tell where the flesh began and the liquid ended. Its mane was a green-brown color, dripping and matted with bits of stone, broken shells, and a few small bones. Its breath was cold and smelled like damp earth.

"Hey, there," I said.

The Nightmare leapt over the rim of the stone pool, landing on the ground a foot away from me. As its hooves touched the earth, they solidified, but still retained a liquid quality. It shook itself vigorously, and I tasted salt water.

The creature examined me for a moment. Then it reached out and took the apple from me, halving it with a loud crunch. I could see its teeth working to tear the apple flesh intos pieces. Its front incisors were black and sharp, like a row of thin stalactites.

"How are we supposed to ride them without saddles?"

"Just wait. They'll show you."

I waited for my Nightmare to finish chewing its apple. It paused for a few seconds, as if to savor the meal. Then it slowly lowered itself to the ground, dropping to its haunches. I climbed shakily onto its back, which was wet and smooth. Its fur reminded me of damp sand.

"I'm really not sure about—"

Before I could finish, the Nightmare rose in one fluid motion, forcing me to grab onto its mane. My fingers curled around the hair, which felt more like plant fibers, soft and slightly sticky.

Lucian had already mounted. He smiled in my direction. "You did great."

"Sure. But I have no idea how to ride a horse."

"You don't really ride them, per se. You just tell them where to go, and they do the rest. Like this." He leaned forward and whispered something into the Nightmare's ear. It made a small sound in reply that could have been a whinny, but more closely resembled a bubbling coffeemaker.

"Just say, 'Nightingale's court,'" he said. "That should be enough."

Still holding on to the wet mane, I leaned forward and whispered, "Nightingale's court," into my Nightmare's ear. It made no reply, but I got the impression that it understood what I was saying.

"Now what?" I asked.

"Just hold on."

I felt the Nightmare's body tense underneath me. Then there was an odd pinching sensation, somewhere in the back of my brain, which reminded me of that feeling when a headache is about to blossom.

Suddenly everything shifted. The clearing went black, then white, as if it had been buried in snow. I felt a penetrating cold. I tried to grip the horse's mane tighter, but I couldn't move my fingers. When I breathed in, it was like swallowing ice.

Something pushed me forward. I was sailing through empty space, my stomach suddenly in my mouth. Every atom in my body seemed to be unable to decide whether it should stay together or fly violently apart.

I saw a stream of disconnected images: snakes, rabbits, the mouth of a cave, fire, dark waves, a bridge swaying back and forth, metal dripping blood, and a dog spitting as it barked, louder and louder.

For a few seconds, I felt as if I was being buried underneath tonnes of earth, and I couldn't scream or even move. The sound froze into icicles within my throat.

Then the world blinked back into focus.

I was breathing hard. I realized that we were on an entirely different road. The Nightmares had vanished completely, and the sudden lurch of standing up made me stumble forward, tripping from vertigo. Lucian's hand steadied me. I turned around and stared at him.

"What the hell just happened?"

"Sorry." He smiled ruefully. "I was going to warn you, but I thought it might only be worse if you were expecting it."

"Where did the horses go?"

"Back to the pool. In a sense, they never actually left." He kept his hand on my shoulder. The slight pressure was reassuring. "Nightmares can move at the speed of thought. Instead of galloping along the ground, they travel through people's fears. In order to reach a place, they have to jump from fear to fear. That's why you probably saw a lot of strange images."

I frowned. "I saw rabbits."

"A lot of people are scared of rabbits."

"But they weren't like the *Holy Grail* rabbit. They were cute and cuddly."

"Some people are scared of cute and cuddly things."

I shook my head. "Traveling through people's nightmares is disorienting. I felt like I was trapped in a horror movie."

"It takes some getting used to."

"I'd much rather ride a hopes-and-dreams horse. Something that shows you cotton candy and winning the lottery."

"Unfortunately, they don't exist. But traveling by Nightmare is quite efficient. We crossed at least five miles in less than a few seconds."

"Will we have to ride them back to the market as well?"

"Probably."

"Great."

I followed him down the unfamiliar road, which was lined with trees. The fog was here as well, but it seemed slightly more cautious, gathering along the sides of the path without encroaching on it. This time, I resisted the urge to look back.

After a few minutes, the road ended abruptly at the foot of a stone wall. The wall was surrounded by trees and undergrowth, so it was difficult to get an idea of its exact size. But there was a sense of gravity to it. I could feel the hairs on my arms and the back of my neck stirring slightly as we drew nearer. There was definitely an active materia cluster here, and it seemed to extend in all directions, like a nebula.

We followed the wall until we came to a set of double doors. They were made from what looked like a curious red iron. The metal was heavily oxidized, and etched with symbols that I couldn't quite make out. I took a step forward, but Lucian grabbed my arm lightly, holding me back.

"Wait," he said.

As I watched, a dark mass began to spread around the edges of the portal. It flowed like tar, and I realized that it was actually hundreds of spiders, all moving in unison. The spiders completely blanketed the doors, covering every inch of the metal with their small bodies, all of which had green and gold markings. It looked as if someone had hung a tapestry of arachnids before us.

I heard the sound of metal scraping.

A section of the undergrowth surrounding the wall parted, and two enormous spiders emerged into view. They were both twice our size, and their legs looked like furred tree trunks moving across the ground. Each leg was encased in silver plate armor, which was the source of the scraping noise. The plates clicked against one another, making the creatures seem more mechanical than natural. Not that a ten-foot-tall spider looked natural, exactly.

The spider on the left opened its mouth, and I saw that its teeth were also gilded in silver. It looked like it could tear through a bus with those fangs. Its eight eyes regarded me, trembling slightly, like red gelatin.

"Arañas," Lucian whispered. "Spider demons. Try not to move too much when you're talking to them. And be polite."

Of course. Spidergate. Why couldn't it have been Kittengate?

"Guardians," Lucian said politely, "We have an audience with Lord Nightingale. May we pass?"

The Araña didn't answer. Its legs moved. Click click click.

Suddenly, I remembered something that the Iblis had said to Lucian. "I shooed the spider demons away from you." I couldn't imagine anyone "shooing" the Arañas, given that they could probably eat me in a single bite. But maybe an Iblis could. They were probably from neighboring dimensions.

The Arañas seemed to confer with each other, moving their silver-plated legs and clicking their teeth together. Finally, they both moved to the side. The carpet of arachnids covering the door scurried in all directions, vanishing into cracks and crevices within the stone, until the iron was visible once more. I heard a low boom, like a bolt being pushed forward. Then the gates slowly opened.

"Thank you," Lucian said simply.

I followed him through the entrance, taking one last look at the Arañas. They were watching me with all of their eyes. It made me shiver.

"What exactly is Lord Nightingale trying to keep out?" I asked.

"Everything."

We walked down a corridor lit by stone basins. I held my hand close to one of the flames, and was startled when frost appeared on my skin.

"Don't touch it," Lucian said simply.

We followed the corridor, which opened gradually into a kind of arcade with arched pillars. Vines and leaves crawled up the pillars, some flowering, others bearing black fruit. I followed Lucian, treading lightly over the shadows, until we came to a set of stone doors that had been carved with flowers. I could see green light spilling from the crack beneath the doorframe.

"We're about to enter the court proper," Lucian said. "It's a bit unnerving the first time you see it. Just remember the rule."

"No eating," I said. "And no touching."

"Perfect." He smiled. "You'll do fine."

He touched the surface of the doors, and they opened silently.

The room beyond was an open courtyard, with low stone walls and no ceiling. The night sky moved overhead, full of stars and almost frightening in its clarity. The green light seemed to be coming from the walls themselves. I looked closer, and realized that the stone was covered with hundreds of glowing green shapes, all clinging to its surface and wriggling their small, plump bodies. Lampyrid larvae. Their twitching tails illuminated the entire courtyard.

There was a stone table in the center of the clearing, with eight seats, all carved from stone as well. The seats were empty. Behind the table was a raised dais, covered in moss and vines. A chair made of bone seemed to be growing directly out of the undergrowth, its smooth, white edges draped with thorns.

A young man sat on the chair. "Lounged" was probably a better word for his posture, since he looked slightly indolent. He wore black armor that resembled the Lampyrid's chest plates, black and reflective, its surface etched with unfamiliar designs. His hair was dark and close-cropped, and he had sharp green eyes. A circlet of iron rested on his head. It was so thin, it almost looked like braided wire, black and tipped with silver.

He rose from his chair. "Lucian. Well met."

"Well met, my lord." Lucian inclined his head.

Lord Nightingale walked over to where he was standing, and kissed him lightly on both cheeks. Lucian returned the kiss. Then he turned to me.

"You must be Tess." He extended his hand. "Welcome to my court."

I remembered what Lucian had said about touching Lord Nightingale. I wasn't sure if he wanted me to kiss his hand, or just shake it.

"Nice to meet you," I said.

I reached out and brushed his fingers, just for a second. I didn't feel anything. His touch was surprisingly warm, and his pale skin was soft. I drew my hand away.

"You're here about Luiz," Nightingale said. "So sad. His death was a great loss to the Dark Parliament."

"We're a bit baffled by his death, actually," I admitted. "We don't know what killed him, or why he died wearing a suit of armor."

"The armor was stolen. From my private collection." Lord Nightingale shook his head. "Sad, really. Ordeño was probably going to sell it offworld."

"Why would he do that?"

"Because he was an addict." His eyes seemed to flash purple for a second. Then they were green again. "Trino-vantum has a number of hallucinogenic substances to offer, and Ordeño sampled nearly all of them. He owed a tremendous drug debt. We had to parcel off his entire estate in order to pay it."

Lucian touched my arm. I couldn't tell if the gesture was protective, or possessive. But it felt reassuring all the same. "We found something of his in the Night Market," he said. "A Polybius Book."

I noticed that he didn't say "half of a Polybius Book."

Lord Nightingale smiled. "Yes. They're pretty, aren't they? I imagine someone will pay top dollar for it."

"We spoke to a merchant," Lucian continued, "and he claims to have gotten the book from one of your Than-atars."

"Why would a Thanatar deal with a merchant?"

"I don't know. I was hoping you might have some idea."

Lord Nightingale chuckled. "I'm afraid I don't have a clue, Lucian. I didn't personally oversee the dissolution of Ordeño's estate."

"You certainly liquidated it quickly enough."

"Lucian. I know that Luiz was one of your favorite teachers. But you understand how these things go. Business is business."

"He served the Dark Parliament for centuries."

"Yes. And now he's dead. Permanently." Lord Nightingale returned to his chair, looking slightly annoyed. "There's no sense in having a funeral. This whole city is already a graveyard. Ordeño is dead, and his seat at the table needs to be filled. For the moment, that's my only concern. Continuity."

"Actually—" I cleared my throat. "Speaking of continuity, the merchant that we talked to said something else about your Thanatar. He was told that Ordeño died a week ago. But that's not true. All of our tests confirmed that he died less than a week ago."

His eyes hardened. "I'm not sure I see your point."

"It's just confusing. Why would he sell the merchant something that belonged to a member of the Dark Parliament—a respected civil servant—and then lie about when he actually died?"

"I have no idea."

"Maybe Ordeño was as good as dead already."

He leaned forward. "What do you mean by that?"

"I mean that he could have been targeted for assassination."

Lord Nightingale smiled. "Assassinations aren't carried out unless I approve them, Miss Corday. Luiz Ordeño may have been murdered, but he was murdered in your world—not in ours. The responsibility, therefore, falls to you."

"But people can move between the worlds. It's just as likely that someone from your court did the deed, then returned seeking asylum."

"That sounds quite circumstantial."

"So does your claim about Ordeño's drug debts."

"Excuse me?"

"Tess—" Lucian warned.

But I was already on a roll. "Do you have any receipts? Where are these druglords that he owed money to? How do we know that his estate wasn't liquidated in order to erase his presence from the city?"

"I'm telling you that it wasn't. That should be enough." His voice had a dangerous note to it. A smart person would have definitely heeded that warning. But I could be a slow learner sometimes.

"I'm not convinced about the armor, either. Why would he steal it? And why was he wearing it at the moment of his death? What was it supposed to protect him from?"

"I can't imagine what his motives were. And I hardly care. As I said before, the matter is now beyond our jurisdiction."

"Ordeño was a political activist. He must have had enemies in the court. Maybe he was running for his life."

"Perhaps. But why does any of that matter now? He's dust."

"But his legacy isn't."

"How do you mean?"

"I believe," Lucian interjected, "that Tess is talking about Ordeño's work as a litigator. He did have a fairly influential role in designing the latest treaty."

"Yes. And now his duties have been taken over by another member of the Parliament. The treaty will go ahead as planned."

I didn't believe that for a second.

"Who's finishing Ordeño's work?" Lucian asked.

"That's not important."

"But I'd like to know."

"I think you've shared enough already with Miss Corday." Lord Nightingale stood up. "I'm sure she's a lovely person, but she's also an offworlder. We can't discuss politics in front of her."

"Politics seem to be what got Ordeño killed. I'm only

trying to figure out why, so that my agency can see that justice is done."

"That's interesting. I've never heard one of your people talk about justice before." His green eyes surveyed me with the calm of a superior animal. "You deal in chemicals, computer programs, and mathematical formulae. You think you can analyze and deduce what causes a murder. But it's not that simple."

"Of course it isn't. We know that."

"Do you?" He shook his head. "Magic doesn't sit inside of a computer. It doesn't reside in powders or chemistry, and it can't be read with a laser. Magic is what holds the universe together. And no matter how closely you study it, you're never going to be able to record enough data to understand its purpose, or its will."

"That's why we don't look for intentionality. We focus on evidence."

"But you used the word 'justice.'" He smiled. "Maybe you think justice is at the heart of magic. Like a soul. But it's just as likely that what you call 'materia,' what you try to control, is actually just a wild animal. Ancient, amoral, and unstoppable."

I swallowed. "I think materia is about as complicated as the rest of the universe. That's why we have to focus on physical evidence."

"But you have no evidence in this case. Isn't that the problem?"

"We have the armor. And a name."

Lucian looked at me strangely. "What name?"

"Indeed. What name? Tell me."

"El alquimista," I said.

Lord Nightingale laughed. "A fairy tale?"

"Isn't that all your city is?"

His smile turned to a scowl. "Are you finished, Miss Corday?"

"Almost. I just have one more question."

"What's that?"

"Why did you send one of your Thanatars to attack me?"

His eyes widened. "Are you serious?"

"I've got the cracked ribs to prove it."

"Why would I send someone offworld to attack *you*? You're nothing to me. You barely even exist."

"Maybe so. But someone in your Dark Parliament has a broken Vorpal gauntlet. And I'm going to find out who."

"Very well. Keep searching. But this audience is over."

"Actually—" Lucian grimaced slightly. "We need to ask a favor first."

Lord Nightingale rolled his eyes. "Oh, by all means."

"We need a container to transport something offworld."

"Let me guess. The Polybius Book?"

Lucian nodded.

"Fine. If it gets you away from here, so much the better." He held out his hand. A latticework of ruby light flowed to life above his palm, taking the shape of a glowing red cube. He handed it to Lucian. "This reliquary will keep the book alive for a few days, but after that, it will vanish unless you return it to the city."

Lucian took the cube. "Thank you for indulging us."

"Yeah, thanks." I smiled. "It's been fun."

After the door to the courtyard closed behind us, I turned to Lucian.

"I know you want to yell at me, but I actually think that went really well. He's obviously lying."

"Of course he is. Everyone lies here. About everything."

"But you saw his face when I mentioned the Vorpal gauntlet. He definitely sent that guy after me."

Lucian sighed. "It's starting to seem more and more likely."

"So you believe me."

"I always believed you. I just had to be sure that I wasn't crazy."

"Or that I wasn't crazy."

"No." He smiled. "I already knew that."

"Thanks."

"Now that you've offended my monarch, are you ready for the Nightmares?"

"No. I think I'm going to throw up."

"That's okay." He led me back down the corridor. "They won't mind. They're mostly made of water, remember?"

18

For a moment, it felt like the darkness was never going to go away. It pressed on me from all directions, and when I reached for Lucian's hand, there was nothing there. Just a void where he'd once been standing. I opened my mouth to call his name, and ice crystals filled my throat, choking me.

Then there was light. Fluorescent light.

I blinked and looked around. I was standing in the trace lab, which was empty, at least for the moment. Lucian was standing next to me, looking like he'd just gone for a brisk walk. I swallowed down my nausea and took a deep breath.

"Are you okay?" he asked.

"I want to stay in my apartment for the next week, with all of the lights on. Other than that, I'm good." I saw the reproduction of *Las Meninas*, which was still sitting on a light table. "Did we come out of the painting?"

"Yes. I thought you'd like to come to the lab directly.

Once you know how to travel by speculum, you can negotiate the entire network."

"How come we didn't end up on the table?"

Lucian frowned. "You know, I'm not quite sure. I think it has something to do with particle spin, though."

"Thanks. I completely get that."

"I figured you would." He grinned slightly.

Cindée chose that moment to reenter the lab. She was carrying a box full of files, and she almost dropped them when she saw us.

"Tess? How did you get in here? I was only gone for a second."

"We came out of *Las Meninas*."

She stared at me. "Are you drunk?"

"I wish. But no. It's a long story involving necromancy." I reached into my coat and drew out the bone knife, which was sealed in an evidence bag. "Right now, I need some dental stone to make a plaster mold of this. If I don't do it within the next hour, the whole thing's going to disappear."

Her eyes narrowed. "You're sure you're sober, hon?"

"She's fine," Lucian said. "I promise. The knife is from Trinovantum, and it can't be away from the hidden city for long before it vanishes."

"Is that were y'all just came from?"

I nodded. "It's pretty. And frightening."

"That's what I've heard." Cindée reached into a drawer under a nearby counter. "What kind of dental stone are you looking for? We've got gypsum-based, ADA type-three, type-four—"

"Just the pre-measured stuff. The bone is porous, so I'll need to use some of the Mikrosil casting material to capture all of the grooves and little holes."

"I believe they're called lacunae." She smiled and

handed me a white container, along with a plastic mold. "But 'little holes' are the same thing."

I placed the bone knife inside the mold, positioning it so that the serrated edge was slightly elevated and facing toward me. Then I mixed a pound of the dental stone with six ounces of water. I would have used more for a tire-track impression, but the knife was small and delicate, so it required less casting material. Lucian watched the process with some degree of fascination. It was strange that spider demons didn't faze him, but this was suddenly capitvating.

"Can you stir this?" I asked him. "It's just like pancake batter."

He stared at the pink material. "It really doesn't look like it."

"Just stir it, please. I'll be right back."

"Where are you going?"

"I have to make a call." I turned to Cindée. "Is Selena still here?"

"She went home an hour ago." Cindée was watching critically as Lucian mixed the dental stone. "Honey, maybe you ought to let me do that."

"He's doing fine. Can you page her at home?"

"*Tess.* She's gonna bite my head off."

"Just tell her it's about the Ordeño case."

"Why don't you call her?"

"I don't have her home number. You've called her before."

"Yeah, but—"

"Thanks so much." I ran out of the lab before she could protest further. Delegation was a fine dance, and my balletic abilities sucked. But I did know how to leave a room at the perfect moment. It was a secret I'd learned from my mother.

I called the house. Derrick picked up after the first ring.

"Are you okay? Where are you?"

"Back at the lab. Did you honestly think I'd get reception in Trinovantum?"

"Maybe. It's only a matter of time before the iPhone goes multidimensional. When did you get back?"

"A few minutes ago. I need you to come to the lab. Is Miles with you?"

"He's watching TV with Mia and Patrick."

"You got the closed captioning to work?"

"Yeah, Patrick figured it out. I don't know if we'll ever be able to turn it off again, though. There was this crazy sub-menu under SAP—"

"That's fine. I need you to bring everyone with you. Miles, Patrick, and Mia. If Mia argues, tell her it's non-negotiable."

"What are you planning?"

"It would take too long to explain. And I'm barely holding on to the idea as it is, so I don't want to jinx it. Just get here as soon as you can."

"Okay. Wait—" I heard him saying something inaudible. "Patrick wants to know if he can drive."

"Only if you sit in the front seat with him. And if he doesn't obey the speed limit, you have to make him pull over."

"He's probably going to complain about that."

"He owes me a favor. Just remind him of that, and it should be fine."

"All right. We'll be there soon."

"Thanks, hon."

I closed the phone and walked back into the lab. Cindée was in the middle of talking to Lucian. She saw me, and her eyes narrowed.

"You called her?"

"I did."

"And did she bite your head off?"

"She said she's changing her cell number."

"That's an empty threat. She's said that dozens of times."

"She said you'd say that, and I should tell you that she really means it this time, and that you owe her a coffee the size of her head."

"Wow. She was pretty articulate. Usually she just swears."

"At any rate, she's on her way."

"Good." I turned to Lucian. "Done stirring?"

"I think so. It's gotten much more solid."

"It's faster than most dental stone. We've been experimenting with injecting semisolid earth materia into the gypsum."

"I'm not really sure what that means."

"Don't worry about it. You're just here to look pretty."

It came out before I could stop it. Cindée raised an eyebrow, but didn't say anything. Lucian just smiled.

I took the plastic mold, sealed it, and put it in the fridge. "Just like Jell-O. In a few hours, we can send it down to the morgue, so Tasha can take a look at the casting. I'm willing to bet that the serrated edge of the bone shear matches the wound-track left in Ordeño's neck. Even if the weapon disappears, we'll still have the impression."

"I guess the killer didn't count on that," Lucian said.

"No. They never do."

"What's next?"

I heard footsteps in the hallway. Selena emerged into the lab, wrapped in a full-length trench and looking a few shades away from pissed.

"Jesus, how many red lights did you run to get here so fast?"

She hung her coat up. "I took a cab. At one point, we

were driving so fast down Cambie, I thought we might go into orbit."

"You got here in one piece, though. That's what counts."

"No." She folded her arms. "What counts is the story you're about to tell me. It's going to be riveting. It's going to involve concrete physical evidence, and an amazing reason for dragging me back here."

"Actually, you're right on nearly every count. I'm not sure I can deliver fully on the physical evidence part, though. Our murder weapon is dissolving as we speak."

"I already don't like where this is going." She turned to Lucian. "Did you take her to Trinovantum? Did she wreck anything?"

"Yes to the first, and no to the second." He inclined his head. "She was actually quite professional."

Selena blinked. "And then what happened?"

I stepped between them. "It was nothing important. I may have insulted Lord Nightingale. And I almost puked while riding a Nightmare. But I'm pretty sure that I made friends with a glowworm."

Selena looked at Cindée. "Is she drunk?"

Cindée shrugged. "I already asked, and she said no."

"There's some delicate trace evidence in the fridge," I said. "Once the dental stone hardens, we'll have an impression of the weapon that—possibly—killed Ordeño. But the weapon itself is like one of Cinderella's pumpkins. It won't last."

Selena sighed. "I'll admit it. I'm slightly intrigued. But you'll need to give me more than a casting impression."

"Oh, we've got more. Lucian?"

He looked at me. "What?"

"Get out your pipe. We're going into the evidence closet."

"Sure. *Tu eres el jefe.*"

"No," Selena said, "I'm *el jefe*. That does mean 'boss,' right?"

"It does." Lucian smiled. "You speak Spanish?"

"My husband's from Uruguay. Mostly, I just know profanity."

"And how to make *milaneses*, I'll bet."

Her eyes softened. "God. They're amazing, aren't they? But I always end up with bread crumbs all over the kitchen floor."

"The secret is to—"

"Can we stop talking about food?" I asked. "All I've had to eat today is a blueberry bagel, since someone wouldn't let me have anything in Trinovantum."

Lucian rolled his eyes. "Did you want to end up as a slave to the city forever? I was only trying to save your soul."

"Maybe I was willing to sell it for one of those black watermelons."

"They are pretty good. They kind of taste like licorice."

Selena turned to me. "Fine. Why are we going into the evidence closet? I don't want to have to clean it afterward."

"You've got half of a Polybius Book in there. Now that we've got the other half, we can put them together. Cindée, can you unlock the door?"

She chuckled. "Why not? This is the most interesting thing that's happened all night. Before you arrived, I was cataloguing fiber evidence."

We all filed into the secure evidence locker, which was really a museum-style room exhibiting several precious artifacts. The most recognizable was Ordeño's suit of armor, with its wings and eyes, sitting sedately under glass. Next to it was the first half of the Polybius Book, still smoking within its own glass cage.

Cindée closed the door behind us, then punched a code into a keypad on the wall.

"I've turned off the chemical sensors. Otherwise, the alarm will sound if there's a one percent change in the atmospheric composition of the room. It's designed to keep out everything, including materia."

"I'm not even sure this falls under that classification," I said. "What exactly would you call a Polybius Book, Lucian?"

He was already taking out his bone pipe, delicately carved into the shape of a blooming lily. "Dangerous. And not to be read lightly."

"I've heard of them," Selena said. "We weren't sure that Ordeño's book was one of those. It could have been any number of unpleasant things. But this isn't the kind of book that tries to eat you, right?"

"No," Lucian said. "I promise it won't eat you."

"And you took the second half of it from Trinovantum?"

"It's not going to last," I replied. "But Lord Nightingale gave us a crucible to hold it in, so I think we've got a few hours at least before—" I paused. "I was about to say before it goes up in smoke, but it's already made of smoke. Before it evanesces?"

"I'm not sure you're using that word correctly," Lucian said.

"When did you become such a grammarian?"

"I'm not a grammarian. I'm just a perfectionist."

Selena gave me an odd look. This was definitely descending into overly familiar territory. We needed to pull it back.

I reached into my bag and pulled out the second half of the book, which was encased in the glowing red matrix of Lord Nightingale's crucible. Its tendrils of smoke moved silently against the invisible barrier of the cube. The smoke didn't smell or taste like anything. I'm not sure what I'd expected. It was a grimoire, not BBQ.

"I don't think we're insured for this," Selena said. "Cindée, do you have a fire extinguisher handy?"

"Don't worry. Lucian's done this before."

"Right." He sprinkled some tobacco into the pipe. "No pressure."

"None at all."

Selena's eyes widened. "Are you doing what I think you're doing?"

"Just watch," I said. "It's actually pretty cool."

"Your definition of cool is exactly the sort of thing that I usually run from. I feel like I should be wearing protective gear."

"I can get you a lead apron," Cindée said. "Would it make you feel better?"

She shook her head. "At this point, nothing will. Just get on with it. We'll figure out what damage forms we need to sign later."

I placed the Polybius Book on an empty pedestal. "How do I release the crucible again? I don't want to lose a finger."

"Just breathe on it," Lucian said. "That should be enough."

I blew on the glowing crucible like it was a bowl of soup. The lines of light shivered, then vanished. The Polybius Book began to curl and expand. I saw points of light flickering within its depths. Its tendrils moved toward the glass case, where its other half was resting.

"Can I lift the case?" I asked.

Cindée punched in a code. "There. Security's off."

"Just don't lean too close to it when you remove the lid," Lucian said. "You don't want to get a mouthful by accident."

Gingerly, I lifted the glass case. Both clouds of smoke

began to swirl and roil, as if a storm had awakened inside of them. As I watched, they hovered in the air for a moment, and then flowed into each other.

Lucian lit the pipe, and the tobacco burned orange. He inhaled. I thought of Gandalf. I couldn't help it.

A long tendril of smoke from the unified book rushed into the bowl of the pipe. Lucian closed his eyes, taking a long, luxuriant hit.

"Is this legal?" Cindée whispered.

"Of course," I replied. "He's only smoking the words."

Selena shook her head. "I should have stayed home. Why can't I just learn to stop answering the phone when you call?"

"It was Cindée who called, not me."

"But I knew you were behind it. You're always behind it."

"And that's why you love me. Because of the intrigue."

"You're giving me an ulcer. I'm almost sure of it."

"I thought I had an ulcer once, but it was just gas pains."

Lucian exhaled a large ring of green smoke. It trembled in the air for a few seconds, revolving slowly. Then it spread out, like a transparent sheet of paper. Those familiar serpentine characters began to glow within the smoke.

"Should I take a picture?" I asked. "Maybe we could read it later."

Lucian coughed. "It won't show up on film. Not even digital." He scanned the Polybius script. The runes moved before my eyes, flicking their calligraphic tails and dancing with one another.

"What does it say?"

"I'm not sure yet. It's a kind of journal, and it's written in shorthand." He frowned. "There's a lot that doesn't make sense. Weird measurements and calculations. Almost like a recipe."

"A recipe for what, exactly?" Selena asked.

Lucian stared into the smoke. "I'm not sure. Some of the notes are written in Catalán. I can barely read them. Other parts are in Old Castillian, mixed with Latin and Old French. I think he was trying to make it as illegible as possible."

Lucian passed his hand in front of the smoking book. The characters trembled and shifted before him. I guess it was the equivalent of turning the page.

"There's a refrain that keeps repeating," he said. "But it doesn't make sense."

"What's it say?"

"*Ve por ella*. It means 'look through her,' or 'see right through her.' But I don't know who the 'her' is that he's talking about, or even if it's a real person."

"I think there's a way we can find out," I said. "But first we have to call Becka. We need her to prep the Nerve."

Selena stared at me. "What are you going to use the simulation room for?"

I smiled. "Art appreciation."

19

The Nerve was full of people, and its egg-shaped white walls made it appear as if everyone had been trapped inside a genie's bottle.

Mia and Patrick were talking to each other, probably ironically making fun of everything while unironically trying not to be freaked-out by their surroundings. Miles and Derrick were signing back and forth to each other, but their fingers moved so rapidly that I couldn't quite get the gist of what they were talking about. Whenever Miles talked to me using ASL, his gestures were slow and deliberate, in the same manner as one might talk to a six-year-old. But when he was speaking with Derrick, all bets were off, and I always felt bad about asking them to slow down. I didn't want to interrupt the conversational flow.

Even Baron had come along. He slept curled next to the door, his tail thumping the ground slightly as he dreamt. Probably he dreamt of Miles, who was the center of his canine universe. Lucian stood near the dog, watching him sleep. Their minds were equally unfathomable. But at least Baron was trained not to run away.

Becka and Selena were standing on the mezzanine level, where the controls to the simulation room were located. Through a mixture of arcane energy and sophisticated computer graphics, the Nerve could reproduce nearly any type of virtual reality. It worked on the same principle as a forensic total-mapping system, which recorded crime scenes digitally using a 360-degree bank of cameras. The only difference was that the Nerve used alternating materia flows to create images that you could actually touch, and it could even see through physical substrates using infrared light.

At the moment, we weren't using this priceless technology to re-create a crime scene. Not yet, anyway. First we were doing something completely different. And if it didn't work, I'd probably get fired. But that was nothing new.

"I've loaded both simulations into the computer," Rebecca said. "We have to wait another minute for the lens to calibrate. We just installed a new emerald laser, and it's a bit persnickety."

"It also cost nearly as much as this building." Selena grabbed Becka's extra-large coffee and moved it gently away from the screen. "So I don't care if it's persnickety or not. Let it warm up, and don't spill anything on the controls."

"I am a professional, you know."

"Is that why your blouse was on inside out when you got here?"

Becka looked chagrined. "I was sleeping when you called."

"It's fine. Just make sure the machine keeps humming smoothly." Selena turned to me. "Where did you get this idea from again?"

I smiled. "An article by Frederic Chorda on computer-aided painting analysis. Becka was the one who made me think of it, actually. She was talking earlier about computer techniques being used to analyze paintings like *Las Meninas*."

Becka inclined her head. "Happy to be of service."

"Where did you find the article?" Selena asked.

"JSTOR."

"I didn't know we subscribed to that database. And I just approved our electronic licensing agreements last week."

"Sorry," Becka said. "I may have slipped that one in."

"Did you slip any others in?"

"Just a Shakespeare archive. And the *Women's Studies Index*."

Selena stared at her. "What do those have to do with forensics?"

"Nothing. I like blank verse and feminist theory. Is that a crime?"

"It might be in Texas," Mia said.

"Oh, snap." Becka grinned at her, then returned her attention to the monitor. "Okay, this is almost ready. I'm going to dim the lights."

"Is there popcorn?" Mia asked.

"You'll have to ask *el jefe* over there," I said, pointing to Selena. "She approves all the refreshment decisions in the lab."

Selena sighed. "Let's just get on with this, okay? I'd like to get home at a decent hour, if that's still possible."

"Why did you take this job again?" I asked her.

"Honestly? The dental is superb."

The walls began to hum softly as the circuitry within the white ceramic panels came to life. I smelled the tang of ozone, and I could feel an active materia field stirring the hairs on the back of my neck.

"I'm running the simulation," Becka said. "Now."

There was a pulse of white light. I felt static electricity move over the length of my body, like an invisible spiderweb.

When the light cleared, we were standing in *Las Meninas*.

The reproduction of the artist's studio in the Alcázar palace was perfect. The white walls of the Nerve had become dark wood, terminating in a high ceiling. A door with recessed wooden panels stood ajar, revealing an entryway where natural light streamed through, and a flight of stairs that led up. There were paintings on the walls, and I recognized them now because Derrick had explained them to me. Mostly, they were copies of scenes from Ovid's *Metamorphoses*. Everything was a copy of a fable, or a fable of a copy, the whole scene wrapped within a devious *simulacro*.

A small mirror hung on the far wall, reflecting nothing. It was supposed to offer up the image of the king and queen, but Becka had erased that. Now it was blind and dark, adrift and waiting for an impression of any kind.

Velázquez's easel was positioned in the far right corner of the room, so that we could see the frame, but not what was painted on the canvas. That, too, had to remain blank. It was one of those unanswerable questions.

The artist himself was absent. All of the people had been erased from the painting, leaving only a pure landscape behind. It was beautiful and still. I could see the light dancing as it filtered through the high windows of the room. I knew that if I touched the easel, it would feel solid and reassuring, even if its true substance was far closer to that of a dream.

What had the fairy Puck called the human world again? *This weak and idle theme / no more yielding than a dream*? It was hard to tell, as always, where magic ended and technology began. The boundary was no more than a flickering cursor that vanished if you looked at it too closely.

"Okay," I said. "Everyone needs to get into position. Becka, can you illuminate the coordinates?"

"Sure thing."

Becka entered in a stream of code. The room shimmered again. Ten sets of floating crosshairs appeared in various positions, each a different color. Glowing letters drifted next to the marks: *Velázquez*, *Infanta*, *María Augustina*, and even *Dog*. For Baron's benefit, of course.

"Mia, you're the Infanta. Take your position."

She sighed. "I wanted to be Velázquez."

"Tough. Just stand next to the coordinates."

Mia took her place. "Should I do a dance now?"

"No. Just stand still."

"Am I allowed to talk?"

"Whatever. Just don't move."

"Not even—"

"Mia."

She rolled her eyes. "Okay. Geez. No moving, I get it."

"Good. Patrick, you're Velázquez. Go stand next to the easel."

He did so. "Is the canvas supposed to be blank?"

"Yes."

"Can we paint something on it?"

"No. Just keep still."

He muttered something, which I chose not to hear.

I scanned the room. "Hmm. Derrick and Miles, you're going to have to be the *meninas*. Take the two marks on either side of Mia."

"So gay," Mia said. "I love it."

They both took their positions.

I'm the pretty one, Miles signed to Derrick.

"You're deluded," he replied.

I remembered Lucian in my dream, standing at the door. I turned to him. "You get to be Don José Nieto, the chamberlain. Go stand in the entrance."

"Am I coming or going?" he asked. "I can never tell from the painting whether he's arriving or leaving."

"I guess we'll never know." I kept seeing him as he'd been in my dream, wearing the shattered mask, his face bloody. Even though I knew that Braxton was the one who'd attacked me, I still saw Lucian's eyes behind that mask.

I blinked to clear the image. "Right. We're going to need everyone to pull this off. Selena, can you take the place of Mari-Bárbola? Behind the dog."

She did so, standing three feet to the right of Mia. "Is this okay?"

"Yes. Perfect."

"I don't think we're supposed to talk," Mia stage-whispered to her.

Selena chuckled, but didn't reply.

They were all going to drive me crazy.

"Okay. Becka, can you stand to the right of Selena? You're going to be Nicolas Pertusato, the other little person."

Becka took her position. "Should I be doing anything special?"

"Yes. We need Baron first, though."

Miles whistled, and Baron was instantly awake. He snapped his fingers and pointed to the space in front of Selena. Baron trotted over and sat down.

I turned to Miles so that he could read my lips. "Is it okay if Becka rests her foot lightly on him?"

"She could sit on him, for all he'd care. It's fine."

"Okay. Becka, put your foot on Baron's back."

She did so. Baron glanced at it for a moment, then promptly fell back asleep.

"What about the remaining two figures?" Lucian asked.

"We don't have enough people. We'll have to shuffle."

"It's okay," Becka said. "I've set the controls to re-mote, so I can shift the image parameters from where I'm standing."

"Perfect. Can you call up Ordeño's apartment now?"

"Yes. One second."

Becka hit a button on a slender white remote. The room shimmered, and I felt another wave of static electricity.

Then we were standing in Ordeño's living room.

"My God," Selena said. "It fits perfectly."

She was right. Even though Ordeño's apartment looked nothing like Velázquez's studio on the surface, it was spatially an exact duplicate. Everyone retained their positions without interfering with a single piece of furniture. The entire room had been designed to accommodate exactly this scene, as I'd suspected. Even the windows were in the right place, and the ceiling was just high enough. The only difference between the open doors was that Ordeño's entry-way still had yellow scene tape attached to it. Otherwise, their positions were identical.

"The painting is a map," I said. "All we need to do is figure out what perspective we're supposed to be looking from."

"*Ve por ella*," Lucian repeated. "'Look through her.' But who do you think he's talking about? 'Her' might even refer to the room itself, if Ordeño was feeling truly diabolical when he wrote the instructions."

"I don't think he was being that arcane. There are five women in the painting. Six, actually, if you count the queen's reflection. But we can check that later. For now, let's try the perspectives that we can actually see."

"I've programmed in image maps for the other rooms in the apartment," Becka said. "All you have to do is say the name of each figure in the painting, and the program will provide their perspectival data. It'll fill in the visual details for the parts of the room that are currently blank."

Selena shook her head. "Tess, what made you think of doing this?"

"It's actually kind of logical. I remembered Becka saying how computer programmers were using these complex algorithms to try to map out all the lines of perspective in paintings like *Las Meninas*. They wanted to literally peer behind the canvas and see what only the painter himself was able to see."

I walked over to the blank space, where Velázquez's canvas had once been.

"Ordeño used the painting as a kind of transparency, in order to hide something within his own home. Obviously, it's hidden somewhere in plain sight, but in a place where nobody would think to look. In order to find it, we have to locate the right perspective. I think."

Selena looked at me. "You think?"

"Yeah. I mean, I'm pretty sure. I came up with all of this while I was getting dragged through an undead garden. I haven't exactly had the chance to test my hypothesis out until now."

"Why don't we try looking from the Infanta's perspective first?" Lucian asked. "She's often seen to be at the center of the painting."

"Okay," Becka said. "Activiating the Infanta's perspective now."

"Mia, what do you see?"

She squinted. "A hallway."

Indeed, the interior hallway had appeared, leading toward Ordeño's bedroom. It was empty and silent.

"Right." I turned to Becka. "What about the nun, or *doña*, or whatever she's called? The one who's supposed to be standing behind Mia?"

"I believe she's Marcela de Ulloa," Lucian said. "The Infanta's chaperone. She's talking to some anonymous *guardadamas*, or bodyguard."

"Whatever. Let's see what she sees."

"I'm loading her perspective now," Becka said. "Go stand in her position."

I walked over to where the woman's shadow was. "I can see farther down the hallway. A little bit of the bedroom, but that's it. Let's try the *menina* on the left. That's you, Derrick."

He sighed. "Always the *menina*, never the Infanta."

"How long have you been waiting to make that joke?"

"Possibly my whole life."

"What do you see?"

"The door to Ordeño's room. And a bit of the carpet."

I shook my head. "It has to be something obvious, but still hidden." I turned to Selena. "Okay, Mari-Bárbola. What about you?"

"I'm activating her perspective now," Becka said.

Another patch of the hallway appeared, this time leading in the opposite direction, toward the bathroom.

"I don't think it's in the shower," Selena said.

"Shit. There's nothing else in the hallway?"

"Just the A/C."

My eyes widened. "Wait."

I walked down the phantom hallway. Set into the wall, just as Selena had described, was a state-of-the-art A/C unit. I stared at the panel.

"Four pounds of snow for Mari-Bárbola," I said softly.

Lucian stared at me. "You're not serious."

"I don't get it," Selena said.

"It's something that Duessa said to me. Supposedly, Mari-Bárbola was promised four pounds of snow every year, and nobody knows why. Maybe an A/C unit is the modern equivalent of her four pounds of snow. We need to go to Ordeño's apartment."

"And you're convinced that the secret to his murder is hidden within the air-conditioning unit?"

"I think it's probably not the most insane thing I've ever come up with."

Selena blinked. "That's actually true. All right. We'll take separate cars."

"And no," I said, before Patrick could even ask, "you're not driving. You and Mia are staying here with Becka."

"That sucks!" Mia glared at me. "We always miss everything!"

"You can play Nintendo Wii in the simulation chamber," Becka told her.

Mia and Patrick exchanged a look.

"Have fun, Tess," she said. "We'll see you later."

We met Selena in the underground parking of Ordeño's building. It was cold, and the ceiling had that fluffy white insulation that seemed to be standard-issue in every subterranean lot. I could hear air ducts hissing.

"Did Ordeño drive?" I asked Lucian as we both got out of the car.

"No. He liked transit."

"You don't have a car either. Is it a necromancer thing?"

"I think it's more of an environmentally conscious thing. And I used to have a car, but I sold it when I moved here."

"From where?"

"That's a conversation for another time."

"You always say that when you're about to get to the good stuff."

"Maybe that's a necromancer thing."

"Hah."

Selena emerged from a black sedan, which she'd borrowed from the lab. She clicked on the alarm, then turned to me, shivering beneath her coat. "I really didn't think I'd end up here tonight."

"I don't think any of us did. Especially me."

"But you're the one we're all following this time."

"Right. But when's the last time one of my hunches was actually correct? I thought this was just going to be another flash in the pan."

"I seem to remember you having some premonitory dreams."

"Yeah, but that's pretty erratic."

"I never remember my dreams," Derrick said, following Miles out of the backseat. "Except for the nightmares."

I thought it best not to mention my dream about *Las Meninas*. A dream was less convincing than a scholarly article, at least to this crowd.

Selena had brought Ordeño's keys, and she used them to unlock the parking garage door. Stale apartment air washed over us. We filed into the elevator, and Selena pressed the button for Ordeño's floor. It was one of those new elevators that was so quiet and still that you could barely tell if you were moving or not. Sometimes my life felt like that. I was never quite sure if I'd forgotten to press the button.

We emerged on Ordeño's floor. The yellow caution tape was still drawn across his front door. Anyone walking past, including local authorities and the building superintendent, would see an incomplete unit still under construction. The veil would last until the cleaners arrived to erase any lingering traces of materia in the air. Then the scene would be released. Most likely, the unit would rent again in record time. Everyone wanted to live in the fancy building with the tree on its roof. It had a beautiful view of English Bay, and nobody had to know that a necromancer had died here.

Selena drew aside the yellow tape, and we entered the apartment, making our way down the silent hallway. Everything was as we'd left it. There were still dishes in the sink, and none of the furniture had been moved. I looked one more time at Ordeño's degrees hanging on the wall. Like most paranormal folk, he'd managed to get through post-secondary education without arousing any suspicion. He must have been lonely, though. Could you use necromancy to cheat on a test? It didn't seem likely, unless you planned on de-fleshing your TA.

"It's weird," I said, apropos of my own thoughts.

"What's weird?" Lucian asked.

"This case. We've all devoted so much energy to solving the murder of a person we know virtually nothing about. No pictures on the walls. No family. Did he even leave behind a will?"

"It's being contested by the Dark Parliament. I haven't seen it yet."

"I thought you were Fifth Solium, or whatever."

"Seventh Solium. And that doesn't mean I get to see every document. I'm not in Lord Nightingale's inner circle."

"But Ordeño was."

"Sure. He could have ruled the Dark Parliament someday."

"How did the two of you meet?"

"I don't really see how that's relevant."

"Right." I turned around. "Can I see a show of hands? Who'd like to know how Lucian and Luiz Ordeño met?"

Everyone slowly raised their hand, including Selena.

Lucian sighed. "He was one of my teachers."

"What subject?"

"History. He was very passionate about the origins of the hidden city, and the ancient customs of necromancy. A little obsessed, in fact."

"I didn't notice a school when we were there."

"You only saw ten percent of the city. Half of it is underground."

"Ah. That makes sense."

"He was a great teacher. We became friends."

"What was his favorite color?"

"Tess."

"Come on. I've got nothing on this guy. Give me a point of interest. What was his favorite color? Did he like animals? Was he straight, gay, asexual? He seemed to live the life of a perpetually single academic."

Lucian seemed to consider this for a moment. Then he shrugged. "I suppose you're right. Luiz was a very private person. Even I didn't know much about him. Like most people who've lived for more than a few hundred years, I think that he was bisexual, or at the very least open-minded. But I never saw him with a partner of either gender. He didn't have pets. He wore a lot of blue. And he collected vinyl."

I brightened at this. "What kind?"

"Weird bands, mostly. Folk music. Zappa. The Incredible String Band."

"Wow."

"He read a lot of Maria Zambráno. She's a philosopher."

"Oh. I've read her in translation," Derrick said.

We were all silent for a minute. There wasn't much else to say. No matter how many anecdotes we traded, we'd never know anything more about Luiz Ordeño. He'd left an empty vessel behind, and it was locked in a morgue freezer. He seemed to have poured most of his personal energy into creating a puzzle that we were on the verge of solving. Or maybe we weren't even close. Funny how the positions of absolute certainty and folly are so similar when you're standing on the border between them.

I followed Lucian down the hallway that led to Ordeño's bedroom. The A/C unit was compact, about the size of a small kitchen cupboard. It was made of buffed metal, so smooth that it virtually disappeared into the wall. I held my hand in front of the vent. There was no air coming from it, cold or otherwise.

"Miles?" I asked. "Are you picking up anything?"

He approached the wall and held out his hand. "I'm not sure," he said softly. His eyes narrowed. "Wait. There's . . . something. It's really faint, though. It might just be some defrayed materia left over from when the necromancer died. Or it could be microwave static. I can't tell."

I turned to Lucian. "What about you? Any necroid materia?"

He frowned. "I agree with Miles. There could be something behind there, but it's like a dim echo. The barest suggestion of power. It could be anything."

"Step aside," Selena said. "I've got power tools."

She used an electric drill to unfasten the bolts that held the A/C unit to the wall. When she was done, she dropped the screws into a labeled evidence bag.

"Lucian? You want to do the honors?"

"You're just afraid that there's a booby trap."

"You're the necromancer. You've got the highest chance of survival."

He chuckled. "You OSIs really know how to charm a guy."

"It's called pragmatic romanticism," I said. "Or romantic pragmatism. One of those, I can't remember which."

Lucian gently removed the A/C panel from the wall. A dark alcove full of wires lay behind it. He reached in and felt around the hole for a few seconds.

"Anything there?" I asked.

"Nothing that I can feel. But . . ." He frowned. "I don't know how to explain it. Like when you've got a sneeze caught in your nose. There's *something* in here, something not quite there, and it's rubbing on the edges of my awareness."

"That's how I felt," Miles said. "Can I take a look?"

"Go ahead." He stepped back.

"Wait." Selena handed him a pair of plastic gloves. "Put

these on first. We may need to dust whatever you find for prints."

Miles put on the gloves. Then he reached his hand into the gap.

"Please be careful," Derrick said. "I love all of your appendages. I don't want you to lose anything."

"I'm not going to comment on that," Selena said.

Miles kept digging around in the dark space. "Yeah. There's something here, but it's under the spatial dermis. Almost like a splinter. Just give me a second."

He closed his eyes. A pale blue light began to emanate from the hole in the wall. I felt a slight stirring of my own power as Miles reached into the fabric of space, as if throwing a baited hook into a vast ocean.

His eyes opened. "Got it."

Something clicked in the back of my head. I looked at Derrick, and he simply nodded. It was the curious feeling of two types of space merging, one terrestrial, the other paradimensional. Neither of us understood how the process worked, but we could both still feel it.

Miles pulled a small, carved wooden box out of the wall. It was made of polished black oak, and had an image of a tree on its lid.

"Is that one of the trees from the Grove of Souls?" I asked Lucian.

"I believe so. Miles, can I see it?"

"Gloves!" Selena snapped. She withdrew a digital camera from her purse, taking three pictures of the box from different angles. "We really should have a ruler for scale, but there's no time."

Lucian put on the gloves. "Can I open it now?"

She examined the pictures on the digital readout. "Sure. Slowly."

I leaned in close. Lucian opened the box.

The inside was lined in black velvet. A small glass vial lay within. It was filled with a red liquid.

"Is that blood?" Derrick asked.

"I don't think so. But we'll need to do presumptive tests first." I drew out a large evidence bag. "Let's just put the whole thing in here, and we can spray it with luminol and phenolphthalein once we get back to the lab."

Lucian stared at the vial curiously.

"What do you think it is?" I asked.

"I really have no idea."

I didn't believe him. But that was nothing new. He closed the box and handed it to me. I placed it gently in the evidence bag.

"I'll take that," Selena said. "Let's go before this thing explodes."

"Nice find, by the way," Derrick said to Miles. "You solved the mystery."

"Tess solved it. I just dug around in a crawlspace."

"Babe. You reached into invisible space. That deserves some credit."

"It was pretty sweet," Lucian confirmed.

Miles shrugged. "Thanks."

I dialed the extension for the trace lab. I wanted to make sure that Mia and Patrick hadn't destroyed the Nerve.

The line picked up.

"Cindée? We're on our way back. We've got it."

"That's wonderful news, Tess. Exactly what I wanted to hear."

It wasn't Cindée's voice on the line.

My blood turned to ice. I hadn't heard that voice in more than two years. I'd hoped that I wouldn't ever hear it again.

"Sabine?"

"That's right, sweetheart. I've got both of your kids here. And if you want everyone to get out of this alive, you're going to do exactly as I say."

My heart fell.

I looked at Lucian. He'd heard me say her name, and I could see the fear in his eyes. Real fear. Sabine Delacroix had nearly killed me once before. Now she had both Mia and Patrick, and their lives meant absolutely nothing to her.

I swallowed. "What do you want?"

20.

The plan was simple.

First: Make sure that Patrick and Mia didn't get killed.

Second: Make sure that I didn't get killed.

Third: Make sure that Sabine Delacroix did get killed. No do-overs.

"I hate her," I said, guiding my car into the lab's parking lot. "I really hate her. I mean, what's she even doing here? Where has she been hiding for so long, and what does she want from us this time?"

"It seems pretty clear," Derrick said. "She wants the armor. Otherwise, she wouldn't be negotiating with us. She's been waiting for this."

I shut off the ignition. "Bitch should have stayed exiled. If she lays a hand on Mia or Patrick, I'm taking her out."

"It might not be that easy."

"I've got a gun loaded with silver-nitrate rounds. She's

got a withered, centuries-old heart, just waiting for a bullet. It seems simple to me."

"If it was really that simple, she would have been dead a long time ago."

"Why does this vampire hate you again?" Miles asked.

I opened the driver's-side door. "It's a long story involving Mia, my old boss, and the former magnate. And some GHB. But that's just a side note."

Selena's car pulled into the space next to us. She got out, adjusting her shoulder-holster. We'd stopped by one of the CORE's hidden armament depots on our way here. Selena flashed them her ID badge, and they made sure we didn't leave empty-handed. Personally, I hated guns. They killed a lot more people than magic ever did. But in situations like these, you needed all the firepower you could get.

"Lucian's in position?" Selena asked.

I nodded. "His painting at home gives him access to the speculum network, so he's waiting for our signal. If things get hairy, he can teleport himself into the lab."

"That must be how Sabine got in. Through *Las Meninas*."

"Which means she's got a necromancer in her pocket." I shook my head. "Fucking Braxton. I'm going to feed him that Vorpal gauntlet."

"Easy, tiger." Selena put a hand on my shoulder. "You're worried about Patrick and Mia; I get it. But you have to treat this like any other hostage situation. At least try to give her what she wants."

"What she wants is a world-class beating. She just doesn't know it yet."

"Tess."

I sighed. "Calm and coolheaded. I promise."

"I don't believe you."

"Really? And I have such an honest face."

Selena turned to Derrick. "How's the sensor on your gun working?"

He squinted along the sight line. "I'm pretty sure I can actually hit something. It might take me a few tries, though."

"That's better than nothing. And Miles? You're ready to go?"

He drew his Sig Sauer. "Ready as I'll ever be. I'm using the Glaser rounds that you suggested, which mushroom on impact. So if I get a clear shot, the vampire's definitely going to feel it."

"Make sure to stay in the rear. If Sabine starts whispering to any of her companions, you'll be able to read their lips."

"I am more than a closed-captioning service, you know."

"Of course. But right now, it's kind of like a two-for-one deal. Interpret first, and shoot later. If bullets start flying, we're probably screwed anyways. So at that point it won't really matter."

"Sometimes it's hard to tell climax from FUBAR," I said.

"Sometimes it's like you're not even speaking English," Selena replied. "But you're right. I do keep you around for the intrigue."

"I knew it."

We made our way through the parking lot. Selena used her card to let us in through one of the maintenance doors, and we found ourselves in a deserted hallway. She pulled out her PDA. "I'm syncing this with the main network. Sabine may have disabled some of the building's security features, but I should be able to reactive them. With Becka's help."

"I hope she hasn't figured out what Becka's job is."

"For once, her age will work in her favor. She looks far too young to be an expert at anything. Sabine will probably just mistake her for an intern."

"And Cindée?"

"She can take care of herself. There are a lot of nasty toys in the weapons locker that she can use, if she manages to gain access to it."

"Shouldn't we be calling in a SWAT team or something?" Miles asked. "Surround the place and demand her surrender at gunpoint?"

"You've been watching too many movies on TNT," Selena told him. "Sabine's an immortal, and she's halfway to crazy. She wants to deal with us and only us. If she gets wind of any kind of armed operation going on outside the building, she's going to kill the hostages and cut her losses."

"You're sure?"

"Trust me. Everyone's still alive because Sabine thinks that she can still get whatever's in that vial. If we eliminate that possibility by trying to capture her, she'll go nuclear. I want to avoid multiple homicides wherever possible."

"I think that's in the handbook," I added.

"But what if someone else calls nine-one-one?" Miles asked. "This is the night shift, right? There must be other technicians in the building."

"It was a half day today. Becka and Cindée are only here because we called them in. Even the cleaning staff has gone home."

As we passed by an elevator, an idea occurred to me. "Wait. What about Esther? She's always here, right?"

Esther worked downstairs, in the guts of the lab. She may have been a living computer, or a bio-mechanoid, or something along those lines, but nobody was certain. She controlled all the data keys and secret files that this branch of the CORE had on everyone, including me.

Selena started to dial an extension on her PDA, then stopped. "It's possible that she's monitoring the lines. I'm not sure I want to risk it."

"Can't we e-mail her?"

"Sabine could have access to the whole network. We have no idea how much tampering her necromancer friends have done already."

"I can go downstairs and see if she's here," Derrick said. "I'll need your security badge, though. The elevator won't take me to her floor without it."

Selena gave him a look. "You're not planning mutiny, are you?"

"If I was, I'd like to think I'd be a bit more creative about it."

"Fair enough." She handed her ID badge to Derrick. "Be careful. If you see anyone, don't engage them."

"Run and hide. Check."

"You're more use to me alive than in pieces. So, yes. Run and hide."

He nodded. "I promise."

Selena pressed the button on the elevator, and the doors opened. Derrick stepped inside. He inserted Selena's key-card into the security slot, and the panel indicating the basement floor lit up.

"See you all soon," Derrick said.

The doors started to close. Miles blocked them with one hand.

"Wait. This is the part where I kiss you for luck."

"What do you think this is, *Die Hard*?"

"Shut up."

Derrick grinned. "Fine. But make it quick. My boss is watching."

Miles leaned in, kissing him lightly on the mouth.

"Luck," he said simply.

"Thanks."

The doors closed.

"Let's go," Selena said. "I already can't believe I let that happen. We have to get to the trace lab."

We continued down the hallway, then went up a flight of stairs. The fire door opened onto another corridor, which led to the reception area. Most of the fluorescent lights had been shut off, but a few were still flickering. I could feel cold air from the ceiling ducts. In the distance, I heard voices.

"Keep your weapons lowered, but don't holster them," Selena said. "No matter what, keep your finger on the trigger. She moves fast."

We made our way slowly forward. The door to the trace lab was ajar. I walked in, scanning the room. All the machines were humming away contentedly, but there was no one here. The door to the evidence locker was open. I walked over the entrance, and saw that the glass case holding the armor was empty. A yellow Post-it had been affixed to the space where the armor recently resided.

We're in the egg. Come join us for tea.

"I really hate her," I said. "Did I mention that already?"

We headed for the Nerve. I kept seeing grim scenarios in my mind. Patrick and Mia already dead. Becka and Cindée incapacitated, or worse. The Nerve somehow turned against us, like that episode of *Star Trek: The Next Generation* where the holodeck gets taken over by an alien probe, and Data's wearing the creepy sun mask. Wait. Why did I remember that? Derrick must have been rubbing off on me.

The door to the simulation chamber was open.

"Let me go first," I said. "I'm the one she's looking for."

"We'll go in at the same time," Selena replied. "I am *el jefe*, after all. It would be bad form to enter behind you."

I grinned slightly. "Thanks."

"Just keep thinking about the dental, and it'll all seem worth it."

At the moment, all I could think about was how I'd been trained to kill vampires since I was a teenager. I knew a variety of techniques for putting down Sabine like a rabid animal, and I wanted to use all of them at once.

The first thing I saw when I walked in was Mia, and my heart unclenched slightly. She was unhurt and sitting on the floor. Patrick was a few feet away from her, unconscious. He didn't appear to be hurt in any way, but he was slumped across the ground, eyes closed.

"Tess!" Sabine was standing on the mezzanine floor, next to the controls. "It's so nice to see you."

"Fuck you, Sabine." I scanned the room quickly. Becka was sitting in a swivel chair close to Sabine, her arms tied behind her back. Cindée wasn't there. Maybe she left before Sabine arrived, or she was hiding somewhere.

Two familiar figures were standing next to one of the monitors. One I'd expected to see again, but the second was a surprise.

"Cyrus?"

He grinned at me, smoothing his bleach-blond hair. "Hey, Tess."

"You're working for this piece of trash?"

He shrugged. "What can I say? Not every vampire agrees with the treaty. And Sabine pays top dollar. She's, like, independently wealthy or—"

"Stop talking, Cyrus." Braxton was standing next to him. I couldn't believe it had taken me so long to recognize his cold, reptilian eyes before. He met my gaze, and I tried to find a spark of human, or even demihuman, compassion behind those eyes. But there was none. It was the same expression of casual malice that my old boss, Marcus Tremblay, had fixed me with just before trying to kill me.

"I really should have killed you in the parking lot," he said.

"Yeah. Likewise."

"What were you trying to accomplish by visiting Trinovantum? Did you honestly think that Lord Nightingale would listen to you?"

"It was worth a shot. And I found a nice bone dagger, the same kind that you used to kill Luiz Ordeño. Once the Jell-O mold around it hardens, we'll have some sweet impression evidence to use against you."

That wasn't strictly true. But something told me that Braxton wasn't going to be around long enough to see a court date, so I figured there was no harm in angling for a confession. Sometimes, you really could get something out of nothing.

He just laughed. "Those knives are a dime-a-dozen at the Night Market. You won't be able to prove anything."

"Care to wager on it?"

"Not really. I'm done dealing with you." He turned to Sabine. "I'd like to kill her now, if you don't mind."

She shook her head. "Simmer down. You've waited nearly a hundred years to take Ordeño's place on the Dark Parliament. You can wait a few more minutes to get your revenge on."

Selena frowned. "I thought Deonara was next in line for Prime Solium. How is Braxton going to take the seat?"

Sabine rolled her eyes. "You're too slow, darling. Deonara's not going to live through the night. Not once I send Cyrus through the painting and into her living room. That's the problem with speculums. Once you gain access, privacy becomes a bit of a moot point, really."

"My money's on Valesco in that fight," I said. "She'll kick his ass."

"Yeah, I would have said that, too," Cyrus piped up.

"But I'm not going to fight her. I'm just going to drug her and then burn her house down."

I stared at Sabine. "I see you haven't changed."

"And neither have you, Tess." She made an annoying clicking sound. "Can't dress, can't fight, and can't form an independent thought to save your life. Did you honestly think I wasn't watching you from the very beginning?"

"Did you honestly think the two vampires you sent after me last year could take me down? That was a weak gesture."

"Of course it was. And you forgot about me, didn't you? You didn't pay me a second thought after that."

Right. I saw where this was going now. A Miss Havisham revenge tragedy. Sabine really did need her own genre at this point.

"I didn't forget anything," she continued. "Not the pain of exile. Not the various shitholes I had to crawl through in order to survive as a banished creature. And certainly not the weapon you deprived me of. And by that, I mean little Mia."

Mia stared at her coldly. "I still owe you for killing my parents. And if you get too close, I'm going to rip your eyes out, bitch."

Sabine chuckled. "I doubt that. Or haven't you realized yet that those drugs you're taking are suppressing more than the virus in your blood? They're also diluting your powers. Making you into a nice, useless doll for the CORE to control." Her face fell theatrically. "Or hadn't Tess told you about that? Doesn't seem fair to keep you in the dark, especially when she's supposed to be your guardian."

Mia looked at me. "Is that true?"

I honestly didn't know. It was altogether possible that the CORE was suppressing her powers for their own gain.

It made sense. But nobody had ever told me anything, as usual. It was my turn to look at Selena.

"I don't know. Is it?"

She shrugged. "If it is, then it's been done without my knowledge. I just pick up the drugs from the pharmacy counter. They're supposed to be retrovirals."

"They're trying to manipulate you, sweetheart," Sabine said. "Just like they do to everyone else. That's their game. They control all the magic, all the weapons, and eventually, they control your head as well. What do you think telepaths are for?"

"Are you honestly trying to turn her against us?" I asked. "This whole plan seems pretty lame, Sabine. Nobody here trusts you. Braxton only wants to kill me, and Cyrus is only in it for the money. What are you trying to accomplish?"

"Terrorism calls for strange bedfellows," she replied. "They've all been useful to me, just like Marcus was. Braxton got me into the hidden city because nobody else would listen to his conservative rantings. And Cyrus was bored and looking for something to make his blood boil again."

"Also, I knew it would piss Modred off," Cyrus added.

Braxton scowled at her. "Is that how you think of us? Accessories to the fact?"

"Oh, honey. Of course not." Sabine smiled. Oh, man, did I ever know that smile. "Not at all. You're so much less to me than that. You're like an afterbirth. At one time, you may have had some value. But now you're all used up and—well—just gross."

"You fucking—"

Two things happened very quickly. Braxton raised his right hand, which was sheathed in another Vorpal gauntlet. But Sabine moved in a blur. She grabbed his arm and snapped his wrist. The sound of it made me shudder. Braxton cried out, falling to his knees. Sabine sighed.

"Cyrus. Drain him, please."

"Wait." I reached into my coat, withdrawing the evidence bag with the carved wooden box inside. "Let's do this first. Braxton may be an asshole, but he doesn't necessarily have to die. I'd much rather see him rotting in a paranormal institution."

The truth was that Braxton was desperate, angry, and in considerable pain. That made him a wild card, and I needed to keep him in play as long as possible.

Sabine extended her hand. "Open the box and take out the vial."

"I hope I don't drop it. I can be superclumsy sometimes."

"Drop it, and the girl dies. It's that simple, Tess. You know how fast I can move, and I know that you're not completely retarded. Just do what I say, and everyone gets to keep breathing tonight."

"I've heard that promise before."

She smiled again. It was like the visual equivalent of nails on a chalkboard. "Maybe I didn't mean it before. But now I do. Give me the vial, and I walk out of your life for good."

"Is that a promise?"

She rolled her eyes. "Do you think I want to keep shadowing you? I have better things to do. It'll be a pleasure to leave you and your pathetic drama behind. Now, take out the vial and walk it over to me."

I turned to Selena.

Her eyes widened. "*Now* you're acknowledging my authority?"

"I thought it might be an interesting change."

"Just give her the vial. It's not worth two lives."

"Listen to your boss," Sabine said. "Mia's fine for the moment, and Patrick's just sleeping. We had to knock him out so that he wouldn't call for backup with that annoying vampire sonar of his. But we can do something far more permanent to both of them. It's so much easier to cooperate."

I drew the vial out of the box. Its contents sparkled, like cranberry ginger ale. It definitely wasn't blood. I crossed the room slowly, and as I approached Sabine, I saw two things. The first was Ordeño's armor, which was sitting on the chair next to her.

The second was Sabine herself. This close, I could see how tired she looked. She was positively haggard. Her eyes were red-rimmed, and there were odd scratches on her arms. What sort of creature could leave scratches on an elder vampire?

"It really does look like you've been through hell," I told her. "I guess I should apologize. But I'm really not sorry."

"I'd only be disappointed in you if you were."

"What's in it, by the way?"

"A tincture. Like a fine paint made out of what you call 'materia.' Luiz spent his life perfecting its creation. That's how he earned the title *el alquimista*."

"Most people think that's just a myth."

Sabine grinned. "And us? Don't most people think that we're just a myth?"

She held out her hand.

I gave her the vial.

Then the lights went out.

The Nerve began to hum. Someone was loading a simulation, but Becka was still tied up in the corner. Nobody else had gotten to the controls, and Braxton didn't even know how to operate them.

Derrick. He must have found Esther.

"This is a pretty lame trick," Sabine said, her voice carrying through the darkness. "You're only endangering your loved ones."

"I didn't do this. Honestly. I don't know what's happening."

"And I'm supposed to believe that?"

"Believe whatever you want. You've got your magic potion now."

A pale blue light appeared, coming from the ground panels. A patch of air near the doorway began to shimmer.

Marcus Tremblay appeared.

Sabine actually laughed. "Seriously? Is this supposed to frighten me?"

The room flickered. Then we were standing in a familiar alley. A blond-haired boy lay propped up against a Dumpster. He was dressed like a mild-mannered accountant. There wasn't a mark on his body, but we all knew that he was dead. Marcus stood next to him, staring at Sabine.

I saw her eyes harden in the dim light. "This is idiotic. You think I'm still grieving over Sebastian? He was a thrall. He meant nothing to me."

"I don't believe that," I said. "I remember how your eyes changed when you talked about him. You cared for him, Sabine. Just like he cared for you."

"Shut your mouth," she hissed, "before I rip your tongue out."

Ah. The Sabine we all remembered was back.

Sebastian's form shifted. His eyes opened. I remembered how blue they'd been in the photograph taken of them together. He looked sadly at her.

"Fuck you," she whispered. "This is meaningless. It's all meaningless."

"Actually—" The lights flicked back on. Derrick was standing in the doorway, his gun leveled at Sabine. "I think it's pretty gripping. A tearjerker."

"Ah. Your maggot's here." Sabine smiled. "How's it feel to be the diversion once again, little man?"

"I'm not sure. How does this feel?"

He fired at her. Sabine moved too quickly, but she'd forgotten about Miles, who was still waiting in the background. He fired from the opposite direction, and the bullet slammed into her shoulder, blossoming on impact. She screamed, staggering a bit, grabbing onto the wall for support.

Selena drew her athame. It shivered beneath her hand, then turned liquid, elongating into a saber that burned like green glass.

"Take them out!" she cried.

Cyrus leapt at me, but I was already moving. I touched the point of my athame to the ground and drew a spike of earth materia. He slammed against an invisible wall, like a bug hitting a windshield. He glanced off the plate of materia, snarling. I leveled my gun at him, but I was one second too slow. His form blurred, and the silver-tipped bullet struck the wall of the Nerve, shattering one of the ceramic plates.

"Careful!" Selena swung her athame at Sabine. "We're not insured for this!"

Sabine dodged the blow. She was bleeding from her shoulder, but that barely slowed her down. She struck Selena across the face. Selena managed to deflect some of the blow's force, but it still threw her across the room like a rag doll. She landed on the floor with a grunt, dropping her athame.

Sabine rushed her. I tried to throw something offensive at the vampire, but she was moving too fast. Then Selena surprised me. Still on one knee, she leapt into the air. Her athame flew after her, gliding into her hand. She hung in the air for a moment, then spun around, pointing the blade at Sabine. A column of force burst from the athame, striking Sabine and sending her stumbling backward.

Selena landed on the ground in a crouch. She raised her

athame, and it began to glow, first blue, then incandescent white.

Then it sang.

The sound was deafening. I felt it stabbing my head from all sides, ringing in my ears and making my teeth chatter. And Sabine's hearing was much better than mine. She screamed, covering her ears.

Something hit me like a truck from behind. Cyrus. I slammed against the wall, losing my grip on the Glock. I tried to rise, but the vampire pinned me to the ground. I could smell the garlic and onions on his breath. He smiled at me.

"You know, you're kind of a bitch. I'm not even going to drain you before killing you. I think I'll just—"

A bullet tore through his eye socket, spraying me with hot blood and clear vitreous fluid. I gagged. Cyrus screamed something incomprehensible, and a second bullet tore most of his scalp off. This time I managed to get my arm up in time, so the blood just doused the sleeve of my jacket.

Miles kept firing until he cut the vampire's spinal cord. Cyrus gave a great, shuddering lurch, and black purge fluid poured from his mouth. Then he stopped twitching, and was still.

Thank you, I signed.

My pleasure, he signed back.

That was when I heard the growling.

Sabine was back on the mezzanine floor. She'd opened up the vial, and was pouring its contents onto the suit of armor. Gold smoke rose from the plate mail, and with it came a sound halfway between leonine growling and metal foundations twisting beneath an enormous weight.

"That's never good," Derrick murmured, coming to stand beside me. Miles helped me up, and we both stared at Sabine. Smoke was rising all around her, and somewhere within its depths, I could see a form emerging.

Sabine laughed. "You're all fucked now. *La manticora* is on her way."

"Tess!" Selena was bleeding from a cut on her forehead, but she'd managed to stand halfway up. She pointed to my Glock. "Aim for the armor!"

I started to crawl across the ground, but then something hot sizzled past me, like a small meteor. The gun went spinning away. I looked up, and saw Braxton with his hand outstretched. He was smiling.

"You're not going to harm it. Not until *la manticora* has fully arrived."

I stared at him. "How dense *are* you? That thing's going to kill us all."

"No." I saw that he'd placed the Vorpal gauntlet on his uninjured hand. "It's just going to kill her."

The armor had become a pool of hot liquid gold, swirling faster and faster as it threw off smoke and sparks like a naked singularity. I could see the manticore beginning to emerge. It had the body of a lion, with bloodred fur and dense musculature beneath its hide. Its tail resembled a scorpion's, but it was divided into three segments, each one with a giant barb, like a fishhook made of bone. The tail moved left and right, hypnotic, its bone shears trembling.

It also had wings like a bat's, only much larger. The wings had three sets of eyes, gold and reptilian, staring at me without blinking. But the manticore's face was what scared me the most. It was human—the face of a withered old man with wiry black hair—and its wrinkled mouth was full of needle-sharp teeth. Its pink tongue tasted the air. Then it howled.

"*La manticora!*" Sabine raised the empty vial. "You're free! Now serve me as you served the necromancer!"

"No!" Braxton stepped between her and the rapidly expanding manticore. "She knows nothing about you. She only wants to control you. If you serve me, I promise to feed you more souls than you can count. You'll drink the blood of worlds. We'll conquer every living realm together!"

"Get out of my way!" Sabine grabbed Braxton by his bad arm. But he was ready for her this time. The gemstones on the Vorpal gauntlet began to glow. He laid his gloved palm against her chest.

"You deserve this," he hissed.

Red light tore across her body. Sabine howled, and the sound of her voice was somehow more shattering than the manticore's birth-cry. She withered before my eyes. The necroid materia devoured her from the inside, irradiating her, making her bones glow ruby and hot. I saw every vein in her body. Her eyes grew impossibly large, and blood sprayed from them, blood that was also burning light.

Her scream became a kind of groan. Then her body collapsed in on itself, crumbling into embers and calcined flesh. She shrank until she was nothing, just a dark, ash-choked stain on the floor.

"That's real power," Braxton said. He turned to the manticore. "You must recognize it. And you respect it. So serve me. Be my paramour. Do what I say, and I'll let you have whatever you desire." He pointed at me. "Starting with her."

Oh, fuck.

The manticore stared at me. It was growing more solid. I couldn't tell what it was considering. But then it opened its mouth, and spoke. Its voice sounded like a plague wind tearing through the room.

"She belongs to another."

Braxton's eyes widened. "I don't care! Kill her! Tear her apart! She's nothing to a creature like you."

Its ancient, impossible eyes held me absolutely still. I could hear it breathing. Then it turned back to Braxton.

"No. She is something. But you—you are nothing."

Its mouth opened wide. Braxton screamed. The manticore snapped its head forward. Its pink tongue wrapped around Braxton's head.

He kept screaming. Even when his head came off. I looked away.

"Tess!"

I turned, trying to ignore the nausea. Lucian was standing in the doorway.

"It's about time!" I snapped.

"You have to destroy the armor. The two are symbiotically linked."

"Tell me something I don't know." I stared at the rapidly liquefying disk of molten metal, still spinning beneath the manticore. "I can't get close to it. That thing will take me apart in a second. And a bullet's not—"

Then I remembered something that Lucian had told me about the Nightmares. I can't say why I thought of it at that moment. But I remembered his gentle look, and the way that he touched my shoulder, reassuring me when I thought I might be sick.

It's fine. They're mostly made of water, remember?

Water.

"Becka!" I screamed. "The fire alarm!"

Becka, managing to free herself, had crawled across the mezzanine floor to the control panel. She reached up and pressed the emergency button.

The sprinklers came to life.

The Nerve was a priceless device, and so a great deal of technology was invested in protecting it. The entire ceiling was loaded with sprinklers, and they all released their water in unison as the fire alarm began to clang.

A curtain of water fell onto the molten disc. It hissed and steamed. The gold started to clump in places, like amber slime.

"Selena! We need ice!"

We both pointed our athames at the bubbling, seething mass that had once been a beautiful piece of armor. There was a lot of materia lining the walls and circuitry of the Nerve, and we drew on all of it at once. Two cones of liquid nitrogen shot from the blades, coating the gold metal in ice and frost.

The manticore screamed.

Lucian grabbed my Glock. He leveled it at the materia beneath the manticore, which now looked like a kind of alchemical soup.

"Shoot! Everyone shoot the armor!"

Miles, Derrick, and Lucian fired in unison, while Selena and I kept the ice concentrated on the bubbling liquid, now brittle, like glass. As the bullets tore through it, the armor shattered.

The manticore howled. All of its eyes were on me, and I felt like every inch of its immortal malice was aimed in my direction. I could hear something, a word, maybe, trapped within its scream. But I couldn't make it out.

Everyone kept shooting.

The armor dissolved into countless fragments, charred and smoking. The manticore became golden smoke once more, still screaming as it began to dissipate.

Becka switched on the overhead fans. There was a powerful rush of air, and what was left of the manticore was sucked into the vents, screaming all the way.

The fire alarm wouldn't stop. I stared at the black patch on the floor that used to be Sabine. Braxton had left only his head behind, mouth gaping, staring at nothing. The rest was somewhere in the manticore's spectral guts.

Lucian put his arm around me. "Are you okay?"

I looked at Mia. She seemed torn between two realities. She wanted to run to me, like I was really her mother. But a part of her held back. I could see the misgiving in her eyes now. She didn't trust me fully anymore.

And all I could hear were the manticore's last words. About belonging. About power, and what it promised.

"I'm something," I told him simply.

Afterthought

Three things happened after we cleaned up the Nerve.

Luiz Ordeño's treaty between the Dark Parliament and the Vampire Nation was ratified by Deonara Valesco, the new Prime Solium. With Lord Nightingale's blessing. Mia started locking the door to her room. To keep me out. And I called up an old ally named Mr. Corvid, who knew where my father was.

He said it would be his pleasure to help me.

About the Author

Jes Battis was born in Vancouver, British Columbia. He teaches and writes in Regina, Saskatchewan. Visit his web-site at www.authorjesbattis.com.

M224G0909